"You were married?" he asked.

"Our styles were too different." Much like hers was with Theo's. Worlds apart. Except right now she felt... "My style was casual, fly-by-the-seat-of-my-pants sort of thing. I wasn't really suited for fancy, structured boardrooms and partner lunches."

"Are you always so honest?" Theo asked.

No. If Josie were truly honest, she'd admit she wanted to move even closer to him and dare to test their attraction. "Pretending to be what you aren't can be exhausting."

A shadow of a smile passed across his face. "Then, tell me, who is Josie Beck?"

"A woman determined to succeed on her own." Josie locked her gaze on his. "I don't want help from anyone who feels sorry for me."

"So, Josie Beck is dedicated, proud and hardworking." He reached up and tucked a curl behind her ear. "Anything else?"

Josie's pulse accelerated, sending her feelings into the express lane. She quickly headed for a detour. "I'm late for an appointment." *And much too late to start listening to my heart.*

Dear Reader,

I grew up in a house where the door was always open. Guests were welcome to stay a night or months. Our dinner table was full at every holiday. These shared moments with our family and friends became a special part of our lives.

The holidays are one of my favorite times of the year. Especially because it's a chance to reconnect with those people in your life that have come to mean so much. *In Love by Christmas* is a celebration of family at the holidays and, of course, romance. Josie Beck and Theo Taylor overcome a lot to discover feelings for each other and share perfect moments with the ones they love.

Wishing everyone a great holiday season!

I love to connect with readers. Check out my website at carilynnwebb.com to learn more about my upcoming books, sign up for email book announcements or chat with me on Facebook (carilynnwebb) or Twitter (@carilynnwebb). Remember to hug your friends and family for making these times special.

Happy reading!

Cari Lynn Webb

HEARTWARMING

In Love by Christmas

USA TODAY Bestselling Author

Cari Lynn Webb

HARLEQUIN® HEARTWARMING™

If you purchased this book without a cover you should be aware that this book is stolen property. It was reported as "unsold and destroyed" to the publisher, and neither the author nor the publisher has received any payment for this "stripped book."

Recycling programs for this product may not exist in your area.

ISBN-13: 978-1-335-51095-2

In Love by Christmas

This edition published by arrangement with Harlequin Books S.A.

For questions and comments about the quality of this book, please contact us at CustomerService@Harlequin.com.

HARLEQUIN®
www.Harlequin.com

Printed in U.S.A.

Cari Lynn Webb lives in South Carolina with her husband, daughters and assorted four-legged family members. She's been blessed to see the power of true love in her grandparents' seventy-year marriage and her parents' marriage of over fifty years. She knows love isn't always sweet and perfect—it can be challenging, complicated and risky. But she believes happily-ever-afters are worth fighting for. She loves to connect with readers.

Books by Cari Lynn Webb

Harlequin Heartwarming

City by the Bay Stories

The Charm Offensive
The Doctor's Recovery
Ava's Prize
Single Dad to the Rescue
A Heartwarming Thanksgiving
"Wedding of His Dreams"
Make Me a Match
"The Matchmaker Wore Skates"

Visit the Author Profile page
at Harlequin.com for more titles.

To my creative and talented nieces,
Kayla and Lexi. Have faith. Keep believing.
And always reach for the stars.

Special thanks to my writing tribe. To my family for their endless patience, support and letting me write on vacation. I love you guys!

CHAPTER ONE

"WE'RE THIRTY MINUTES into the workday and no one is at their desks." Theo Taylor wove through the open-concept offices of Coast to Coast Living's San Francisco headquarters. He glanced at his sister, who was beside him. "Was there a meeting I wasn't told about?"

"Looks like Mother is holding another one of her impromptu employee-wellness sessions." Adriana pointed at the crowd gathered outside a corner office and frowned. "Wonder what it is this week—parrot yoga, IV drips or detox teas?"

Employee wellness was fine and, in fact, encouraged, but not during work hours. Theo had explained that to his mother last week after he'd interrupted her crystal-stone-therapy session, and the week prior after he'd unplugged the blender and dismantled her charcoal-and-celery-juice presentation. Theo shook his head and veered toward his mother's office.

His assistant VP of marketing and his human-resources manager noticed Theo's approach and scurried away, avoiding his gaze. Several well-placed shoulder taps alerted their employees to his arrival and the crowd thinned.

"Ladies and gentlemen, perhaps lunchtime

would be more appropriate for this." Adriana's voice drifted from behind him.

Theo reached the glass wall of his mother's office and gaped. No time would ever be appropriate for this. *Ever.*

His mother stood on the cherry-wood coffee table, her cell phone perched in her hand and angled high above her head. Not unusual—his mother always had a firm grip on her cell phone. And the jeweled crown pinned in her black hair—even that could be overlooked. But…

Unease latched onto Theo like an extra shadow—the feeling was dense, cloying and unshakable. His mother wore a wedding gown. A very familiar, custom-made Linden Topher wedding dress that belonged to…

His sister reached his side and gasped. "She's wearing my gown."

Theo managed only an uncomfortable nod.

"Tell me this isn't happening." The sudden silence amplified Adriana's abrupt command.

Theo's words lodged in his throat.

"I won't wear the same wedding dress as Mother." His sister's voice lowered, as if they were standing in a crowded elevator. "Remember last Easter? She showed up at the charity egg hunt in the same dress I had on. I bet she already tried on *my* sample veil and shoes from Linden Topher, too."

That wasn't a bet Theo would take.

"She's not even engaged and she's already glowing like a new bride," Adriana snapped. She moved toward the closed office door. "Look at her blushing."

Theo set his hand on his sister's arm, stilling her and silencing the alarms clanging inside his head. "I'll take care of it."

"Mother declared at dinner last night she had to find the perfect dress for her next wedding." Adriana lifted her chin, the stiff movement not enough to hide the tremor in her mouth. "I didn't think she meant now, before she's even found her next groom."

Theo eased around Adriana, gripped the door handle and glanced back at his sister.

"I can't do it, Theo." Anger creased Adriana's forehead, making her eyebrows crinkle, but dismay wrinkled her voice. "I can't have her make a mockery of me."

His sister's waterlogged words undid him. Growing up, they'd ended many phone calls from their boarding schools exactly the same way: Adriana holding back tears and Theo promising to fix whatever needed fixing. He'd failed his sister back then. He refused to let down Adriana now. She deserved her own dream wedding—it was time for her to be the unique person she was, not a copycat. "You won't have to. Mia is waiting for us in your office. Meet her while I deal with this."

Theo never waited for his sister's agreement. He rushed inside his mother's office, slid his arm around her waist and helped her off the coffee table. "Mother. What are you doing?"

"Taking pictures of my partial wedding ensemble." Lilian Rose Taylor pressed a button on her cell phone and stretched her smile to radiant. "I saved the veil for later."

His mother had retained her beauty like a priceless piece of artwork that now required protection and delicate handling to ensure its value. "You're not engaged." His tone lacked the softness of white gloves.

"I've decided to change that." She paused to check her reflection in the glass. "Your sister shouldn't be the only one granted the magic of the season and a Christmas wedding."

Yes. Adriana should be granted all the magic she could grasp. This was his sister's moment. No one should steal it away, especially not their mother. Their mother had stolen their childhood. Now she lived in the in-law suite attached to Theo's house and expected to be obeyed like the parent she'd never wanted to be. "It's too late to plan a second Christmas wedding. There isn't enough time."

There also wasn't time for his mother's latest spectacle at the corporate headquarters for the lifestyle brand Theo had built. Too bad he couldn't simply edit out the wedding madness dominating his life. He had a business to grow and his mother—the wild card—made that difficult.

"Your sister is *still* planning her wedding." She tapped her crown back into place as if Theo's harsh words had knocked it askew. "Adriana has plenty of time to make her wedding happen."

Theo stared at the ceiling tiles, noted the tranquility posters his mother had tacked up there sometime that morning and tempered his voice. "Adriana also has a fiancé."

"I will, too." His mother took one measured step at a time along the length of the glass wall. As if she was walking the aisle of the city's oldest cathedral.

The glass walls made a stunning architectural statement, but they also put the occupants on constant display to the staff and visitors. And Theo's business associates—the ones from the TV network who were arriving any minute—would be very interested in his mother's current performance. Had that been his mother's agenda all along?

He wanted to believe his mother was only having a momentary lapse into wedding euphoria. But he'd learned as a child to trust his gut. And every cell inside him knew his mother never suffered momentary lapses into anything. She always jumped in with both heels and little consideration for the impact on everyone else.

He touched his mother's elbow, guided her away from the wall and any possible spectators and led her into the far corner. Then he willed his admin assistant to take the TV producers straight to his office and bypass the coffee bar that had a clear view into his mom's office.

His mother tilted her head and aimed her welcoming smile at the empty leather chair behind her desk, as if she was greeting a wedding guest. "I hired a discreet matchmaker."

Discretion wasn't part of Lilian Rose's makeup. "Was one of your potential match requirements 'must have wedding vows already memorized'?"

"I'm lonely, Theo." She cradled her cheek in her palm, her frown fragile. "Don't be insensitive."

Theo flinched. *As if claiming your own daughter's wedding gown for yourself wasn't insensitive enough.* Still, she was his mother.

And putting out fires wasn't just what he did at the company. "What matchmaker did you hire?"

"Daphne Holland." His mother swiped a clear, shimmery lip gloss across her mouth, supporting her sudden smile. "Holland Matchmakers was featured in last year's August edition. I thought I could be the featured cover story for next August's edition." His mother preened, her loneliness forgotten. "I've always wanted to be a cover story."

And apparently a Christmas bride, too. Theo ground his teeth together. "The August edition—"

"Can be changed," she interrupted. "For your own mother."

His own mother hadn't changed for her own son or daughter. Boarding schools and distance had been Lilian Rose Taylor's response to parenthood. Resentment smashed against his clenched teeth. Thanks to his parents, he'd grown up to be independent and self-reliant. More than comfortable standing on his own. *Being on his own.* Why, then, did he still want his mother's approval? "I want to meet with Daphne Holland."

"Wonderful." His mother pressed her hands under her chin and sighed as if he'd agreed to escort her down the aisle. Her voice was delicate and dreamy. "You could sign up, too. Then we could have a double feature in the August edition."

There wasn't going to be any Taylor featured in the August edition or any future magazine edition. There also wasn't going to be any matchmaking for himself. One Taylor on a love hunt was more than enough. Although his mother never mentioned love. But she looked more than camera-ready. "Between Adriana's wedding and running the company, I have enough on my plate."

"You're right. There's my wedding, too." His mother set her lip gloss into her purse and snapped the clutch closed. "After the holidays, you can sign up with Daphne. Then you can have your own Christmas love story next year."

The only thing Theo wanted for Christmas was a flawless wedding for his sister and a profitable year-end.

His admin, Fran, opened the office door. Her face never twitched at his mother's bridal outfit. Fran was a consummate professional. "Your nine o'clock is waiting in your office. Should I tell them you're running late?"

"It's Tuesday. Today is the meeting with the TV producers." His mother's unwavering gaze pinned Theo in place. "I'm just in time."

Theo blanched. He knew that nothing good

would happen if his mother joined him for the meeting. "I'll be right there."

His admin slipped out of the room and disappeared. Now Theo needed his mother to disappear. At the last production meeting with the network, Theo had insisted the Taylor family was nothing to showcase on the company's new TV series. His mother in her wedding paraphernalia could prove just the opposite.

Theo left his mother's office and searched the hallway. Mia stepped from Adriana's office, a camera clutched in her hand. He forced himself to lessen the panic in his tone. "Mia. I have a small situation and need your help."

More like an all hands on deck situation to distract his mother.

Mia Reid, one of his best contract photographers, waved and headed toward him.

Theo adjusted his smile. He was certain from the slight tilt of Mia's head that desperation widened his eyes and distorted his face. He ushered Mia into his mother's office and stationed himself in the doorway. "Mia, I was hoping you could take several pictures of my mother in her wedding gown."

Mia's eyebrows pulled together in slow motion as her sharp gaze shifted from his mother to Theo.

"I'm not in my full ensemble," his mother protested. "What about my veil?"

"But you should see the gown from all angles. You might want to pick a different length, or style of veil." Theo scrambled to latch onto reasonable arguments, then glanced down the hall at his closed office door. What if it opened? What if one of the TV producers stepped out for more coffee…? His words tripped out in a rush. "Mother, you want the perfect veil."

"You don't want your gown to command the entire frame—it'll take away from you, the bride." Mia jumped in as if *accomplished mind reader* was listed on her résumé. "After all, it's your wedding day, not the gown's."

"That's a valid point." His mother smoothed her hands over her waist and straightened. "Where should I stand?"

Theo owed Mia a bonus. If she hadn't already returned from her honeymoon last week, he'd have offered to pay for it. He mouthed a silent thank-you to Mia and slipped out.

Twenty minutes later, Theo stopped believing he'd convinced the TV producers that the Taylor family was nothing to showcase on the new series.

Caitlyn, one of the younger producers, who probably considered 80s music ancient, slipped on a pair of trendy reading glasses. The tortoiseshell frames that flared at the temples gave her a cat-woman vibe. "The show needs drama to push it to the next level."

Theo sat forward in his chair. "You all agreed the design elements speak to the show's aesthetic." And protected the brand he'd worked hard to build. A brand that did not include showcasing the shaky foundation—the imperfect side—of the Taylor family.

"It's still flat." Cat Woman narrowed her gaze on the slides spread out across the table. "We don't want the Coast to Coast Living program to be like every other design show on TV."

"There's little profit or longevity in that." Foster, the oldest producer, barely had five years on Theo. But the gentleman always wore a well-tailored suit and bow tie, and was fluent in numbers.

Turning a profit was Theo's skill. The TV network had assured Theo a TV series would benefit his company's profit line. Theo intended to hold the network to their word. "So, how do we make the show unique and make a profit?"

"We infuse the show with the Taylors." Cat Woman grinned, revealing all her very white, very straight teeth. "The real Taylors. For instance, Adriana has had quite the whirlwind romance—one reportedly not without its hiccups."

Theo folded his hands together and slowly

set them on the table, waiting for his abrasive response to stop whiplashing through him. Settled, he stretched his smile wide and lied. "The Taylors are already reflected in the show's products and room makeovers. We are the brand."

"Yes. Of course." Foster adjusted his bow tie. "But audiences like the behind-the-scenes peeks into families like yours. An inside view into your world."

This time a curse whiplashed through Theo. An inside view—*reality*—would ruin everything that Theo had built. Reality would prove their brand wasn't flawless and shrink their profits, not build them up.

After all, the Taylor family hardly lived the lifestyle the Coast to Coast Living brand embodied. The Taylor family was everything the brand was not. And everything Theo had always wished they'd been. He'd built an entire company around his childhood daydreams. From the positive response, customers wanted the same things: witty throw pillows, fast-paced game nights and harmony inside their homes. "I never agreed to a reality TV show."

"It's not a reality TV show per se." Foster fiddled with the end of his bow tie.

"We'll do preliminary footage here at the offices and around town to help determine the full cast," Cat Woman purred. "Then meet later this week to review the footage with you."

"You can set up that meeting with my admin." Theo stood. "If you'll excuse me, I have another meeting."

A meeting with a certain photographer and his mother. He needed his mother off the premises before she gave the producers even more ideas. Or, worse, proved their suspicions correct. Theo walked toward his mother's office and rubbed his forehead.

He'd transformed his father's local lifestyle newspaper insert into a national magazine and expanded the brand into over a dozen successful retail stores across the country. Surely he could control one TV series and capitalize on the audience to widen their brand's reach. And all without succumbing to the usual reality-TV mayhem. He had to.

He'd been pretending his family was perfect, like a sitcom, since he was a child. He'd built a business on those same fabrications, creating an image of the ideal family he'd been deprived of and transforming the Taylor family into a household brand. If he misstepped now, the brand would suffer. But success was all that mattered. All that people wanted from Theo.

Don't make me regret giving you the family business. The weight of his father's expectations still snagged into Theo's shoulders like iron hooks. It was a daily reminder that everything he did was for his family.

Theo stepped into his mother's office. Only Mia remained. She was sitting on the couch, her feet propped up on the coffee table. Worry seeped through him. "Where's my mother?"

"She stepped out." Mia focused on her camera. "And agreed to use the back stairwell to keep from revealing her wedding attire to even more of the employees. She promised to return quickly."

Theo stuffed his hands in the pockets of his dress pants. He'd give his mother five minutes, then start looking for her. "Sorry about this."

"Your mother is entertaining."

Exactly what the producers would love. And exactly what Theo would hate. "She can be."

Mia changed lenses on her camera. "Adriana told me that she now needs to find a new wedding-dress designer and rearrange all the other details of her wedding, too."

Theo pressed his arms into his sides, restraining his irritation. How could his mother be so selfish?

Mia shifted her camera and eyed him. "I know a designer."

Theo studied the photographer. He'd already

promised to help his sister. "That's rather convenient."

"It is, since you need one willing to work on a tight timeline and meet your sister's requests." Mia grinned at him.

Impatience scratched against his neck like an overstarched collar. He wanted Adriana's wedding over. He wanted his sister—the creative director of Coast to Coast Living—back full-time. He never wanted two brides. At the same time. Theo let his skepticism cut through his tone. "Your dressmaker can do that?"

Mia nodded. "She is up-and-coming."

"Is she any good?" Theo persisted.

"You'll find out that she's fabulous if you give her a chance," Mia said. "Josie just needs a break."

How many times had he heard that line? Theo rolled his shoulders, testing to see if he could handle one more person stepping over him to climb their own ladder of success. He hadn't blamed his past two girlfriends for their dreams. He wouldn't blame Mia's dressmaker, either.

"By the way, your mother went to pick out several wedding veils from your sister's sample collection in the second-floor workroom." Mia checked the time on her fitness tracker. "She should've been back already."

Theo strode to the door, once again intent on

intercepting his mother. He wasn't certain the TV producers were even out of the building. He glanced back at Mia. "One meeting. Only an hour. I'll look at your dressmaker's work. Set it up with Fran."

Surely he could find a better solution—a designer more qualified than Mia's friend. After all, an unknown designer could ruin his sister's perfect dream wedding. That wasn't a risk he was willing to take.

CHAPTER TWO

"I TOLD MOM that Chloe and Connor shouldn't be in the Christmas play with me." Seven-year-old Charlotte sat on Josie Beck's work stool in the back of The Rose Petal Boutique and spun herself in rapid circles. "The twins can't sit still. Ever."

The entire Cunningham family couldn't sit still.

Josie captured a curly-haired little boy around the waist, earned a squeal of giggles and hauled the four-year-old back onto the platform. She swiped the tie-dyed mouse pincushion from Chloe, her matching blond curls bouncing, and twirled the little girl beside her twin brother. Mrs. Cunningham used her hip to nudge a baby stroller around the photograph display at the front of Josie's boutique. The woman tossed toasted cereal to her eight-month-old baby with one hand and pressed her cell phone to her ear with the other. All without skipping a word in her animated conversation.

Josie wanted to skip all her appointments with the Curtain Call Children's Theater group if the Cunninghams foreshadowed her afternoon. The pint-size chaos ruined Josie's focus and kinked her patience.

But she'd drained her account to make December rent that morning. January's payment loomed like a personal rain cloud.

Every alteration mattered. Every costume design mattered. Every client mattered. But every family mattered, too.

Josie positioned Connor on the platform in front of the floor-to-ceiling mirrors and lifted his arms. Resolved to do her best for the troupe, she said, "Stand like an airplane."

"Airplanes don't stand." Charlotte stretched her arms out in her Mrs. Claus costume and her mischievous grin even wider. "Airplanes fly."

The twins lifted their arms as if on cue and zoomed off the platform, weaving around Josie. Josie clenched her measuring tape and squeezed her shout back inside of her.

Charlotte spun the stool in the opposite direction and tilted her head back to ogle the ceiling. "The twins love airplanes and ice cream."

Josie loved clients that stood still. Appointments that stayed on schedule. And harbored a soft spot for a certain seven-year-old girl, who refused to take off her Mrs. Claus costume.

Connor clipped Josie's dress form, his chubby fingers catching on a strapless burgundy winter ball gown. The one waiting for Josie to hem and add sparkle to with a jeweled waistband. The one her client intended to pick up later that week, as promised. Josie settled the dress form and steered Connor up onto the platform. She tacked sincerity and confidence into her voice, then improvised. "I bet if you stand really still and let me take these measurements for your costumes, your mom will get you ice cream."

Chloe crash-landed into the back of Josie's legs.

Charlotte chanted, "Mayday. Mayday."

That was the same chant of Josie's checking account. Utility bills were due in ten days. Josie had to complete the costumes for the children's theater production of *Rudolph*, Somerset Playhouse's *Scrooge* performance and an expanding pile of alterations. If only that was enough to turn a profit. Worry sheared through her, weakening her knees and sapping her hope. Rent in San Francisco was high, but it meant she had easy access to more clients.

Josie shook the bells on the curved end of a sample elf hat, locked her knees and shifted her attitude. Gloom never quite fit her—it was like a poorly tailored dress, cinching in some places, sagging in others. "Let's skip the measurements and try on fun hats instead."

"Chloe won't put that on." Certainty pushed out Charlotte's chin.

Josie jingled the bells again, seeking her holiday cheer and best smile for the spirited little girl. Josie's favorite foster mom, Mimi Sims, had never forced her smiles and had always hugged without restraint. "Can I just set this on your head? One quick second."

Chloe grabbed the elf hat and smashed it under her faux-fur boots. "No hat."

Josie rubbed her temples and slid her gaze to Charlotte. "Will Connor try it on?"

"He does what Chloe does." Charlotte crossed her legs and tapped one glitter-painted fingernail on her chin. "But they might put it on for bubble gum."

"Bubble gum." Josie quickly ran through the contents of her purse. "I don't have bubble gum."

Charlotte shrugged. "They aren't allowed to have it, anyway. Last summer, Chloe stuck her bubble gum in Connor's hair. Then Connor chewed a bunch of pieces and smashed it all in Chloe's hair."

Josie sank onto the platform. She'd almost started another bubble-gum war. Clearly, she needed to be better prepared—and equipped—for children clients in her boutique. Yet this was the happy chaos of a big family. A chaos she'd always wanted. An ache curled through that soft spot.

"Mom had to smear peanut butter in the twins' hair." Charlotte warmed to her story. Delight flashed through her voice. "Mom even used the whole jar. But the gum never came out."

Josie might never finish this appointment. Then she might never become a custom dressmaker. All her hard work as a daytime housecleaner and evening waitress for almost two years, all the overtime shifts and every missed meal to save enough money to open the boutique, would be wasted. And her ex-husband's family would be right: she didn't have what it took to be more than a seamstress in a strip mall.

Josie swiped her hand over her eyes, attempting to wipe away the obstacles of the past and focus on the obstacles in front of her. If she failed now, she'd prove more than her ex and his family right. But Josie wasn't *that* foster kid anymore, either. She concentrated on Charlotte, raising her voice over the stinging taunts of her childhood. "What did your mother do?"

"Both the twins had to have their hair shaved off." Charlotte leaned forward and patted her own head. Regret tugged down the edges of her bottom lip. "Chloe had to wear a hat forever, even though it scratched her naked head."

No wonder the poor child hated hats. "Is there any way to make them stand still?"

"Chocolate." Charlotte never hesitated. Never blinked. Her tone contained only authority.

The kids were already walking sugar rushes. "Can they have chocolate?"

"No." Charlotte pointed at her chest, her blond eyebrows rising along with her grin. "But I can."

Josie eyed the girl, appreciating the child's crafty negotiations. Josie could use the seven-year-old's skills. "If I give you chocolate, will you help me with your brother and sister?"

"That depends." Charlotte adjusted the white apron of her Mrs. Claus costume. "What kind of chocolate do you have?"

One year, Josie had refused to take off the princess costume Mimi had sewn for her on Halloween. Every day after school, Mimi had a full tea party, complete with minicakes and cider, and her princess gown ready for Josie. Mrs. Cunningham offered a distracted wave aimed more at the empty dressing room than her oldest daughter and nudged the stroller in the opposite direction. Once again, she never missed a word in her phone call. No full tea party waited for Charlotte at home.

"I have a king-size chocolate-and-almond bar." Josie had stuffed the candy bar in her purse that morning for lunch. The twin cause was worth the sacrifice. "And a new bag of chocolate drops."

Charlotte glanced at the front of the store. "I can help for chocolate drops."

"Deal." Josie jumped up. She had no tea party prepared, but she could provide an all-you-can-eat chocolate experience. "Why don't you change behind those curtains and I'll fill up the candy dish?"

"I can eat them now?" Wonder widened Charlotte's eyes.

"As many as you want, as long as you change." Josie pointed at the pristine white apron of Charlotte's costume. Mimi had convinced Josie that grass stains on the playground would ruin the princess costume. Josie had relented and worn the dress only after school. "You might be Mrs. Claus and known for baking all sorts of treats for the elves, but you don't want chocolate stains on your outfit before your big stage debut."

Charlotte disappeared behind the thick velvet curtains of the dressing room. Josie grinned at the twins. "One more round of airplane."

The twins took off, increasing their flight pattern to include a full circle around one of the rolling wedding dress racks and a flyby of Josie's bridal accessory wall. Josie dumped the bag of chocolate candy into a glass bowl and set the candy dish on the small table next to the vintage fainting couch. She reserved the candy for tired brides, coming in after long work shifts for their final wedding dress fittings.

If the candy rescued her now, she'd stock up for future fittings for children and brides alike.

Twenty minutes later, Josie waved the twins goodbye and earned a big chocolate-infused hug from Charlotte. Their mother covered her phone with her hand and thanked Josie for her time and hard work.

Josie walked to the bridal fitting area and dropped onto the fainting couch. Tin-foil candy wrappers crinkled underneath her. She tipped her head and checked the pocket-watch wall clock hanging from a chain on the wall. Fifteen minutes until the next family arrived for their costume fittings. Could she make it to the corner store and back for a candy-dish refill? She also had to finish the burgundy ball gown, suit pants and six other alterations for clients to pick up tomorrow.

The bells on the front door chimed. A familiar voice shouted, "Josie. Where are you?"

In an alteration abyss. Josie called out, "In the back."

Mia Reid—formerly Mia Fiore—and Josie's friend and business roommate spoke over the chiming bells. "The front door is sticking again. We need to get it fixed."

Josie added the door repair to the bottom of

her to-do list, after paying the bills and finding more clients. Josie had welcomed Mia and her start-up photography business into her boutique a year ago. In the past few months, Mia's business had grown from portraits to events like society weddings and corporate gatherings and, most recently, still-life photographs for the global lifestyle magazine *Coast to Coast Living*. Josie celebrated Mia's success and wanted her good friend to thrive.

She just wanted to celebrate her own success, too. But Josie's bridal boutique and custom-dressmaker services had stalled somewhere between formal gown alterations and resizing everyday work wear.

Mia dropped her camera equipment near her photography displays and skipped toward Josie. Mia had been skipping since she'd recited her wedding vows three weeks ago. She punched her arms over her head like a cheerleader celebrating her team's game-winning touchdown. "I have the absolute best news ever."

Josie brushed candy wrappers onto the floor and dropped her arm over her eyes. How could she be so exhausted from only one kid appointment? She had more than a dozen to go—she was going to require a warehouse of chocolate. "Unless it involves a wealthy Prince Charming sweeping me off my feet, it can't be the absolute best news ever."

"You always tell me you can stand fine on your own two feet," Mia argued. "No sweeping required."

Josie peeked at her friend from under her arm. "Maybe I changed my mind."

Mia laughed, the sound infectious and bright. "You're telling me you've given up your dream to be the city's go-to dressmaker, become wealthy on your own and live happily-ever-after exactly as you want?"

Josie frowned and wished the candy bowl wasn't empty. The foster-care system had taught her the only person she could rely on was herself. Her disastrous marriage had reinforced that lesson. She hadn't forgotten. "Not exactly."

"Then listen to my best news ever." Mia tugged on Josie's arm, pulling her to a sitting position.

Josie rearranged the ends of her long silk scarf and rolled her shoulders—the ones she relied on that hadn't failed her yet. "Let's hear it."

"Adriana Taylor needs a new wedding-dress designer." Mia plucked one of Josie's consignment wedding gowns from the rack and held it in front of her.

"Adriana Taylor has fired more than a dozen designers." Josie crossed her arms over her chest and eyed the dress Mia held. If she removed the long sleeves, added a deep side split and sweeping train, she'd transform the gown. Lace appliqués and a sheer back would upscale it. Was that fashion-forward or fashion-yesterday? A bride would likely alter Josie's vision. It was better to let the bride decide on the modifications, using the original vintage gown as the base. "That isn't a surprise about Adriana."

Mia stuck the dress on the crowded rack and faced Josie. "Will you be surprised when I tell you that *you* are going to be Adriana Taylor's new wedding-gown designer?"

Josie finally understood the purpose of the antique fainting couch. A burst of joy shook her, but just as quickly, fear frayed her excitement. *What if she wasn't…?* "Me?"

Josie could hardly tame a pair of four-year-olds. How was she supposed to handle Adriana Taylor, rumored to be one of the city's leading bridezillas? Word had spread through the fashion industry about the Taylor sibling, reaching even Josie's small-time boutique.

"Yes. *You.*" Enthusiasm infused Mia's movements and voice. "Theo Taylor's assistant is going to call you to confirm a time this week for you to show the Taylors your designs."

"This week." Doubt and unease soaked through Josie's words.

"I don't know your schedule so I couldn't just set up the appointment." Mia twisted her long hair into a bun and fastened it with a jeweled clip Josie had created. The only original thing Josie had created in the past six months.

Anytime this week was too soon. Josie lacked inspiration. The last few months she'd been upscaling used wedding gowns for budget-strained brides, not creating her own fashions. She doubted Theo's sister wanted a used gown, however updated it was. "Why do the Taylors want me?"

"Because I told them you're the best designer in the city." Mia looked herself over in the floor-to-ceiling mirror and grinned at Josie.

Josie absorbed her friend's compliment like a cat curled in the sunshine, grateful Mia believed in her. If only Mia's confidence could chase away Josie's uncertainty. "That was kind."

"And the truth," Mia said. "You're up for this, right? You know what this means?"

She could pay next month's rent on time, and the month after that. Launch her custom dressmaking business rather than suffocating one alteration at a time. "I'm stunned. I'm still processing."

"Well, process faster. If you design an original gown for Adriana, I get to shoot the June wedding edition, cover to cover." Mia swung around to face her. "And you'll get billing and your own spread in the issue."

"That's…" Josie faltered. If she failed, she'd let down Mia, too. Her friend—one of her only friends. How would Josie ever forgive herself? How would Mia ever forgive her? Josie touched her forehead as if that would stop the sudden spinning.

"Incredible. I can't wait to tell Wyatt." Mia pumped her fists. "This can launch your business and mine to the next level."

Josie wanted the next level. Needed the next level. Now wasn't the time to discover a sudden fear of heights. Still, worry swept through her and her stomach swayed.

"And you can come with me to the Coast to Coast Living holiday gala," Mia said. "It's the networking event of the year."

Josie concentrated on Mia's composed voice and optimism to counterbalance her own fear. The Coast to Coast Living holiday gala was one of the premier events in the city. The Taylor family invited every vendor, retailer and contractor who'd helped make their global magazine and lifestyle brand a success. Invitations were coveted. Opportunities to meet other business leaders were exceptional. That disquiet slowly returned.

There are no shortcuts to success, Josie. And the climb isn't always comfortable, either.

Wise words from Mimi. Josie had pricked her finger on a needle during their sewing lessons. A glittery Band-Aid, sugar cookies and a trip to the fabric store had righted Josie's world and convinced her she'd master sewing, the same as Mimi.

Josie poked a stray pin into the mouse pincushion on the side table and popped the doubt bubble inside her. "Looks like I need to start designing a wedding gown."

"Any chance you could design dresses for us, too?" Mia swept her hands over her waist as if she was wearing a formal ball gown, not jeans and a sweater. "We could arrive at the gala in Josie Beck originals and be walking billboards of your work."

Josie had chosen her studio apartment for the unexpected large walk-in closet—a closet she'd filled with clothes she'd designed and sewn between shifts and many sleepless nights the past few years. Dresses, pants, jackets—all designed for a specific occasion and yet never worn. Josie hadn't actually been invited to any of those special events.

Until now.

So far, she'd created her clothes for her own joy. Every hand stitch, every embroidered thread, every hand-dyed fabric made those hours between midnight and sunrise a little less lonely. “I need to concentrate on the wedding dress first.”

“That wasn’t a no. I’ll take it.” Mia gave Josie a quick and easy hug. “This is ranking up there to be one of the best days ever.”

Josie had to find inspiration and fast. Or this would become one of her worst moments ever.

CHAPTER THREE

"I'M ALL BOOKED UP, Mr. Taylor, until next fall. Best of luck to you." The dial tone ended Theo's conversation.

His prior conversations had circled around variations of the same theme.

Oh, this is for Adriana? I just noticed there's a conflict on the schedule.

Even for that price, Mr. Taylor, I cannot find more hours in the work week. And I would need infinite hours to meet Adriana's exacting standards.

I fear Adriana and I would clash, Mr. Taylor. Our aesthetics do not align, as it were. That can be very unpleasant.

Each phone call had been a dead end. Each one an unavailable wedding-dress designer. That totaled nine well-established designers unavailable or unwilling to work with Adriana. Theo was two hours into his workday and already things were descending into the discouraging and disappointing column.

If the designers on both coasts knew about Adriana's reputation as difficult and micromanaging, then the TV producers likely knew, too.

A city bus shuddered to a stop on the street

corner behind Theo. The gasping squeal of the brakes ratcheted his headache to another level. Theo's phone rang. "Fran, tell me you found someone."

Fran's bluntness cut through the speaker. "No available dress designers."

He rubbed his forehead. "What about my mother?"

"She's refusing to let me return the exclusive Linden Topher wedding gown. She's intent on getting married, Theo." Fran's tone was resolute.

Theo switched his phone to his other ear and pulled a business card from his pocket. He checked the address printed on the card and continued down the sidewalk. Frustration quickened his strides. "Tell me something good, at least, Fran. What did you find out about Josie Beck?"

"Josie is the sole owner of The Rose Petal Boutique." Fran paused. The sound of her rapid typing drifted in the background. "It's a unique consignment wedding-dress shop for every bride."

Good news would've been Josie Beck had earned a bachelor's degree in fashion design or apprenticed in top fashion houses in Europe. Theo clenched his phone and stared at the vintage exterior of The Rose Petal Boutique drooping in front of him.

He was anything but charmed.

The boutique reminded him of a neglected stepchild. The run-down building was smashed between two vibrant, profitable older sisters, their buildings renovated and restored. The boutique signage was simple and faded. The paint around the wood molding on the front windows was cracked, chipped and dingy.

If he was interested in an instant makeover, he'd paint the exterior lavender to help the small building blossom like a vibrant, rare rosebush on the block.

But his sister needed a wedding gown.

And Theo needed to know an unknown designer was worth his trust.

Theo tugged on the door handle. The warped front door never budged. Perhaps that was all the proof he required about Josie Beck. Certainly, if the boutique owner wanted more customers, even sidewalk window-shoppers, she would have repaired her door. Wedged as it was in the door frame, the welcome sign in the window should've read Go Away.

Theo yanked harder and forced the door open. A set of bells chimed and a woman's voice called out from the back of the store, "Welcome to Rose Petal. I'll be with you in a minute."

There was nothing bland about the woman's cheerful acknowledgment. Her voice, crisp and colorful, like the holiday celebrations featured in the December edition of *Coast to Coast*, invited Theo to linger and explore the boutique. Too bad she wasn't outside on the sidewalk, greeting window-shoppers and drawing in potential customers.

Familiar photographs on a maze of wire-rack displays, stood before Theo and he frowned. The space was completely misused. Even worse, Mia's talent as a photographer wasn't being highlighted. That wasn't the point. Theo was well-versed in Mia Reid's talent. It was Josie Beck that concerned him.

Theo wove through the wire-rack maze, following the sound of voices in the back. He paused in front of a framed photograph of a blond woman and a mixed-breed dog, given its patchwork of brown, black and white fur. The dog's paws rested on the woman's shoulders as his pink tongue swiped across her cheek. The woman's head was tipped back, her smile calling.

Theo leaned forward, then caught himself. He glanced around, prepared to argue—*of course, I hadn't been edging closer to see if I could hear the woman's sunny laughter. That would be impossible*. Still, he lingered until he scowled. He'd never been charmed by a picture before.

Theo stepped around the last row of displays and glanced toward the floor-to-ceiling mirrors.

A tall brunette stood on the platform, facing the mirrors. A woman, her blond hair tied back with a frayed piece of plaid fabric, wrestled a gown's enormous white bow into submission, revealing the one redeeming element of the dress—a low-cut back. Then she gathered the bulky white skirt to tighten the outdated wedding dress around the brunette's curves.

"Do you see it, Shanna?" The blond woman flattened one of the puffy white shoulders the way Theo used to smash a toasted marshmallow between graham crackers at summer camp.

Theo tilted his head. All he saw was that obnoxiously large bow popping free of the woman's grip like a broken jack-in-the-box and an excess of ribbons. How had the woman convinced the bride-to-be to try on such an unappealing gown?

The blond woman folded the bow in indignant pleats, forcing it out of sight. She rattled off a series of alterations, her free hand sweeping gracefully along the woman's side. "Can you envision the dress you described to me? The one we drew together."

"I see it, Josie." Hesitation slowed the woman's words.

Josie Beck.

Everything slowed and rolled inside Theo as if he'd tripped over a speed bump. His focus locked onto the blonde with the colorful voice, but she couldn't stop his fall into captivation.

"That's wonderful." Josie rose on the tips of her boots and peeked over the shoulder of the woman she'd called Shanna. "It's enough if you can see it in your mind right now."

"But I can't afford all these changes to the dress, Josie."

Josie released the heavy skirt and stepped around the cascade of fabric to face the Shanna.

The brunette's height concealed Josie's face, but not the tremor in her voice.

"The dress itself is in your budget, right?" Josie asked.

The woman nodded.

Josie moved closer to Shanna, her face still hidden, but her sure voice more than clear. "Then that's all you need to pay for."

Theo rubbed his chin as if he'd done a face-plant, after all. At the very least, Josie should've inquired if the woman had any woodworking skills. Then Josie could have gotten her front door repaired in exchange for the dress alterations. A business arrangement should always benefit both parties. *Always*.

Complimentary services had a place, but not if the business suffered more loss than profit. From the drab exterior to the dated interior,

Theo guessed The Rose Petal Boutique was more in the red than the black.

"Penny told me you were an angel. She told me you'd help me out." Shanna covered her face, her shoulders trembling. Tears splashed against her cheeks, her voice barely a whisper. "I never expected..."

Theo never expected compassion and generosity—it was a compliment and a criticism. A kind heart had no place in business. The weak allowed their emotions to guide their decisions. Theo had stopped being weak in grade school—the summer after his grandmother's death. The same summer his parents had refused to let him come home. *Life rewards the self-reliant, Theo.*

Theo backed away.

Josie could keep her kind heart. If she wanted to thrive in the business world and even survive in the upheaval produced by the Taylor family, she needed to develop a harder edge.

"This is the start of your new life." Josie moved around her client, gathered the bulky train and guided the woman off the platform. Sincerity and resolve fused her words into a convincing argument. "Your wedding day has to be everything you ever dreamed, including your dress."

Shanna offered Josie a watery thank-you before they disappeared inside the dressing room.

Theo had given his sister the very same promise. A wedding to surpass her dreams. He narrowed his gaze on the thick velvet curtains of the single dressing room.

Could Josie transform the chaotic mess of a dress the woman wore into her dream gown? Could she keep her promise? Theo wasn't sure.

Josie would need to create an original gown—one that met Theo's standards—and deliver it finished and ready to wear in less than three weeks. But if the woman insisted on giving away her services for free, word would no doubt spread. Then she'd be stuck in a backlog of charity work. Surely Josie wanted more than to recycle old wedding gowns at a steep discount. Surely Josie valued her work. Unless the dressmaker wasn't that good.

A tic of irritation pulsed along his jaw. Theo glanced around the space, skipping his gaze over the worn Victorian violet-print couch, the bridal accessory shelves and twin rolling racks bursting with secondhand wedding dresses. Certainly, Josie wouldn't be so careless with her own creations. If she had any.

Disappointment settled in. He wasn't seeing anything original. Surely Josie wanted her work displayed. That would give her clients confidence in her skill and ability as a custom dressmaker.

That would reassure him, too. He pulled out his cell phone, certain there were other designers he hadn't considered. He'd given his word to Adriana. He couldn't rely on a timid, softhearted dressmaker who doubted herself.

The women emerged from the dressing room. The bride-to-be tugged a knit cap over her long brunette hair. "Josie, you have to come to the wedding. You have to be *in* the wedding."

"That's very kind." Josie handed Shanna a thick wool scarf. "You have more to think about than me and I need to concentrate on getting your dress ready for your wedding day."

Josie also needed to concentrate on turning a profit. Wasn't that the point of a successful business? That was how a business owner earned respect and discovered their value.

Shanna faced the floor-length mirrors and wrapped the long scarf around her neck. "What now?"

Theo should leave and continue his search to find a designer he believed in. One capable of creating and completing an exclusive gown for Adriana in a tight time frame. A gown worthy of the Coast to Coast Living brand.

Josie carried the wedding gown out of the dressing room. Her one arm was completely concealed within the dense layers of ribbons and lace, much like the uncertainty that camouflaged any guarantee in her voice. "I'll call you for the next fitting in about two weeks."

About was very indefinite. *About* invited suspicion and doubt into a client's mind. That was never good. Would Josie call the woman in ten days or closer to three weeks as both dates fell into the about time frame? Theo never liked sliding time frames. Too much room for error and misinterpretation. He preferred to work with people who committed to a specific date and delivered on their promise.

"I can't wait." The bride-to-be brushed past Theo, her face bundled up to her eyes, and disappeared outside.

Theo returned his attention to the photograph of the woman and the dog. Once again, he searched for the reason this one simple picture fascinated him. It was more than the perfectly placed lighting. Or the backdrop. Or the vibrant subjects. If he'd been asked to give a definition for *carefree*, he'd have chosen the picture. But he'd never been carefree in his life. Never considered such an impractical sentiment until now.

"Sorry to keep you waiting. Mia's work is exceptional." Josie appeared beside Theo and pointed to a photograph. "Are you thinking about hiring her?"

"I already have." It was the woman beside Theo that worried him. He turned toward Josie, extended his hand and, for the first time since middle school, stumbled over his own name.

Her blue eyes were too round, her smile too honestly genuine, her face too guileless. And those wisps of blond hair brushing against her pale cheeks—he'd bet anything the soft curls were natural. She was too natural. Too refreshing. Even more distracting than the photograph. The photograph *she* was featured in. The one that now seemed to be laughing at him. "Theo Taylor," he finally managed to say.

She reached for her scarf, rather than his hand. The silk fabric loosened around her neck as her fingers tangled in the frayed ends, as if she was struggling to hide something. "This is an unexpected surprise. I wasn't aware we'd confirmed a meeting time."

She was an unexpected surprise. Theo avoided surprises. He never liked the disruption that surprises caused in his routine. Knowing what to expect in any given situation gave him the advantage and that was often the difference between winning or losing. He followed her toward the fitting area. "Can I offer you some business advice? You really shouldn't give your services away for free."

Josie draped the measuring tape around her

neck, letting the ends twist around her scarf. Disapproval twisted through her voice. "You really shouldn't eavesdrop on conversations that don't affect you."

He shrugged. "Free services are not a sustainable business model. There is no profit in *free*."

She walked into her workroom and rolled a dress form in front of her. She eyed him as if he was more distasteful than Shanna's secondhand wedding dress. "You probably haven't heard of Penny's Place."

The annoyance in her tone set him back. She dared to judge to him. Dared to make herself even more appealing. He centered his focus on her, letting his gaze narrow. "Coast to Coast Living has donated to Penny's Place every year for the past decade. Penny is well-known for the sanctuary she provides to women in need of a safe place to recover and rebuild their lives."

"But you've never spent time inside Penny's Place," she said. "Never met any of the women who live there."

He didn't have to stand inside Penny's Place to understand the value of Penny's nonprofit organization. The Taylor family and Coast to Coast Living supported many charitable organizations in the city and around the country. He wouldn't defend himself to her. "I have not."

"Shanna Jennings—the bride-to-be that just

stood on this platform—recently moved out of Penny's Place." Josie set her hand on the body form as if to find her balance. Anguish creased her forehead, pulling her eyebrows together. "Her story isn't mine to share. Shanna has more than earned a fairy-tale wedding. I have the opportunity to be a small part of her new life. That means something to me."

She had an opportunity to turn a profit, too, and chose not to. Josie acted as if she was being granted permission to work for Shanna, not doing Shanna a large favor. A *very large, very free* favor.

Josie Beck was obviously a good person. But charity should never stand in the way of profit. Everything had its place. Charity was separate from the daily tasks and standard practices of any business.

He couldn't recall the last time he'd done something for free. Something for the simple pleasure it gave him. He always considered the business first. Always considered the corporation's bottom line. *Always*. And he wouldn't go soft now because of some selfless, misguided wisp of a dressmaker no matter how much she charmed him.

He picked up the design book that was lying open on the corner of the platform. The drawing was similar to how she'd described the alterations to Shanna. He could almost envision the finished dress. *Almost.*

He flipped through more pages. Nothing sparked inside him. Nothing leaped from the page and commanded his attention. He wanted more for Adriana. He needed more for his sister's wedding. His sister might be getting married, but Coast to Coast Living would be reflected in every detail of the day. Perfection was expected.

Josie might be appealing, but Theo feared she lacked the experience and sophistication required for such an event. "I'm sorry for interrupting your morning, but I don't see anything suitable for my sister."

She yanked the book out of Theo's hands. Her fingers clutched the binder and it seemed as if she was debating whether or not to bash him on the side of the head. "These designs are for my current clientele, modest and affordable." He could hear the irritation in her voice. Her words came out like finely sharpened tacks.

Theo crossed his arms over his chest, blocking her barbs. He refused to be swayed. "And not original."

She pressed her design book into the seat cushion of the couch and held her position.

"You're using the base of consignment dresses to build from," he accused. He couldn't back down. He'd given his word to his sister. Not to mention the other promises he'd made. He had a family and company to protect. "Rather than the dresses being your own work from start to finish."

She straightened and faced him. Anger lit her gaze. "When I'm finished, you won't be able to tell where the vintage dress ends and the current one begins."

He doubted that. He didn't doubt that Josie Beck was much too interesting.

"Come back for Shanna's final fitting." She lifted her chin, straightened her shoulders and met his gaze: challenge for challenge. Nothing timid about her. "Then you can judge me."

"I might just do that." Not because he wanted to see her again. Only because he wanted to prove her wrong. "But I don't know when that fitting will be. About two weeks isn't a very definitive date. Now if you'll excuse me, I have scheduled meetings to attend."

She blocked his path. "I only need to meet Adriana and I can design an exclusive gown for her." Her voice dipped into that hard-nosed, implacable business edge he often relied on to get the results he expected.

Theo gaped at her. Why wasn't she backing down? This small-time boutique owner, more concerned about her goodwill deeds than ensuring a profit. "Excuse me."

"I'd like to meet Adriana before you dismiss

my work," she repeated in that same inflexible tone. She stretched out her words as if she were stretching out her backbone. Theo approved and moved toward her, certain she wouldn't back away. He hadn't enjoyed a business meeting this much since...

He stopped abruptly. Business was business. Not fun. Not playful. Definitely not joyful.

Still, one meeting was all she was asking for. She was talented, at least reflected in her drawing book. Besides, he already had an idea stirring for Josie Beck. One that would boost her boutique and career without jeopardizing his sister's perfect wedding. He could be kind when he chose to. And make a profit. "Lunch tomorrow at Jasmine Blue Café. Eleven thirty." He motioned to her sketchbook on the couch. "If you have original designs not inside your book, bring those, too."

Theo detoured around her and walked out of the boutique. A smile tripped across his mouth. Josie Beck intrigued him. Lunch couldn't arrive soon enough.

CHAPTER FOUR

JOSIE STOOD OUTSIDE Jasmine Blue Café. A familiar man exited a cab across the street. *Theo Taylor.* Her gaze sealed on his charcoal gray topcoat, she noted how he'd perfected his top executive image. Theo's height refused to allow him to blend easily into the crowd on the sidewalk. Confidence flowed from his sure stride and straight back. Theo seemed to broadcast to every stranger around him that they could rely on his sturdy shoulders for whatever they needed.

That was only an illusion. Josie straightened her own shoulders.

Solid financial reports, obtainable budgets and high profit margins inspired men like Theo. Josie recognized his type. She'd been married to the same kind of man for four years. Her husband never understood her. Eventually, she understood she'd never be treated as anything more than an expense line in his world.

Josie, please keep your handmade clothes in the downstairs bedroom closet. Hobbies are for amateurs and best kept to oneself. After all, there's no profit in a hobby.

Being a starving artist wasn't Josie's goal. Her

ex had considered himself a hero for rescuing Josie from her waitressing job and agreeing to marry her. Perhaps if she'd earned that business degree and made money on her clothing line, then he'd have accepted her. But she'd wanted more than acceptance in her marriage and that had been her error.

The hope Mimi had put into Josie as a child had been doused with a dose of reality from her ex. But Josie believed she could move on and prosper. She clutched her design book and the new sketches she'd spent most of the night drawing. She refused to let Theo Taylor take that away from her.

"Josie Beck." Theo stepped toward the entrance to the café and unbuttoned his jacket. The formality never gone from his tone. "Right on time."

"Mr. Taylor." Josie tried to use the same stiff detachment. She adjusted her design book under one arm, then the other. The book poked into her side, triggering a flinch in her bravado. "Thank you for arranging this lunch."

Theo nodded, opened the café door and motioned her inside.

Josie passed by him, inhaled a trace of his crisp cologne and her reserve slipped. She wanted to linger, right there beside him in the doorway like the infatuated girl she'd never been. Hardly professional. Business meetings required more decorum. She held her breath and walked toward the hostess counter.

A waitress guided them to a private table tucked near the back of the restaurant, but offered an outdoor view. Across the street, a cable car rolled to a stop. Locals jumped off and even more tourists climbed on.

Theo pulled out a chair for Josie, then sat in the one right beside her. Specials of the day were recited. Drink orders placed. After a promise from the waitress to return for their lunch orders once their other guest arrived, Josie and Theo were alone.

Theo nodded toward her design book. "Shall we get to the designs?"

"Should we wait for Adriana?" Or wait until Josie's confidence stopped slipping through her fingers like silk thread.

"My sister is running late." Irritation twitched across his thin mouth, pinching into the edges of his cool gaze. He eyed Josie, his eyebrows lifted as if he recognized Josie wanted to stall and dared her to try.

Josie slid back in the chair and propped her back against the plump cushion.

Judgment waited. Right beside her. Worse, he smelled so good, like the last breath before the sun dipped into the bay. Why did she have to notice that? Now every time she inhaled the ocean breeze, she'd recall this moment. Relive this moment.

Keeping her breaths shallow, Josie pulled two sheets of paper from her book. The top corner bent on the second design like a bad omen. Josie tried to smooth out the crease as if that might unwrinkle her own unease.

Theo gently tugged the designs out of her grip. That unease accelerated, sweeping anxiety from her fingertips to her toes. Her cute suede booties were useless against the assault. She needed steel-toed boots for this task.

So much hinged on this moment: her future as a dress designer. Mia's success. The boutique. Her chin quivered, sinking toward her chest.

Now Theo held her work. The silence suffocated Josie. Or perhaps that was the impending rejection. Had she created a dress for any bride, or something special enough for Adriana? She should've never added the ombré tulle. Or the cap sleeves.

Josie pressed her damp palms against her legs, stilling the urge to flee on a passing cable car. She had often wondered if that A- in math had given away the truth: she hadn't been—and still wasn't—perfect. Families she'd come in contact with, looking to adopt, had only wanted perfect children.

Theo Taylor wanted perfection.

Her pulse chased through her body like short-circuited Christmas lights, igniting every nerve inside her. Her gaze fixed on a corner of the restaurant, the space empty and wasted. She blurted, "Fountain."

"Excuse me," Theo said.

"Sorry. Bad habit. I've been working on a mental filter since grade school."

"How old were you when you decided you needed a mental filter?" The slight curiosity in his voice echoed the obligatory interest of so many distracted caseworkers she'd met with throughout the years.

"Seven. I was at an adoption fair." Those fair days had always made her heart race and her stomach queasy. Like right now.

"You were at an adoption fair?" Theo set the designs on the table and shifted toward her. His gaze settled fully on her, his interest no longer cursory.

Josie's stomach turned inside out. "Several. I grew up in the foster system."

Theo's gaze searched her face, unblinking and somber.

Josie rushed on, skimming over the inevitable pity he was sure to aim her way. Business luncheons had no place for pity. Or outbursts. Or distressing backstory. That filter failed her again. "I brought my report card and artwork with me to the adoption fair to show potential families."

To prove to those potential families that she was more than a reserved little girl. More than the label of being withdrawn that had been stuck on her.

Now she was only showing Theo her insecurities. Her words kept spilling out. "A woman picked up my paperwork. I panicked, grabbed my artwork and yelled, 'bathroom.'"

Josie had escaped into the girls' bathroom, unwilling to wait for the disappointment and the forthcoming rejection by another stranger. Before Theo could react, she added, "A fountain would be nice in that empty corner over there."

Preferably a fountain large enough for Josie to sink herself and her mortification into.

"I'll mention the fountain to the owners when I see them next." His voice was gruff, as if charred by an iron. "And, Josie, those families that didn't adopt you—they lost out."

Josie nodded, realigning her focus. Tears had no place in business luncheons, either.

He returned his attention to the designs. Tension moved across his face, from his firm jaw to his thin mouth. Deep concentration perhaps. Or the look of displeasure.

Josie adjusted the copper brooch on her hand-knit royal blue scarf. She should've worn her only business suit, a leftover from her marriage. The appearance of power might've stiffened her shoulders.

Years ago, she hadn't been enough. No family had adopted her. They'd rejected her heart, her love and her artwork. Worry slumped over her.

"I've seen this before." Theo sat back and drummed his fingers against the design on top.

Despair drummed through Josie. Not from his words, but from the snide laughter of her inner critic chanting *told you so.*

Theo had passed judgment. His nose had already turned down, to better look over her. He tapped his finger against the first drawing. His tone was careful and even. "This gown is quite nice."

Nice. The word tumbled through Josie. He might as well have used *bland* or *boring. Nice* created no impression. Offered no viewpoint. There was nothing unique or special about *nice.*

Josie had also been dubbed *nice* on her foster paperwork. *Nice* hadn't gotten her adopted or helped her find a family who wanted her. As for her clothing designs, her ex had often reminded her that it was *nice* to have a quaint hobby, but her designs should be tucked away, not worn. Or, even better, donated to charity.

Pull yourself together, Josie. Crumpling the

designs and hiding under the table wasn't an option. She had to compete on Theo's level. She had to fight. "Can you be more specific?"

He studied her. "There is nothing wrong with nice."

"There is nothing exceptional about nice, either." She stayed there, beside Theo, as if this was about more than Theo liking her designs. As if this was about Theo liking *her*. "You're just being kind using the word *nice*."

"I'm not kind—not in business." Theo rocked back in his chair. "What do you want me to do? Be blunt."

"Yes. Tell me the truth." *Tell me why you don't like me. Tell me why I'm not good enough.* No one could ever answer that question.

He reached over and slid the ombré-inspired design toward him. "It is a nice gown."

Josie groaned. How many times had she heard? *It was nice to meet you, Josie.* But it was never nice enough for those prospective families to return for her. To take a chance on her.

"Hear me out." Theo leaned toward her, his gaze pinning her in place. "There's nothing unexpected in this gown. Nothing in the details that captures the attention and holds onto it."

Josie glanced at her monochrome sweater and scarf. She'd never wanted to stand out. She'd wanted to be normal, like all the other kids. To blend in. "The details come from the bride."

"But you're the designer. This gown is yours to create as you envision it." Theo tapped his finger on the paper, his tone firm. "It's your name on the design. It's your brand."

"But it's the bride's wedding. The brides themselves inspire those unique details." Josie unwrapped her infinity scarf. The thick blue seemed to be absorbing the negative, not repelling it. But the color blue was supposed to ward off negative energies. At least that was what Mimi had always told her. "Who inspires all the Coast to Coast Living items?"

"Me."

Josie concentrated on closing her mouth. Surely she'd misheard. Surely the company created for the customer they wished to attract. The image of Theo wrapped in one of their signature fleece blankets, wearing their popular fluffy reindeer socks and drinking their signature hot chocolate from the current season's Santa mug, was impossible to envision. The tension in his jaw spread to his quiet gaze, locking in his serious expression. Now wasn't the time to question him. Now was *not* the time to notice the whisper of pain in his eyes as his gaze slid away from hers.

Now was *definitely not* the time to become

aware of the man beneath the smart dress shirt, slacks and polished business veneer. As for wanting to take Theo's hand and comfort him—that was surely only a bizarre reaction to the stress of this lunch. Still, Josie held her hands together in her lap. "I need to meet your sister."

She needed a distraction. A distraction from Theo. She didn't want to get to know the real Theo Taylor. She only wanted to design a wedding gown for his sister.

He nodded toward the far side of the cafe. "Now's your opportunity."

Josie tucked the designs back into her book and smiled at a tall woman, carrying several large shopping bags and a wide grin. Theo completed the introductions and pulled out a chair for his sister.

"Sorry. I was early so I went to the store. Then I got caught up redesigning several of the holiday tables with the staff and now I'm late." Adriana's sigh didn't deflate her enthusiasm. Shopping bags settled on the empty chair beside her, she pulled out her cell phone, tapped the screen and handed the phone to Josie. "I think the displays turned out quite beautiful."

Josie enlarged a photograph of a rectangular dining-room table, exquisitely set for eight. The natural table runner was stamped with metallic snowflakes and pinecones paired with the royal blue cloth napkins folded inside silver holly-leaf napkin holders. Polished silverware rested on round burlap place mats. Satin chair covers turned ordinary seats into invitations to linger through a five-course meal. Mimi would've adored the dancing holiday images scrolled on the plates. The dinnerware would have blended perfectly with Mimi's collection of whimsical holiday pillows. .

Mimi's house hadn't been large enough for a formal dining room. The dinner table had been converted to a sewing station long before Josie had moved in. Yet Josie had never lived in a house more welcoming than Mimi's unconventional, pillbox-size cottage.

Adriana smiled at Josie. "I'd be happy to help design your holiday table, too."

"No, thank you. The display is lovely though." But not for people who lived in tiny studio apartments, surrounded by more fabric and thread than collectibles. That table belonged in her ex's house. Or the Taylors'. Josie handed Adriana's phone to her. "I'm more of a paper-plate-on-a-TV-tray person."

"Everything we sell is dishwasher- and microwave-safe." Adriana picked up the café menu. "Pretty *and* functional."

Adriana would require a wedding gown much the same. A beautiful, detailed dress that also allowed her to move among what was certain to be a rather extensive guest list. Strapless or sleeves? Illusion or cap? Strapless allowed for easier movement on the dance floor. Although formal dancing—as in ballroom—expected conservative cuts. The gown had to be effortless, like Adriana.

"Perhaps we should focus on your upcoming marriage." Theo clenched his hands together on top of his menu. "And your wedding dress, not holiday tables."

"You're sounding quite dramatic," Adriana cautioned.

Theo stilled beside Josie.

Theo and *drama* were not two words Josie would put together. The Coast to Coast Living brand was accessible to everyone—it was stylish, affordable and obtainable. But there was something remote and stand-offish about Theo now. Something that made him about as inaccessible as if he'd climbed up a tower on the Golden Gate Bridge.

"Weddings cause too much drama." Disinterest and boredom diluted Theo's voice.

Or perhaps that was stress he wanted to disguise.

There'd been nothing dramatic or stressful about Josie's wedding. She'd been married at the courthouse: no veil and a white utilitarian dress.

There'd been nothing messy about her divorce, either. The prenup she'd signed to prove she'd loved her ex more than his bank account had turned the end of her four-year marriage into a cold business transaction. She'd walked away, determined to prove she was good enough despite her ex's claims and the constant echo of the sharp childhood taunts about the poor foster kid she'd once been.

Adriana greeted the waitress. Josie ordered the spinach salad with chicken, despite the knots in her stomach.

Josie had to meet Theo's exacting standards, whatever those were. She had to succeed not only for herself, but also for Mia and her clients, like Shanna Jennings, who were depending on Josie for their dream wedding gowns. A pinch squeezed along her spine, straining against her shoulders.

The waitress collected the menus and disappeared.

Adriana launched back into the conversation. "You know what you need, Theo? You need to have more fun."

Theo squeezed a lemon into his ice glass as if watering down his sour tone. "I have enough fun already."

"Ryan and I are meeting several couples at The Shouting Fiddle later for trivia night." Adriana ignored her brother's comment. "You should join us. And you too, Josie."

Josie envied Adriana's consideration—they'd only just met. The woman most likely gathered new friends around her like a master gardener filled a greenhouse with special early blooms. And here Josie rarely ventured much beyond her wallflower position.

Josie needed to concentrate on her work. Although, Adriana's offer tempted. But that was Josie's former self that still yearned to fit in. To sit at the lunchroom table surrounded by the other girls and *not* because the teacher had forced the kids to be polite and let Josie sit with them. Josie had only wanted to be part of their inside jokes and weekend stories. To be included.

Adriana wanted to include her now. Yet all Josie heard was the keen bite of her foster sister's snub: *Josie, you wouldn't want to go to the party, anyway—you don't even know anyone. What would you do? Stand against the wall all night? You'll have more fun doodling in your sketch pad.*

Josie had graduated from doodles to proper drawings. Now she only wanted her gowns to belong in the design world. Winning over Adriana and Theo was the first step.

Josie stretched her neck, kneading the too-tight muscles and the sting of the past that still pained. "Thank you, but I have appointments this evening."

"That's a rather long workday," Adriana said.

"I like to be available for my working clients," Josie said. "Their budgets are often tight, even for the brides that have chosen to upscale a vintage gown. I hate to be the reason they have to miss work when every dollar matters."

Josie helped women like Shanna Jennings—survivors that had earned a second chance and deserved the opportunity to live their dreams. One of her clients often reminded Josie that dreams came true on their own schedule. But to make her clients' dreams happen, Josie often altered her schedule to accommodate them.

Adriana glanced at Theo. "I'm letting Josie off the hook tonight, but not you."

"Can I take a rain check?" Theo leaned toward Josie, as if pleased he wasn't the only one refusing the offer of fun.

"I've given you enough rain checks to fill your social calendar every night for over a month, Theo." Adriana eyed her brother, her voice pensive. "It's not good to spend so much time alone."

"Alone has its advantages," Josie said. She'd grown up alone. She'd earned expert status on how to be alone by the second grade.

"See. I'm not alone." Satisfaction edged into Theo's voice. He tipped his water glass toward Josie and grinned. "Josie agrees with me."

"Perhaps," Adriana allowed. "But spending time with friends offers its own rewards."

Growing up, Josie had put herself out there for friends. Many times. The results—those had always been the same. *This table is taken. Our study group is full. There's no room in the car, maybe you can come next time.* Eventually, Josie had sought refuge among the books in the library and counted the days until she'd step out of the foster system and into her own life.

But this wasn't the moment to let old wishes interfere. The only old that signified: antique sequined lace. Besides, alone was what Josie knew best. Time to focus on the bride. "How did you and Ryan meet?"

"Through friends of friends." Adriana smoothed her napkin across her lap. "Although it was slightly more complicated. There were missed opportunities to meet. Schedule conflicts. Blind dates, but not with each other. Until finally, everything aligned at a hotel bar in Chicago, oddly enough. He was there for a conference. I was there for a buyers' symposium."

There was nothing complicated about how Josie had met Theo. He'd walked into her store, judged her unworthy, then tried to dismiss her.

Josie had refused to be dismissed. She shifted her gaze toward Theo as the server delivered their meals. Was Theo regretting that decision now?

"Then they fell in love, got engaged and here we are now." Theo waved his fork as if pushing aside the details. "Ready to discuss my sister's potential wedding gown."

Potential. Josie had to work harder. Impress Theo and earn Adriana's trust. First, she needed the details. Those would surely spark her own inspiration. She'd always had a weakness for a good love story. "How would you describe the love between you and Ryan?"

"Don't you want to know her favorite color instead?" Theo asked. "Or if she has allergies to certain fabrics? Or what dress length she prefers?"

Josie frowned at him.

Theo sighed and bit into his sandwich. He gestured with his sandwich, as if giving Josie permission to continue the questioning her way.

Had Josie really wanted to hold his hand earlier?

"It's the kind of love that fills you with starlight and sunbeams. The kind of love that makes you smile even when you're exhausted and at your lowest." Adriana glanced at her engagement ring as if the secret was encased in her round-cut diamond.

Josie had felt that kind of love in every all-inclusive hug from Mimi.

"Have you ever experienced this kind of love?" The sigh in Adriana's voice was the kind that wobbled around good tears…happy tears.

Theo set his unfinished sandwich on his plate and shifted toward Josie as if suddenly invested in the conversation.

"I haven't, but my clients have." Josie shook her head and pushed the spinach leaves around her plate. She'd imagined she had that sort of love when she'd recited her marriage vows. But it had never been real. Only a deceptive wish of her broken heart.

"But you want to find love like that one day, don't you?" Adriana asked.

"I share the experience with my brides." Josie speared a piece of chicken on her fork. A deep numbness had seized her chest during her divorce. Only then had she realized the truth: love required a part of herself that her childhood had damaged. She'd lost a piece of herself in each of the seven transitions to new foster homes. Her two failed adoptions had smashed her childish hope for parents to call Mom and Dad. Finally, Mimi's sudden passing had splintered the last of Josie's heart into unrecognizable pieces. Josie forced herself to smile and added an upbeat note to her voice. “Besides, my work fulfills me. I’m much too busy to even look for love.”

“Once again, Ms. Beck and I agree.” Theo toasted Josie once more.

“Well, I highly recommend falling in love.” Adriana touched her ring and everything about the woman turned blissful, from her green eyes to her soft smile to her relaxed posture. “It’s much better than being alone.”

“I’ll take your word on that.” Josie would let Adriana have love with all its starbursts and sun rays. After all, what did a damaged heart like Josie’s know about a love like that? Josie claimed her knife. “You’re going to be a gorgeous, unforgettable bride.”

“Only if Adriana has an actual wedding dress.” Theo tossed his napkin on his empty plate. A deep frown settled on his face, his focus transitioning from the table to the entrance. “But it appears work has followed us here.”

Adriana turned around and waved at a trio of men. “Barry, Nolan and Timmy recorded their initial footage of me this morning at the offices, then they filmed me at the store. Now it’s your turn, Theo.”

Theo’s frown etched into an even deeper scowl. He stopped the waitress, asked for their bill and stuck cash into the portfolio.

Josie tracked the men. The tallest and leanest held a video camera and an endearing smile. The youngest adjusted a slouchy maroon beanie on his head and worked not to bump his equipment against the other café guests. "Why are you being filmed?"

"It's a possible business venture. Nothing to concern yourself with." Theo tucked his wallet in his back pocket and stood. "You're going to be too busy making the perfect exclusive gown for Adriana. One suitable for a Taylor bride."

Josie looked at Adriana. The woman's bright smile only increased Josie's confusion. Theo had labeled her designs nice and now expected Josie to create an original gown. Josie scrambled to collect her purse and rushed after Theo. He'd already motioned to the men, directing the group back toward the street, his long strides taking him farther away from Josie. Outside, on the sidewalk, she said, "Just to clarify. I'm making Adriana's wedding dress." *You are choosing nice. You are choosing me.*

"I'd like two prototypes by this Sunday." His unwavering gaze landed on Josie, pinning her in place. He added, "Is that feasible?"

"Yes." Sunday was four days away. Sunday was her one day to catch up on her projects. Sunday just became another opportunity to prove herself. To be more than *nice*. "Should I schedule the follow-up appointment with your admin?"

Adriana breezed onto the sidewalk, organizing her shopping bags. She squeezed Josie's arm with her free hand. "We'll come to you for a private fitting. That will be fun." With that, Adriana slipped away to talk to the small film crew.

Josie's gaze collided with Theo's and held. Questions bounced against her teeth. *Why are you playing me? You don't even like me.* "I look forward to Sunday."

Theo nodded, then turned, gathering his sister and the three men like a coach calling together his best players. Josie stood outside the café...alone. Inside, her uncertainty and determination battled for control.

She had only four days and her entire afternoon was already booked. Five appointments for winter formal-gown alterations and one to measure for a business suit. She needed to find more time. And standing in place solved nothing.

Josie headed in the opposite direction of the Taylors and the film crew, working her way through the tourists and local lunch crowd. Ahead of her, a children's store claimed an entire street corner, inviting shoppers of all ages to drop in and look around.

Sequined hats, fancy satin bows and holiday

velvet dresses adorned the child mannequins in the store's window, tempting every little girl to step inside and become their own fairy princess.

Mimi had taken a ten-year-old Josie to similar stores—not to purchase the pretty gowns, but to imagine. To encourage a younger Josie to dream about a different life. Not the one she'd lived—always a short-term visitor in different foster families' worlds.

She wanted her boutique to be more than a short-term proposition. More than a temporary job. Yet the only permanence she truly understood was constant change.

Josie checked the time on her phone and focused on the present. Alterations and clients waited. This was her life—the one she lived on her own terms. As for the dreaming, she'd leave that for the children. She no longer found it useful.

Turning her back on the children's clothing store, Josie upped her pace. If she hurried, she'd have a few minutes before her first client arrived. Back at her boutique, Josie opened her design book on the checkout counter, picked up her pencil and summoned her confidence.

She had to create a runway dress so spectacular Theo couldn't turn his beautifully refined nose up at it. That meant she had to create magic now. Mimi had always believed in magic. The dear woman had hand-stitched fairy gardens into plain, dull fabric and decorated her house with her enchanting creations. Josie had to believe, like Mimi. With the very same soul-deep conviction.

Don't limit yourself. Think beyond the pattern, Josie. Then you'll create magic.

Theo most likely disapproved of anyone who believed in magic. What about love? He'd agreed with Josie that work fulfilled him and occupied his time. But he'd never commented on Adriana's description of love. Did he believe in that sort of love? For reasons she refused to explore, she wanted him to believe. But that wasn't her concern.

She tapped her pencil against the page as if that would release the magic in her foster mother's wand. Nothing happened. She'd been generating replications of her clients' wishes for the past year. Had she misplaced her own perspective? Maybe her creativity had simply expired like a city parking meter. Or like her chance at a real family. That had ended after Mimi's unexpected illness. Mimi had been the one who'd believed in her. Mimi had encouraged Josie.

Sadness tangled with that familiar knot of misery inside her. Josie dropped her pencil and rubbed her hands over her face.

Scenes of Theo and his sister sharing a look

merged with ones of the laughing children in front of the children's store. She booted up her computer and typed *Taylor family* in the search bar, then clicked on the images. In every picture, the Taylors were connected: arms around each other, Adriana's head resting on Theo's shoulder, arms linked at the elbows. What did a foster kid like Josie know about close-knit families like the Taylors?

The flip side of every project isn't ever as pretty as the front. Remember, what people show the world isn't always the full truth. Mimi's best advice about life had always been shared while they'd sat in rocking chairs on the back porch. Fresh lemonade in tall glasses on the wicker table and the sewing basket perched between them.

Still, every image of the Taylor family appeared more flawless than the last. The bylines included appearances at charity balls, Coast to Coast Living-sponsored events and fundraising causes. Nothing scandalous. Nothing that suggested the flip side wasn't as perfect as the front. Theo would expect perfection from the first stitch to the last.

Josie's confidence unraveled, spooling near her feet. What did she really know about exclusive, A-list designs? She knew how to upscale.

How was that ever going to be enough? Could she ever be enough for Theo?

She was more comfortable in secondhand stores than runway shows. Theo dressed like a fashion model clipped from an ad for the smartest business wear. He probably never doubted his choice of attire or his decisions.

The bells on the boutique entrance jangled. Josie closed the case on her laptop, greeted her client and welcomed the reprieve. Surely later she'd find the magic.

As for being enough for Theo Taylor—that wasn't her goal. And nothing more than a stress-induced musing. Besides, recycled shirts and skirts, no matter how trendy, didn't belong beside custom-tailored suits and men like Theo.

Four hours later, Josie rose from her knees and rubbed the knot from her back. She eyed the burgundy ball gown on the dress form, unable to rub away her reluctance to finish her client's requested modifications. The blinding number of crystals and rhinestones Josie tacked onto the gown's waist glimmered as if mocking Josie for bending to her client's over-the-top vision. For keeping silent. Her design book, opened to a blank page, waited on the couch, taunting Josie to create. To release her own voice on the page.

She'd been criticized for her shyness as a child. Skipped over at adoption fairs and overlooked by her peers. Now she must put herself out there again.

Face more judgment.

And the stakes—they were nerve-wrenchingly high this time.

Her past was supposed to have prepared her, not defined her. Those were the parting words of her last caseworker. As if all her experiences had somehow strengthened her. Why, then, did she feel so weak? Her fingers shook. Panic pressed against her chest, dislodging her breath.

The bells chimed at the shop's entrance. Mia's greeting contained the opening lines of "A Holly Jolly Christmas."

Failure wouldn't be only hers this time. This time if Josie fell short, the descent would take down her friend, too.

Josie fixed her focus on the dress form, flexed her back and willed away her panic. She hadn't broken down at the adoption fairs. She wouldn't melt down now, especially not in front of Mia. Her past had taught her the importance of keeping things to herself. *If your mother had wanted to dry your tears, she would've kept you. Trust me, no one here wants any more tears.* Josie's foster brother had imparted that wisdom the first night in her third foster home. Josie had dried her tears then and imprinted that lesson deep inside herself.

As for her silent muse, Josie always preferred to rely on herself, anyway.

She stopped to watch her friend in the floor-length mirror. Mia finished her Christmas song, added a spin and curtsy, then dropped her camera equipment near the couch. She stepped beside Josie, her hands on her hips. “You really couldn’t talk your customer into something different.”

Josie shook her head. But she’d have to convince Theo and Adriana that they wanted her designs. She’d have to speak up. She’d have to speak out. The wallflower would have to step into the spotlight and defend her right to be there. Josie widened her stance, bolstering her balance.

“That many jewels looks like country gone rogue.” Mia’s festive mood had evaporated. She picked up Josie’s design book and sat on the couch. “It was a striking dress. Now it’s edged into gaudy.”

“My customer wanted more.” Despite Josie’s suggestions for a jeweled headband and coordinating bracelet. Despite Josie’s assurance the dress already sparkled enough. Josie had finally conceded to her headstrong client. She threaded her needle and stepped toward the dress form. Sunday she’d channel all her resolve into Adriana's dress. No concessions. "I agreed to give her more."

"More isn't always better." Mia's fingers drummed on the blank page of the design book.

"It's what my client wants." Josie silently apologized to the gown and threaded her needle into the fabric.

"But you're the dressmaker," Mia argued.

In this instance, Josie was the seamstress. And she needed happy customers. Happy customers returned. Happy customers paid and helped boost Josie's checking account. "I'm here to give my clients exactly what they want."

"Speaking of which, where are the designs for Adriana Taylor?" Mia flipped through the design book.

The needle stilled as if Josie had stabbed into metal. Josie pointed at her forehead and stretched the truth. "In here."

"We need to get them on paper first, then fabric." Mia smiled and ran her palm over the blank page as if she already pictured the finished wedding gown. "I'm sure they're fabulous. And I'm certain that Theo and Adriana will love them."

She hoped so. Josie secured the last section of the jeweled belt, knotted the thread and her doubt. *Every project starts with one stitch.*

Mia studied the dress and glanced at Josie. "You don't like it, do you?"

Her opinion didn't matter. Only the customer's happiness. Still, Josie's fingers twitched, wanting to grab her seam ripper and remove the jewels. "That's not the point."

"What would you have done?" Mia persisted.

Josie leaned down, stretched out the full skirt and checked for pins she might've missed in the hem. "She was stuck on adding a belt. A simple sequined sash would add a subtle, but interesting waterfall of shimmer if it draped down the side of the gown and blended with the side slit."

"You should do that," Mia encouraged her. "Once your client sees the finished gown, she'll fall in love."

"It's not what we discussed." Josie shook her head. "Or what she requested."

"But it's so much better."

"I'm not the one paying for the dress." And if her creative choices were wrong? And the customers refused to pay? That was a risk she couldn't afford.

"It's past time you gave your clients more than what they asked for. Give them what they need to shine. What are you afraid of?" Mia picked up Josie's design book. "Your talent exceeds a lot of folks who've been highly trained. Your sketches dance off the pages. And your bridal clients…name one bride who wasn't breathless and amazed at her final fitting."

Josie touched the too-thick jeweled band and avoided looking at the crumpled paper filling the trash can. She'd started over a dozen designs for Adriana, then quit. So many starts and stops in her life—it was something of a theme. She had to finish tonight for Adriana to have something to try on by Sunday. Mia was depending on Josie. "Nothing feels right for someone like Adriana Taylor."

"Then don't think of her as Adriana Taylor," Mia said. "Think of her as your ideal winter bride. The one radiating a love that lights her from within. And wrapped around her in the tulle and lace are the magic and joy of the season."

Winter was a tricky time for Josie. December had been the month Mimi had learned about her diagnosis. It had also been the same month Mimi had taken Josie to get her first public library card—a card she still carried in her wallet. It was a reminder that even seemingly small moments were precious. One year, she'd moved from her second foster home to her third the week before Christmas. Yet Josie could still tap into the delight that had seized her Christmas morning when she'd opened colored pens and reams of paper from her foster parents. They'd urged her to continue drawing, no matter what happened. That was a gift. Even more special was they'd noticed more about Josie than her reserved, withdrawn nature.

"It's dinnertime. One thing I know—nothing ever gets accomplished on an empty stomach." Mia jumped up and zipped up her coat. "I know the perfect place and you should come with me."

"Where?" Josie touched her stomach. She hadn't eaten much at lunch.

"My mother-in-law's house." Mia held up her hands and rushed on, blocking out Josie's argument. "It's only the moms. A small group. Well, not even a group, more like a collection."

Josie squinted at Mia. "A collection?"

Mia grinned. "It's been said that if you own three pieces of art by the same artist, then you have a collection. My mom, my mother-in-law and I are all family now. So, we're like a collection."

Family. How easy the word rolled off Mia's tongue. How safe the word sounded coming from her friend. Josie knew so little about being part of a family. Knew only that she'd always wished for her own. But she realized wishes weren't always meant to come true. Now Mia wanted Josie to spend time with her family. But Josie couldn't even accept Adriana's trivia-night invitation without overthinking the evening. "I should—"

"Come with me," Mia said, cutting her off.

"Eat because Helen and my mother don't know how to cook for less than a dozen people and food that good should never be wasted."

Josie twisted a piece of thread around her fingers. She had designs to create. A deadline to meet in four days. And not a minute to lose not sewing. Her stomach growled.

"My mother is making homemade spring rolls and egg rolls." Mia pointed at Josie. "Don't deny those are your favorite. You order takeout from Ginger Sun at least once a week."

"That's not fair." Josie had already considered placing a to-go order from the Chinese restaurant on her walk home.

"Helen made homemade white-chocolate raspberry cheesecake." Mia picked up her camera bag and laughed. She knew full well that cheesecake was one of Josie's other favorites. "I bet they'll give you all the leftovers you can carry."

Josie could very well disappoint Mia in the next few days. She'd most likely disappoint Theo, too, and confirm that the critical look on his attractive face at lunch had been warranted. But tonight, she could take a small step to being unfettered by debt and expectation and join her friend. "I'll get my coat. But I can't stay long."

"You can eat and leave. The moms are happy just to share their food." Mia grabbed Josie's design book and headed toward the door. "Always good to have it within reach. The muse doesn't always play fair."

The muse disappeared a while ago. As for her insistent worry, she refused to let it affect her right now. She also refused to overstay her welcome with Mia's family. She glanced at her watch and calculated the appropriate length of her stay. One hour and twenty-five minutes. Long enough not to appear rude. Short enough not to forget she didn't belong.

CHAPTER FIVE

THREE HOURS LATER, spring rolls made—thanks to a lesson from Mia's mother, Jin—and devoured, Josie dried off the last sauté pan and handed it to Mia to put away. Dinner was long since complete, but the debate about the best holiday events offered in the city continued through dessert and cleanup.

Helen, Mia's mother-in-law, gathered the scraped-clean paper dessert plates and plastic forks, then dropped them into the trash. "The light exhibit at the Conservatory of Flowers is on the top of my list."

"Evening ice-skating on one of the outdoor rinks." Mia twirled around the kitchen, then dropped into her chair and touched her stomach. "Perhaps not on such a full stomach."

Josie was full, too. The food had been delicious. The secret to decadent pumpkin cookies revealed by Helen: chocolate. Yet the true pleasure came from being surrounded by Mia's family. Josie sipped her hot tea and lingered, cherishing her time with these women. She couldn't imagine Theo on ice skates, but strolling through the lights at the conservatory…perhaps. But only if a business function brought him there.

Jin dried her hands and shook her head. "I'm torn between the annual Dickens Fair, the symphony and *The Nutcracker*."

"The upcoming gingerbread house exhibit at the Silver Monarch Hotel is my favorite," Josie offered. The women approved. Would Theo?

Jin sat across from Josie and grinned. "We have quite the list of holiday events to attend, ladies. We're going to be busy."

"Josie is already busy." Helen picked up the coffeepot from the kitchen counter and returned to the table. "I hear you're designing for Adriana Taylor."

Josie curved her hands around the coffee mug and watched the steam disappear into air. Much like her contentment. Good things never lasted. She avoided glancing at her design book on the chair beside her. Mia had set it there earlier, as if the book deserved a place at the table. Josie cleared her throat. "It's not official yet."

"It will be once the Taylors see Josie's sample dresses on Sunday." Mia squeezed a generous portion of honey into her tea.

Drops of panic oozed through Josie, instead.

"I adore the special-edition holiday dishes at Coast to Coast Living," Jin said. "I was at their store yesterday and purchased the entire merry-

and-bright themed serving set. We can use it at the next Second Winders widow club meeting."

"Christmas paper plates and napkins are just as festive." Helen dabbed the edge of her Santa-print paper napkin to the corner of her mouth as if proving her point.

"I agree." Jin toyed with her napkin. "With less to clean up at the end of the evening, we have more time to visit with each other."

Or more time to avoid awkward personal questions. Yet there hadn't been any awkward moments this evening. With these women. They'd welcomed Josie as if she'd been there the day before and the one before that. As if she'd always been with them.

Jin glanced at Josie, her voice as softly gentle as her smile. "Can we see your designs?"

"They're…" Josie clutched at her tea mug as if grasping for her words. All she pictured in her mind was Theo's censure for reaching too far.

"Not ready yet." Jin refilled her coffee cup, understanding flowing through her quiet voice. "Mia and her father always told me—'it's a work-in-progress, Mom. You can't view the documentary until it's totally ready.'"

But Josie's dresses weren't *in progress*. The dresses hadn't even been started. Josie shifted her focus from Jin to Helen. Kindness wove through both women and it showed in their patience with Josie in the kitchen earlier—she'd never learned to cook—and in their attentive gazes as they listened…really listened. And in their encouraging advice that dropped into the conversation like the surprise bites of chocolate chips in Helen's pumpkin cookies.

Mimi had radiated the very same kindness. Josie missed Mimi so much. Perhaps even more now. She could've used her guidance. Or her reassurance. Josie imagined the fluffy whipped cream as frothy trim on a coat. Would a top designer use food as inspiration?

Josie worked her words free. "It's not that they aren't ready. It's that I have nothing."

"We understand." Helen reached over and patted Josie's arm. "It's hard to talk about your art before it's finished."

The warmth from Helen's hand looped through Josie, curving deep inside her chest. Comforting and considerate. Would Theo's hand feel the same inside hers?

"We're unbearably nosy," Helen continued. "We didn't mean to pressure you."

A pressure built inside Josie. Panic and grief generated. For her lack of inspiration. For all she'd missed growing up. For all she refused to admit she still wanted. Acceptance. A husband. A family like the one she'd seen on the street yesterday. The little girl had held onto her father's hand, and her mother's, skipping happily between her parents. The love had swirled around them like silk ribbon binding them together as one.

Now everything felt like it hinged on the success of her designs for Adriana. Clearly Josie had overstayed her welcome. She should've declined dessert and fled.

Helen's hand remained on Josie's arm like a steadying anchor. Like a promise that all would be fine. Josie wanted to believe her. Wanted to grab Helen's hand and hold on. She had to leave. *Now.* Instead, Josie blurted, "No, really. I have nothing."

Silence circled the table.

Josie lifted her design book from the empty chair beside her, opened it and pointed at the blank page titled *Adriana Taylor.* The truth spilled out of her like an overturned glass of milk. "I really have nothing. *Nothing.*"

Josie's pulse stretched against her skin as if trying to burst free. What had she done? How could she burden these wonderful women like that? Surely Helen would escort her to the door and wish her well. Jin would suggest she keep such heavy worries to herself. *No one wants to dry your tears, Josie.* Josie clutched her sweaty palms together under the table. If she could move her numb legs, she'd run to the front door herself.

The three women around her jumped in as if more than accustomed to spilled glasses of milk and after-dinner confessions.

Mia picked up a clean dessert plate, handed it to Helen and announced, “We’ve got this.”

Helen nodded, her chin firm, her movements steady. She sliced a second piece of white-chocolate raspberry cheesecake and slid it onto the plate.

Jin added two tall dollops of whipped cream beside the cheesecake slice and said, “Of course we do.”

“I’ve solved many problems with extra whipped cream.” Helen motioned for Jin to add another swirl of whipped cream. “I trust you all won’t tell my son.”

Josie rubbed her damp palms across her jeans. She’d just trusted these three women with her horrifying truth. She’d unloaded on them as if she had the right. As if she belonged. And they simply served her another piece of cheesecake with extra whipped cream. Surely she’d disappointed Mia. Surely Helen and Jin considered her an imposter.

“Your secret is safe with me, Helen.” Jin swirled whipped cream onto the top of her coffee with the skill of a seasoned barista. “It’s the best part of my coffee.”

Helen eyed Josie and Mia. The older woman

tipped the end of the whipped-cream can toward them, as if readying to attack.

Mia glanced at Josie and back to her mother-in-law. “We won’t tell Wyatt about your whipped-cream habit if you share your recipe for your pumpkin cookies.”

“Deal.” Helen handed a clean fork to Josie. “Now, where were we?”

“Wedding dresses.” Jin slid another plate toward Helen. “It’s impolite to make Josie eat alone.”

It was even more impolite for Josie to dump her worries on strangers. Then again, Josie had never taken a class in etiquette. And these women apparently preferred their own customs. Josie picked up her fork. The numbness eased. Yet her stomach twisted, not quite convinced all was well.

“Wedding-dress shopping was my least favorite part of the wedding planning.” Helen served Jin a piece of cheesecake and shook her head. “It was my height.”

“You’ve a lovely stature.” Jin swirled more whipped cream onto her plate, making a floral pattern around the edges. “I would’ve given anything for several more inches.”

“You’re a dear, Jin.” Helen beamed at her friend. “The bridal shops were not as kind.”

“What did they do?” Mia took the whipped

cream from her mother and frosted several pumpkin cookies with it.

"Suggested I was too tall and would never find a nice dress." Helen poked her fork into her cheesecake as if poking at a distressing memory. "My limited budget wasn't appealing or worth the effort, either."

"It was the fabric, wasn't it?" Josie asked before she could stop herself. These women drew her back in. Made her feel comfortable. She hadn't felt that…well, ever. Josie took in Helen's elegant, lean frame. Adriana Taylor had the same build and, like Helen, she'd make a beautiful bride. "They would've needed additional fabric to accommodate your height and that altered the cost of the gown."

"I'd think they'd have wanted a sale." Jin shrugged.

"Or to make a bride feel beautiful on her wedding day, no matter what." Josie crammed a bite of cheesecake into her mouth, censuring herself. No one had asked for her personal opinion. *Best to keep quiet, Josie. The parents here yell even more if you talk.*

Yet she believed every bride should shine on their wedding day. Mimi had taught her as much. The one summer Josie had lived with Mimi, they'd assisted more than two dozen brides inside the one-hundred-year-old chapel in Lake Valley.

She wanted Adriana and Shanna to feel the same on their wedding days. It wasn't about how lavish the wedding was or how much it cost. It was about the love between the bride and groom. Josie wanted every wedding dress she touched to showcase that love. Years later, the couple might not remember the details, but they'd always remember how they felt. That was the most lasting memory.

"How I wish you were designing back then. My mother would've adored you." Helen patted Josie's arm again.

Once again, her touch was warm, kind and comforting. Josie wished she could reciprocate, but it never came easy for her. After her third move to a new foster home, she'd skipped the hugs and resorted to simple handshake introductions. Even with her ex-husband, she'd never readily reached for his hand. Always aware of her surroundings. Always unsure of his reaction.

Helen waved her fork in the air and continued her story. "My mother brushed off every negative bridal consultant and took me all over the state. We finally located a tiny family-owned boutique up north."

Mia rose and picked up a framed picture from

the side table. "And you got your perfect wedding dress."

"I took on an extra job as a cashier at the ice-cream shop that summer to pay for my extralong veil and shoes." Helen touched the picture frame. Joy and love softened her face. "I've never forgotten my mother's words. 'Always hold your head up, Helen, and you'll be able to see over the ones trying to look down on you.'"

Josie studied Helen's wedding picture. Was it wrong to take the best parts about Helen's dress and do a modern spin on the silhouette? Was that stealing? She had very little to sway Theo. Panic steam pressed into her skin. "It looks like you were married in a fairy garden."

"The redwood forest was simply magical that day." Helen's eyes widened and lit up as if a dial had been set to dazzle.

There inside Helen's vivid gaze, her breathless voice and unsteady smile was the love—that feeling Mimi had always insisted would be the most precious memory for any couple. Josie wanted to capture that in a gown. Weave it through the beading and pearls. Apply it with appliqués on lace. Extend it from the top diamanté button all the way through to the embroidered train. She wanted to give that gift to every one of her brides. That would fulfill her. That would be enough.

Helen added, "Certainly erased all the tears and stress that led up to our wedding."

"Carlo and I had no stress." Jin set down her fork and picked up Mia's free hand. "We were having lunch at a quaint bistro in SoHo. He reached across the table, took my hand and said in his usual blunt way, 'Let's get married now.'"

"James never really asked, either. He more or less told me we were getting married." Helen and Jin laughed together.

Would Theo plan an elaborate proposal or simply tell his girlfriend? He was too detailed not to propose in an extravagant manner.

"I also laughed at Carlo. Our families didn't much care for each other." Jin traced the large ruby on her wedding ring. "But he never flinched. Instead he told me I was missing one thing and slipped this ring on my finger."

Josie leaned forward and searched Jin's face. That same sort of love glowed inside her dark gaze—the same way Adriana's gaze had glowed at lunch earlier. "What did your families do?"

"We never told them." Jin shrugged. One side of her mouth tipped up and time stepped back.

Josie saw only the young woman, in love and willing to risk everything for one man. Love required a courage Josie wasn't certain she possessed.

Theo's bride would be well-known, capable

of standing on her own in his world. His family's approval—that would be required.

"We filled out the paperwork at the courthouse after lunch and headed upstate," Jin added. "We discovered a tiny historic chapel in a forgotten small town on the backroads. Inside we exchanged our own vows—ones from the heart. A retired minister blessed the union."

Mia crossed her arms over her chest and eyed her mother. "But you were married at the courthouse in the city."

"That was to satisfy the state of New York and our parents." Jin wiped at her damp eyes. "The real occasion was inside the tiny chapel."

Would Theo agree to a secret ceremony? One reserved for only his bride and himself. A romantic moment only the couple shared. Or would budgets and expenses dampen the storybook occasion?

Jin continued, "I wore my pale pink suit ensemble and a feathered hat with a veil that reached my chin."

"You wore the suit at the courthouse, but not the hat." Mia set down her cookie and brushed her hands together. "I have your picture—the one taken outside the courthouse on your wedding day."

"The veil belonged in the chapel." Jin touched her cheek as if feeling the brush of the delicate fabric. “It was perfect. The minister blessed our union, Carlo lifted the veil and kissed the breath right out of me.”

Josie smiled. She’d lost her breath only twice in her life: once after she’d miscalculated the distance to the wall during swim lessons—lessons she’d taken her first and only year of college. And after she’d signed her lease on the boutique space. That day, she’d escaped outside and thrust her head between her knees, gasping around her sudden dread. She’d never risked so much.

But being kissed breathless? Josie wasn’t convinced that was possible. Theo looked capable of that kind of… Josie carved out a large bite of cheesecake and ignored the direction of her thoughts.

Still, she hoped every bride experienced Helen and Jin’s kind of love. But the feelings were up to each couple. As for Josie, she’d add magic to the bride’s day and perhaps give her clients a wedding dress that left them breathless. “Do you still have the hat?”

Jin nodded, a half grin on her face.

“Mom, why didn’t you tell me?” Mia asked. “I could’ve used it in my wedding weeks ago.”

“That was your day, dear.” Jin cupped Mia’s cheek. “Your chance to make your own perfect memories.”

"Can I see the hat?" Mia asked.

"It's boxed up and safe," Jin said. "One day it will be yours. For now, I want to hold onto the memory a little longer. Selfish, isn't it?"

Helen gripped Jin's hand. Two widows who recognized what the other had lost. Who understood the grief and joy in revisiting the memories. Who leaned on each other now for friendship and support.

Mia stood up and hugged her mom. "I like knowing there was more than the courthouse."

"There was so much more." Jin rested her head on Mia's shoulder.

Josie's wedding had been at a courthouse, too. Her ex had explained they were too practical for the expense and pomp of a fancy ceremony. She'd had no guests at her marriage. No secret chapel or fairy-tale forest setting. But she had her imagination, her sketches and her clothes. Josie looked at Mia. "Do you have your parents' wedding picture?"

"It's in the front room." Mia walked out to retrieve the picture.

Josie set her design book in front of her and picked up the pencil she kept stuck between the pages. "Jin, can you describe your hat?"

Jin scooted closer to Josie then used her hands and words to form an image of her bridal hat.

Josie drew the hat on the model, drawing Jin's excited exclamation. "That's it."

Josie continued drawing, covering the sketch model in a fitted gown that flared out at the knees. She added a lace overlay. Wrote the word lavender in the margin. Sat back, studied the gown and drew a fur capelet over the shoulders.

"A muffler," Jin suggested. "Unexpected."

Josie's pencil skipped over the page.

Helen leaned closer. "A bouquet of winter berries and branches. Rustic and enchanting."

Josie started again, drew her model sketch and covered her in the same gown. Only she replaced the capelet with a floor-length veil that fastened at the neck.

Jin sighed. "It's stunning."

Mia clapped her hands. "I want to wear that gown and have another wedding."

Josie laughed and turned to the next page. So many pages—a lot more than she had when she'd arrived for dinner. She kept sketching, outlining another gown. The scratch of the pencil tip silenced the voice of her inner critique. She glanced at Helen. "This one is for you."

Illusion sleeves, a scalloped border at the hemline and a chapel train filled the page. Clear crystals and sequins covered the medallion lace dress. A satin lining would complete the gown. Helen suggested juniper boughs and silver-dipped pinecones for a different wedding bouquet. Jin wondered about crystals to make the bouquet shimmer like snowflakes in the sun. The three women resorted to one-word exclamations. Stunning. Exquisite. Dramatic.

Josie's inner critic countered—*Too basic. Not original.* Had she truly captured Adriana?

An hour—and almost a dozen designs—later, Josie walked to the door, her design book tucked under one arm, a to-go bag swinging from the other. She hadn't given up. What would Theo think of her now?

"Remember to lift your chin on Sunday and stand tall." Helen cupped Josie's cheek. "If you need a hit of whipped cream afterward, you know where to come."

CHAPTER SIX

"THANK YOU FOR meeting me here." Adriana touched a garment bag draped over one of her empty office chairs. "I wanted to give you this since you gave me the idea at lunch yesterday."

Adriana had called Josie before she'd left her apartment that morning and asked her to meet at the Coast to Coast Living offices. Adriana hadn't mentioned anything about a gown. Intrigued, Josie walked closer to Adriana and the chair. "What idea?"

"Sorry. Let me start over." Adriana laughed. Excitement wrapped around her voice, seeping into her bold green eyes. "This is my Grandmother Pearl's wedding dress. And it's in very good condition, too."

"If treated appropriately and cared for correctly, vintage gowns can be worn today." Josie grinned. Finding an unexpected vintage piece always thrilled her.

"You talked about upscaling vintage gowns at lunch. I thought maybe… I think Grandmother's dress would fit me." Adriana reached for the zipper. "I didn't put it on. I just held it up. We were similar in our build. Mother says I got my height and eyes from my Grandma Pearl."

"Can we take it out?" Josie asked. "Look at it?"

"Adriana." Theo's sharp voice ping-ponged around the office, vibrating from the office doorway. "Where have you been?"

Adriana pulled her hand away from the garment bag as if she'd been burned, then stepped forward to address her brother. "I was up in the attic at your house."

"The attic?" Theo repeated.

"I was looking for… Never mind." Adriana shook her head and motioned toward Josie. "I was just telling Josie that I found Grandmother's hope chest up there."

Theo inclined his head toward Josie.

Josie nodded back—a slight tip of her chin, giving away even less than Theo. Although she was certain something sparked in his gaze. Almost as if he liked seeing her. As for her, that race in her pulse was only for Adriana's discovery of her grandmother's dress.

"I forgot we had moved all Grandmother's things to the attic in the main house." Adriana's words and her joy continued to tumble out. "I discovered all her china tea settings and the server table she loved so much. The spinning wheel that belonged to one of her great aunts. I even found her handmade wooden Christmas ornaments. Do you remember those?"

"We have a meeting in five minutes." Theo

crossed his arms over his chest, his stance widened like a bodyguard prepared to deter the uninvited. Clearly, he wasn't interested in joining the vintage club. "You'll have to amuse yourself with a trip down memory lane later."

The edge in Theo's voice startled Josie, pulling her focus to him. Pain flattened his mouth and his tone. That spark was extinguished. She recognized the hurt—she'd heard the same snags in her own voice as she tried to avoid her own past. Memory lane wasn't pleasant, or a trip Theo took willingly it seemed. And Josie guessed his pain was from more than a missed vacation to Europe.

But what could a man as successful and confident as Theo Taylor have suffered? *People only ever show the finished side of every project, Josie. Often, the backside is just too messy.* But there was nothing messy about Theo or his sister.

"This isn't a random trip, Theo." Adriana touched the garment bag as if protecting it from Theo's harsh words. Sadness muted the wonder in her tone. "I was looking for Grandmother's wedding dress."

"Why?" Theo's voice was implacable. Rigid. "You can't wear it."

The bow on Adriana's pale pink 1920s-inspired silk blouse wilted like her excitement. Josie wanted to comfort Adriana and kick Theo. Anger, not pleasure, made her pulse race now.

Couldn't he see that their grandmother's possessions meant something special to his sister?

Adriana set her hands on her hips and glared at her brother. "Why not?"

Josie almost applauded Adriana's boldness. Instead she dipped her chin in approval.

"It's a used wedding dress." Theo glanced at Josie.

How dare he? Josie stepped closer to Theo, not wanting any misunderstanding to be blamed on the distance between them. "If a vintage dress is customized by a skilled dressmaker, a wedding guest would have trouble discerning where the old ended and the new began."

Theo moved closer to her, as if to ensure his low voice reached her. "I won't ruin my sister's wedding with the past."

Stubborn, stubborn man. The dress could never upset his sister.

"A new gown will be the start of new memories for Adriana. She'll look back on her wedding day and want to revisit each and every single moment," Theo said. "To accomplish that, Adriana will need to have a one-of-a-kind dress."

Josie acknowledged that he wanted the best for his sister. She appreciated that and how he wanted to protect his sister—he loved her. But his unfair distaste of used gowns was less than pleasing. "A modified vintage gown could be considered one-of-a kind."

Adriana stepped beside Josie, their shoulders bumped in solidarity.

"Perhaps by the amateur eye," Theo countered. "There is nothing amateur about the Taylors."

And there was nothing professional about a wannabe dressmaker with a hobby. Josie picked up the garment bag as if that would relieve the tension inside the room. "There's nothing wrong with vintage gowns. But your own unskilled eye cannot recognize that."

Adriana's voice softened into a plea. "You haven't even seen Grandmother's dress, Theo."

"She most likely bought it at a five-and-dime store. I've seen the photographs." Theo walked toward the doorway. "It's simply not good enough for you."

"Josie could make it perfect." Adriana smiled at Josie. "Mia showed me pictures of your clients' reworked wedding dresses."

Theo paused. His attention shifted back to Josie, his gaze intense and unsettling. "Josie has promised to make you an exclusive dress, Adriana. Forget about Grandmother's."

How painful was your past that you'd opt for one of my gowns rather than your own grandmother's? Shun your own family. Josie wanted to take Theo's hand and comfort him. No questions asked. No answers required. But she knew little about comforting someone else. Even less about easy, natural affection. She stepped past him out into the hallway.

Theo followed her as she walked away, his deep voice stopped her outside another office. "What is that by the way? In your hands."

Behind Josie, Adriana gasped then coughed.

"This?" Josie met his gaze and tossed his words from their lunch meeting back at him. "It's a possible business venture I wanted to share with Adriana. Nothing to concern yourself with."

Theo's gaze narrowed on her as if he debated whether to believe her or not.

Josie held his gaze and never flinched.

"Theo, dear." A woman's voice splintered between Josie and Theo, breaking the connection.

Theo winced and sighed.

Josie shifted her attention to the striking pair of women weaving around the last desk toward them. She recognized Mrs. Taylor from the online photographs that clearly hadn't needed to be altered to improve on the older woman's timeless beauty. The photographs had only failed to capture Lilian Taylor's movements, which were graceful, fluid and purposeful.

His mother called to him again, revising her greeting to a simple wave. Then she pitched her son's name higher, to float over his employees.

Theo inclined his head in acknowledgment.

Josie gaped at him, certain he'd released another sigh, only this one was curse-infused. He was a man anything but thrilled to see his mother.

"Mother has impeccable timing, as always," Adriana muttered. A scowl transformed Adriana's face. Her gaze tracked her mother like Josie tracked a spider in her apartment—she was annoyed and alarmed.

Josie took a step back. Where was the close-knit Taylor family Josie had read about online and in magazines? Wasn't anyone pleased to see the matriarch of the Taylor family?

"Is that Daphne Holland with mother?" Adriana shifted behind her brother's shoulder as if contemplating a surprise attack. "Theo, what's going on? Daphne isn't on the features' list."

Before Josie could ask what a features' list was or who Daphne Holland was, Theo distracted her again. "Ms. Beck, thank you for stopping in. We'll be in touch."

Back to the formality. Panic infused Josie. She'd never perfected the art of lying. She pushed the garment bag into Theo's chest and whispered, "I can't take this. It belongs to your family."

"I'm Lilian Rose Taylor." The older woman extended her arm toward Josie. "Theo's mother."

Josie stopped shoving the garment bag at Theo and his solid chest. He made no move to take it, anyway. Josie elbowed him in the side to let him know she disapproved, then adjusted the bag to free one hand. She reached out to shake Lilian's cool hand. "Josie Beck. It's a pleasure to meet you."

"What do you do, Josie?" Lilian held onto Josie's hand, but not in the we're-long-time-friends-and-I've-missed-you sort of way. Her grip was too firm and unrelenting, as if she intended to keep Josie right there until she learned exactly what she wanted.

"Mother," Theo said. The warning in his tone dropped between the women.

"It's a perfectly acceptable question. Polite even." Lilian Rose squeezed Josie's hand and released her. "Especially given your lack of manners, Theo."

Josie tucked her hand and her sudden discomfort underneath the garment bag.

"Josie is a local business owner and we're keeping her from her work," Theo explained.

Lilian Rose ignored her son and tipped her head toward the petite woman pacing around Theo's office, her cell phone pressed to her ear, her mahogany hair sweeping across her jaw. "That is Daphne Holland. Are you single, Josie?"

"Mother." The single word was clipped, as if Theo's clenched teeth chipped each syllable.

"Daphne is the premier matchmaker in the city. Why shouldn't Josie know her?" Lilian set her fingers against her mouth and spoke around her hand as if imparting a secret to Josie. "Daphne is also my matchmaker."

"I thought we were keeping that information confidential." Theo coughed and cleared his throat.

"Josie won't share, will you?" Lilian Rose smiled as she eyed Josie. Her gaze critical, her grin challenging. "I'm quite certain Josie has been vetted. Otherwise she wouldn't have been granted a private meeting with you, Theo." She paused. Nothing stilled in her assessing eyes. "My son can't be too careful. It seems everyone wants something from him and they're willing to do whatever it takes to get it."

If only she'd worn higher heels, Josie would've met Lilian Rose eye-to-eye. Still, Josie tipped her chin up, refusing to let Theo's mother look down on her, too. Theo had sought out Josie. Josie should've been the one to do the vetting. Surely Theo would correct his mother's misconception.

Theo never responded.

"Why don't we let Josie get on with her day?" Adriana stepped beside her mother.

Yet Adriana's smile lacked her earlier enthusiasm, was less infectious, more strained. More forced. Nothing like the photographs Josie had glanced through.

"Theo has a full schedule today," Adriana continued. "And I have wedding details to finalize this afternoon."

"If you'd like a meeting with Daphne Holland, please let me know." Lilian Rose applied a shimmery lip gloss to her mouth.

The deep red color reminded Josie of the poisoned apple Snow White bit into. The princess had a charming prince and the power of true love's kiss to save her. What about Josie?

She slid a quick peek at Theo. He closed his eyes and inhaled. There was power and mastery in the simple action, as if he'd practiced the technique often. As if his mother forced him to center himself often.

Josie was on her own.

"I'll be more than happy to arrange one." Lilian Rose added one last swipe of lip gloss, pressed her lips together and winked at Josie.

There was nothing hollow in the older woman's smile. Or insincere in her grey gaze. But Josie searched for the catch behind Lilian Rose's offer. "Thank you."

Adriana stepped forward, wrapped her arm

around Josie's shoulders and led her away and into the safety of Theo's admin, Fran.

Josie handed the garment bag to Adriana. "You should probably take this back."

"I'll be in touch about my grandmother's wedding dress." Adriana gently pressed the gown toward Josie and slid her gaze toward Theo's office. "Thank you, Josie. I have a really good feeling about working with you."

Josie searched for a good feeling among all her confusion. What had just happened? She'd met Theo's mother. Was judged by Theo's mother. Then asked if she wanted a meeting with a matchmaker. All the while, Theo stood beside her, silent and reserved. She'd have to bypass dissecting the Taylor family dynamics and channel her energy into her dressmaking. Still, her curiosity about the Taylors was getting the better of her.

Adriana guided Josie around Fran's desk. "Fran will take you to the elevators."

Fran held her arm out, pointing the way to the elevator bay. "Did your meeting with Adriana go well?"

Josie stared at the elevator call buttons. "I think so."

"I'm so pleased." Fran pressed the down button. "Adriana deserves the most beautiful wedding day."

Theo said he wanted the same thing for his sister. Josie wondered if Theo and Adriana had different visions for what a beautiful wedding day entailed. That wasn't Josie's problem to solve. She had to get sewing. Now. After her early afternoon fittings with the Curtain Call Children's Theater group and the six teens from Somerset Playhouse's *Scrooge* production. Then there were the late-afternoon alteration appointments. No matter. She'd work into the night. One day her sleeplessness would pay off.

Inside the elevator, Josie unzipped the garment bag and peeked at the gown inside. Layers of lace shifted under her searching fingers. She discovered several satin rosettes before the elevator bounced to a stop and the doors slid open. Adriana wasn't the only one excited about the gown. Josie was ready to race back to her shop to see the full dress.

Josie closed the garment bag. Annoyance slowed her steps through the lobby. There would be no gown to reveal. Because of one stubborn man who couldn't possibly know what would or wouldn't look good. A man with an impossible vision. The one who'd accept nothing less than perfection. As if that could be delivered. There was always a first time. And for Josie, it had to be now.

CHAPTER SEVEN

"You didn't have to be quite so rude to Josie." Adriana stepped beside Theo and shoved her elbow into his ribs.

Josie had elbowed Theo earlier. He'd missed what she'd been whispering, yet had barely restrained his smile at her boldness. Now he frowned and walked with his sister toward his office. "I wasn't—"

"Yes," Adriana interrupted. "You were rude. And you need to apologize."

"But I'm not sorry." He'd given his opinion. Expressed how he felt. He'd never apologized for that before. Maybe he could've used different words. Or not been quite so blunt. Theo shook his head. No. He was always blunt. No need to change now, even for the softhearted Josie Beck. As for the wisp of guilt shifting through him, he'd ignore that, too. Right now, they had other things—other people—to focus on. "Mother wasn't kidding earlier. She really is Daphne Holland's newest client at Holland Matchmakers."

Adriana swayed on her heels and squeezed his arm. "That's not funny, Theo."

Neither was giving Josie false expectations.

But he'd done just that at their lunch meeting yesterday. She'd looked at him, gratitude and hope shining in her big blue eyes. Something about Josie Beck stuck to him and made him question himself. There was nothing amusing about that. Or the guilt that lingered. "When was the last time I made a joke?"

Building a national brand required single-minded concentration and dedication. Light moments and laughter, however welcome, offered little return on investment. If Theo dwelled in those lighter moments too long, he feared he'd become content, like his dad.

You'll never build anything worthy if you become content like me, Theo. Love will do that to a man. Make you believe you have enough. Yet when you look back, all you'll really have is an endless list of regrets.

His father had expected Theo to be better. He had to be better. He'd earned his parents love after he'd grown the business. Only then had he been welcomed home, or, rather, welcomed home to the house he'd bought for his parents. The business had brought his family back together. Only continued success would ensure they stayed together.

He had no regrets since he'd accepted control of his father's company a decade ago. Yet watching Josie walk away, her head held high despite his negative words about her vintage dresses, he knew she could be his only regret. If he wasn't careful.

But he'd mastered the art of caution. He hadn't defended Josie against his mother, preferring not to put too much importance on the dressmaker. His mother would've honed-in, and she was already too curious about Josie.

"Mother hired a matchmaker to find a fiancé quickly, didn't she?" His sister's briskness confirmed his belief that she was truly worried.

"So it appears." As for his interest in Josie, he'd learned as a child to be more disciplined with his emotions. He'd perfected that skill as an adult, been determined to prove he was an obedient son and not merely another one of his father's regrets.

"We have to stop her." Adriana glanced inside his office. Their mother sat at his eight-seat conference table and was touching up her makeup.

"We're going to." Theo walked into his office, waited for Daphne to end her phone call and take a seat next to their mother. Then he looked at his sister. "Right now."

Adriana walked to the opposite end of the conference table, choosing a seat the farthest away from their mother. Adriana and their mother shared the same high cheekbones, defined features and dark hair color. The similarities ended there. Their mother preferred to offer advice and criticism to her daughter in the same conversation. Adriana opted to challenge her, yet with actions, not words.

"Thank you for coming in today, Daphne." Theo closed his office door and picked up a remote from the center of the large table. One press of a button and the windows dimmed, blocking his employees from seeing inside.

"I'm delighted to be here." Daphne tucked her dark brown hair behind her ear and smiled at Theo as if he'd agreed to become her client, too. "It's wonderful when an entire family comes together to support their loved one's journey to find companionship and, hopefully, love."

Support wasn't the word either of the Taylor children would use. His gaze collided with his sister's. Adriana rose to cover her sudden cough, opened the small refrigerator and handed out bottles of water. The only support Theo intended to give was for the cancellation of his mother's contract with Holland Matchmakers.

Their mother clicked her compact closed, the distinct snap drawing everyone's attention to her where she'd always desired it to be—on her. "Daphne has brought a list of potential matches for us to look over together."

His mother used the word *us* as if they'd collectively agreed she should hire a matchmaker.

The Taylors agreed on very little. From things as simple as food—his mother preferred chicken, while Adriana maintained a strict vegetarian diet and Theo chose a medium-rare steak, prime rib or bacon-wrapped hamburger any chance he could—to the Christmas holiday, which Theo always worked. Adriana always escaped to Ryan's house. Their mother floated from one social event to another.

"We'd like to begin the initial meet-and-greets as soon as this Saturday." Daphne pulled out a large slate-gray folder.

Saturday. As in two days away. One day before Josie had promised to have two prototypes completed. *Impossible*. He'd given Josie an impossible task. From the looks of Daphne's extra thick folder, her task wouldn't be simple, either. Although, Theo could simplify the list quickly by persuading them that none of the potential matches suitable for his mother.

That would require he stay in his office and look over each candidate. That was also impossible. He didn't have that kind of open time on his schedule. He had actual work to do. A job to perform. A company to oversee.

His office door opened. The film-crew trio spilled into the room. Nolan, wearing his ever-present boyish grin, carried a fuzz-covered microphone. Timmy balanced the camera in one hand and tugged off his usual knit beanie with the other, as if he'd arrived for a sit-down family dinner. Barry—the assistant producer and leader—closed the office door and clasped his hands together as he surveyed the scene like a seasoned director.

Theo stood and shook hands with Barry, Nolan and Timmy. "Guys, this is a bad time."

"There couldn't be a better time." His mother set her cell phone on the table and rose like a queen pleased to take another audience. She hugged each man and urged them farther into the room.

"You won't even know we're here." Barry kept his arm linked with Theo's mother's.

Way too late for that. Theo smoothed out his expression and his irritation. "Mother, we haven't asked Ms. Holland's permission to film her."

"It's no problem." His mother released Barry and set her hand on Daphne's shoulder. "It's just rough footage for our possible TV show. You don't mind, do you, dear?"

Daphne touched her cheek and scanned the film crew.

"There are usually written consent forms involved." Theo returned to the table, gripped the chair back and held onto his frustration.

Nolan slid a piece of paper across the table

toward Daphne. One edge of his mouth tipped up along with his one-shoulder shrug. "We like to be prepared."

And Theo liked to be forewarned.

"This is only footage to determine the final cast for the show." Timmy raised the camera and settled it on his shoulder. "It won't be aired."

Daphne took the pen his mother offered her and signed the paper. Theo rolled the chair away from the table and reluctantly sat down.

"Let's get started then." His mother took a portion of the paperwork and divided the pages into three piles. Eagerness punctuated her movements, delight her words. "There are so many. How should we proceed?"

"We shouldn't proceed." And Theo should've proceeded much differently with Josie Beck.

He should've opened their lunch meeting by informing Ms. Beck that her dressmaker services were not required. Regardless of her *feelings*. Feelings had no place in business. *Ever*. He added, "Daphne, it's not an appropriate time to begin this process."

It would've been an appropriate time at lunch to explain to Josie that her boutique would be renovated and redesigned from the storefront to her not profitable business model on Coast to Coast Living's new TV series. If she agreed to the terms.

"Look at all these potential matches, Theo." His mother's half smile and the blush that tinted her cheeks revealed her pleasure. "Seems like a very good time to start."

Barry stepped forward and grabbed a paper from Theo's pile. "What are we starting?"

"The journey to find my perfect partner, of course." His mother beamed and waved toward Daphne. "Gentleman, this is Daphne Holland, my talented and successful matchmaker. Would you gentlemen like to help us look through profiles, too?"

Theo narrowed his eyes and slapped his hand on his pile of profiles, stopping Barry from seizing more papers. Barry tiptoed back beside Nolan.

If Theo canceled the matchmaking, he didn't trust his mother not to go out and find anyone willing to say yes to her hasty proposal just to spite him. His mother adjusted her phone, nudging it closer to the matchmaker. Nolan and the oversize microphone shifted into Theo's view as if eager to capture Theo's comeback. He pressed his lips together.

Daphne brushed her bangs to the side to reveal her face, as if she was suddenly willing and more than ready to be fully seen on camera. "Lilian Rose wasn't very specific on what she was looking for in a partner."

Theo had wanted to be very specific about the idea of Josie meeting Daphne Holland. Instead, he'd flattened his rapid refusal between his clenched teeth. It wasn't his place to dictate Josie's dating life. Even if the idea of Josie with another man roiled his stomach.

He'd have to get used to the discomfort. Protecting Josie wasn't his priority. Neither was dating. Yet maintaining the family image mattered. "Mother, that surprises me. You're always very particular."

Adriana opened her water and drank, as if washing down her response.

"I want what Adriana and Ryan share." Lilian Rose pressed her ring finger against the edge of her eye, as if smoothing out the age-revealing fine lines for the camera. "But I don't want someone Ryan's age."

Theo wanted to remember that relying on a pair of blue eyes, no matter how captivating, was beyond dangerous. His father had fallen under the spell of a pair of dove-grey eyes. Married young and often lamented about his unfortunate lapse into a life of contentment.

Theo had a lapse in judgment. He'd requested two dress prototypes, not one, from Josie. As if Josie's liquid sky-blue eyes provided a compelling enough argument to hire her sewing skills.

As if Theo always relied on eye color to guide his decisions.

But success wasn't built on daydreams and delusions.

And if he terminated the matchmaking agreement now, his mother's disappointment would trail him like bad press. Theo picked up two stacks of paperwork and handed one to Adriana. "Let's exclude everyone under the age of fifty."

His sister ignored the paperwork and grasped his arm. "*We* are not a part of this."

"Fifty-five," their mother corrected. She leaned toward her cell phone, smiled at Timmy and added, "Sometimes people are still searching to figure out who they are in their early fifties. I'd like someone who knows himself."

"So birthdates from 1964 and earlier." Theo picked up a pen and drew a line through several profile pages, then imagined he could draw a line through Barry's forthcoming film clips, too.

Adriana picked up a profile page to hide behind and leaned toward him. "What are you doing?"

The paper blocked their faces but the frustration in Adriana's voice vibrated between them. Nothing blocked the obnoxious microphone Nolan lowered over their heads.

"If she's dating, then she can't be wedding

planning, too." Theo snatched the paper from Adriana and drew a line across it. "We're diverting her attention."

"For how long?" Adriana whispered.

Their mother was never good in a supporting role, like mother-of-the-bride. Lilian Rose laughed, swirled a large smiley face on one of her profile pages and presented the paper to the camera. The blissful tint in his mother's cheeks made the skin on the back of Theo's neck bristle. How long before his mother's dating life collided with the wedding planning and crashed into the business?

His mother handed the profile page to Adriana. "One of his hobbies is ballroom dancing. Perfect for a first dance."

That happy face his mother drew turned smug, whistling its taunt at Theo. The hairs on the back of Theo's neck shuddered. That was faster than even he'd imagined.

"Perhaps we could meet for a private dance lesson," his mother suggested.

Barry's foot tapped as if the man danced to his own internal music. Or perhaps that was the happy beat of ratings gold.

"We recommend all meet-and-greets occur in public places." The waves in Daphne's hair looked to be sliding off, each strand like an icicle surrendering to the sun. In this case it was

Lilian Rose, and she'd expect Daphne to concede. The matchmaker added, "Casual settings work best."

"Still, we prefer to look out for each other, don't we, Mother?" Adriana tapped her pen against her pile. "That's why my mother called my fiancé with a fake emergency a month after we started dating."

Barry bounced on his heels and leaned toward Nolan. The microphone never wavered. Timmy adjusted the camera lens as his grin widened. Clearly the film trio was more than thrilled by this inside glimpse into the Taylor family.

"I wanted to know how Ryan would handle a crisis." Their mother angled her head and eyed Adriana, as if waiting for a thank-you. "He passed, by the way, and that's the important thing."

Precisely why Theo rarely dated. His mother acted according to her own counsel and rarely considered the consequences. As for other people's feelings, those were their responsibility, not hers. After all, she always had some point to prove, even if her methods were often misguided.

"You want to know that your partner is levelheaded and competent in any situation." His mother crossed off several pages like a teacher grading her students' blank quiz answers. "I want that too—a team player."

"My mother wants a man who knows himself, is a team player and will love her like Ryan loves Adriana." Theo wanted to end this meeting and clear these folks out his office. Now. Before Barry and the crew decided his mother's search for love really would make a hit TV show. "Daphne, could you please refine your search to include those key words?"

Barry raised his hand as if he was one of his mother's students. "Theo, what key words would you use to find your mother's ideal partner?"

No. Not happening. This wasn't a question-and-answer session. Or a producer-led interview. Theo remained silent.

"That's a lovely idea. Thank you, Barry." His mother clasped her hands together and tilted her head at the appropriate angle to radiate genuine curiosity to the camera. "I should know what my own children want for me. What kind of partner they'd like to see me with. After all, he'll be a large part of their lives, too."

Under the table, Theo pressed his heels into the floor to stop the irritation from sending his legs into a rapid shaking rhythm. Finally, he cleared his throat, but not the annoyance. "I want the same things as my mother wants, of course."

Beside him, Adriana finished her bottle of water. "As do I."

There was nothing faint about his sister's tone. Nothing waterlogged about her voice. What was his sister up to? They were supposed to be on the same side.

"Those are things Lilian Rose will discover at their first meet-up." Daphne's smile strained at the edges, as if she was struggling not to scowl for the camera.

"If mother doesn't like her dates, then Theo will be there to take care of it," Adriana added. Her half grin steamrolled over Theo.

Wait. What? Theo frowned at his sister. "I will?"

Barry pulled a notebook from his back pocket and scribbled on a page. No doubt a note to follow up with Daphne on meet-up times and places. More ratings gold.

Theo didn't have time to supervise his mother's dates. He didn't want another diversion. He had a company to guide to the next level and that involved his attention and dedication. What happened to canceling this farce? What happened to his decisiveness?

Theo untwisted the cap from his water bottle and drank. The cool water did nothing to ease his dry throat or his frustration. The wedding planning, the matchmaking and a certain dressmaker dulled his edge.

"We agreed to look out for each other," his mother said. "That's what families do."

His mother's voice was too smooth and a notch too pleasant. Her smile too genuine. He knew that practiced look all too well. His mother had perfected it each year for parent weekend at his boarding school. And now, it seemed, for the TV camera. His teachers had adored her. The other parents had wanted to meet her.

Their family always looked out for each other from a distance. Until Theo had proven himself competent and dramatically raised the Taylor-family status. Then they came together as a family to be celebrated as an American success story in the press. With their brand solidified, no one in the Taylor family bothered to issue a correction.

"First, you need to agree on someone to meet." Daphne clicked her pen. *Open. Closed. Open.* The steady rhythm fell short of tempering the worry in her tone. The matchmaker had made no matches.

A twinge of sympathy for the flustered matchmaker tweaked Theo's conscience. But not enough for him to soothe Daphne's worry.

He had to end this...and quickly. Before Barry offered more insightful questions. Before his mother discovered her starring role.

Theo drew an *X* across several of the profiles in his stack. No smokers allowed. No serial marriages—seven times married was not a badge of honor.

The next one made him pause—"coached little league on Saturdays, widow for six years, favorite meal to cook: pasta. Thankful for a good life and great memories." Profile HJ-62 sounded promising. Theo wasn't there to encourage his mother. He was there to oppose. He crossed a line through Profile HJ-62.

"What else are you looking for, Mother?" Adriana's gaze remained fixed on her stack of profiles. Only a mild interest leaked through her tone.

"As I said, dear, what you have with Ryan." His mother sighed and flipped several profiles into the growing *no* stack. "What I had with your father. That special something."

"But paper cannot reveal that." Daphne gathered the discarded profiles from Adriana and Theo as if collecting lingerie spilling from a suitcase at the airport baggage claim. The exasperation in her tone shifted into a breathless insistence. "As I've explained, that's what the first meet-and-greets are for."

Theo had witnessed "that peculiar something special" every time he saw his mother and father holding hands. A small, insignificant connection to most observers. Yet Theo had noticed the way his mother's smile had always flared up into her gaze, lighting her entire face. His father's grin had always tipped up as if his wife had told him a really good secret.

Nothing more than warmth had ever seized Theo whenever he'd reached for a former girlfriend's hand. Certainly nothing that realigned his core as the urge to hold on longer burned through him. Not that he was searching for "that peculiar something special." Signing up for Daphne Holland's matchmaking program was not happening. As for holding someone's hand, he hadn't wanted to do that until recently. Until he'd stepped into a certain bridal boutique.

But he knew nothing about those special feelings his mother liked to talk about. Most likely his memory had adjusted the recollections of his mother and father holding hands.

Theo tapped his pen against the profile pages, filtering his focus back to the conference table. He was really only interested in the gown Josie Beck produced with her hands. Nothing more.

As for his mother, he couldn't envision his mother holding any hand of her potential matches. Except maybe Profile HJ-62, but Theo had already removed him from the running. Just as he was also removing himself from any kind of running other than a business association with Josie.

"I expect I'll have a feeling. In here." His mother set more profiles on the rejection pile then placed her palm over her heart and spoke into her phone. "I have to honor that feeling when it happens."

Barry raised his hand again. "I'm struggling to decide who has a faster rejection rate—Ms. Lilian Rose or Theo. What feeling are you both getting that is resulting in such a rapid rejection rate?"

His mother tapped her heart. "There's nothing flipping over in here. Nothing good happening."

Except Theo suddenly had a good feeling. A very good feeling that his mother wouldn't have a meet-and-greet this weekend, considering that her rejection rate clearly exceeded his.

Daphne Holland would need to expand her search criteria into zip codes beyond the city. Arranging long-distance meet-and-greets would require planning and scheduling. That alone would slow the process.

That elusive something special his mother expected—well, Theo wasn't convinced she'd ever find that again. Or that Daphne Holland could locate it. Or that it ever really existed in the first place—perhaps it was only part of his boyhood imagination.

Daphne Holland had an impossible task before her. Theo drew a line through a profile page and smoothed out his grin.

Almost as impossible as the one he'd given to Josie. Two prototypes in four days. Two dresses that would meet his exacting standards. It wasn't possible. Just as Daphne wouldn't be able to find a candidate that met his mother's exacting standards, either.

That realization curved optimism through him. He rocked back in his chair, finally feeling like he was back in control.

Josie would have to give in, too. Admit defeat. Of course, he wouldn't judge her. Then he'd offer her a spot on his TV show, keeping attention away from the disputing Taylors and keeping the brand in tact for another day.

As for Daphne, surely he knew several high-profile bachelors to send her way once his mother backed out.

That left the wedding gown. He'd convince his mother that she wanted a different gown. Then persuade Adriana the Linden Topher—the one-of-a-kind custom dress—was the best option.

What could be more simple? He'd negotiated seven-figure contracts and guided disparate businesses into lucrative partnerships. He hadn't faltered in the business world. Surely he could manage his own family.

Theo crossed off the remaining pages of profiles with a renewed flourish and slid the pile to Daphne. He made his voice sound accommodating and interested. "When would you be able to have more profiles available?"

Daphne gathered the paperwork and straightened the stack on the table, as if aligning the conviction in her tone. "As soon as tomorrow."

He applauded the matchmaker's confidence. Confidence that reminded him of a certain bridal dressmaker.

"My next meeting should be only with your mother," Daphne suggested. "Then she can share her choices with you and your sister."

"I disagree." Theo stood and shifted his smile to offer more sincerity. "This group collaboration worked quite well. The next meeting should be at Glass Violet."

Reservations for the exclusive five-star restaurant were often booked three weeks in advance. The current holiday season lengthened the wait time to five weeks, often longer for premium dining times. If he planned appropriately, he could postpone another meeting with Daphne Holland and his mother's groom search until after the New Year.

"Lunch at Glass Violet would be delightful. I can't wait." His mother rose, hugged Daphne and then reached for her phone and pressed a red button.

Suspicion dulled Theo's earlier optimism. He rose from his chair. "Mother, were you recording this meeting, too?"

"Absolutely." His mother tucked her phone into her purse and patted her flawless hair into place. "I'm making a video memory book of my next love story."

Theo paused. "A video what?"

"You won't understand." His mother walked over to him and tapped his cheek. "It's nothing to concern yourself with."

Theo had used those same words with Josie. Josie had thrown those same words back at him earlier. Now his mother. Those words made him concerned. Those words suddenly made him want to get involved—very involved.

"Now, I have errands to run." His mother blew kisses into the room and grinned at Barry. "Would you gentlemen care to join me?"

"They're spending the day with me," Theo said, then slammed his mouth closed. The last thing he wanted was to spend the entire day being filmed. But his mother alone with the trio… Theo added, "I've promised them an exclusive interview and a behind-the-scenes look at the company."

Barry rubbed his chin, smoothing his fingers through his goatee. His assessing gaze shifted from Theo's mother, then back to Theo.

His mother could not be alone with a film crew. Theo launched another volley. "I have a meeting at the Pioneer Stadium with the team owner. He mentioned extra playoff tickets he has to give away."

Nolan and Timmy high-fived. His mother had lost out to the local professional football team and possible box seats. But Theo sensed it'd been a close race. Too close.

His mother preened at Barry and his crew. "Until next time." Then she was gone.

Barry gathered Timmy and Nolan. "We're going to get refills at the coffee bar and talk to a few of your staff."

With that, Theo's office was almost back to normal.

"Mother can be rather particular. I wish you luck." Adriana handed her stack of rejections to Daphne and left the office.

"Particular is my specialty," Daphne muttered. She crammed the paperwork into her tote bag and blinked at Theo as if only then realizing he was still in the office. She straightened, pinned a smile on her face and put positivity in her tone. "The more time I spend with my clients, the more I learn about them. That's always good."

It was also good to be back in control. Why didn't he feel in control? Theo stepped behind his desk and checked the calendar on his computer. One meeting with his editorial staff. A conference call to discuss potential shareholders. He'd have the rest of the evening to get caught up on his work from the morning and regain his footing. "I'm certain my mother would like to spend more time with you."

And Theo would most certainly appreciate the distraction Daphne Holland provided.

"I know it can be hard for children to see their mother with someone other than their father." Daphne crossed the office and stopped on the other side of Theo's desk. "I'm aware that no man will match up to yours."

Perhaps not in his mother's eyes. Theo was counting on that much. At least until his sister recited her vows and her wedding was over. After that, he'd worry about his mother's dates fitting the image for their brand. But that was for later.

Right now, he needed his mother occupied with endless profile pages and her diverted from wedding planning. Theo escorted Daphne to the elevator lobby. "My mother's happiness is important to me."

"I'm glad to hear that." Daphne stepped into the elevator and held the door open. "Perhaps next time you can put her happiness first and not reject every single candidate."

"I'm also quite particular," Theo said. "I suppose I get that trait from my mother. I'm sure you can meet our expectations in time."

"I intend to." Daphne nodded, clenched the handles on her bag and let the doors slide shut.

Theo intended to stop letting dressmakers and matchmaking distract him from his real work.

CHAPTER EIGHT

JOSIE WAS OUTSIDE for the first time since she'd arrived at work eight hours ago. She'd spent the entire day inside her shop. No lunch meetings. No quick stopovers at the Coast to Coast Living offices. Yet it was already Friday and even closer to Sunday's fitting and another encounter with Theo. She wanted to see Theo again and she wanted more time to prepare.

She took a long, deep breath of the cool evening air. Many stores on the block had turned on their Christmas light displays in their front windows. Small trees and more colored lights blinked from the windows in the apartments several floors above the businesses. Across the street, the Christmas lights circling the Pampered Pooch pet-store window chased each other in a cheerful red-green-blue pattern. They were beautiful. Enchanting.

The emptiness inside her expanded into more than a twinge.

Josie hadn't put up a tree or decorations, not inside the boutique or her apartment. She wanted to point her finger at time and blame her lack of extra hours on an already too-full work week. The valid excuse, however valid, fell flat like rain-soaked tinsel. Theo probably paid someone to decorate his house. That would free him up to work longer, harder hours.

Every year, she acted like those Christmas lights and tried to chase down the holiday spirit. Yet she never quite caught it completely. This season, she raced to secure the future of her business. That mattered more than a seasonal feeling—one that faded once the ornaments and garland were put away in storage. Next year, she'd pursue her elusive Christmas spirit, if she wasn't too busy with her work.

A woman called Josie's name from the street corner, pulling away her attention from the Christmas decorations and her holiday disconnect.

Adriana Taylor hurried along the sidewalk, slipping around the couples dressed for an early dinner and the business suits stepping off the bus. Adriana's extralong coat fanned out behind her, revealing a simple shimmery sweater dress and over-the-knee suede boots. Josie envied Adriana's effortless ease. Her snowflake-print shoulder bag proved her connection to the holiday season.

Adriana glided to a stop, steady and poised in her heeled boots. More animated than breathless. "I'm so glad you're still here. I was worried you'd already closed."

"The boutique is officially closed." Josie tugged open the door, welcoming the warmth as if the cool breeze, not her lack of holiday joy, chilled her. She waited for Adriana to step inside.

"I got your message about discussing dress designs." Adriana set her fingers on Mia's framed photograph of the Golden Gate Bridge in the dense fog and smiled. "I could fill my flat with Mia's work and be content."

Josie studied the photograph and searched for her own contentment. But Adriana's unexpected arrival unraveled a disquiet inside her. Even her voice sounded restless and rushed. "We could've spoken on the phone. I didn't mean to disrupt your evening."

Adriana clutched the handles of her purse, holding the festive shoulder bag in front of her as if to hide her shifting steps. Her voice was cautious, her words hesitant. "There's another reason I'm here."

Alarm thudded through Josie like a tipped-over Christmas tree.

Was she going to fire her? Was Theo letting Josie go? Adriana hadn't really looked over the designs. Another designer most likely sent her another gown. A better dress. Surely fashion houses provided Adriana with clothing year-round. Josie couldn't compete. Not on that level. She'd known as much. She'd just wanted a chance to believe. Josie stepped behind the checkout counter and braced her hands on the desk, as if to slow her fall.

Adriana crossed one ankle in front of the other.

But nothing blocked out the awkward stillness.

Adriana said, "I'm wondering if you have my Grandma Pearl's wedding dress here."

"Of course." Josie lifted her unsteady arm and pointed toward the back—her arm wobbled like a broken tree branch. She had stored the garment bag in her workroom beside her upscaled wedding gowns. Within easy reach, in case Adriana wanted to wear a part of her family's history, if only inside The Rose Petal. Josie had blank spaces for her family history. To have something tangible like a wedding gown was rare and not to be discarded or so easily overlooked. "It's in my workroom. I'm sure you'd like it returned."

Adriana set her hand on Josie's arm, stopping her before she disappeared in the back. Once again, Adriana's tone dipped into a quiet reserve. "I'd like to try my grandmother's dress on."

Josie swayed. "Really?"

Adriana nodded.

Delight dashed through Josie, brightening her wide grin. Christmas could keep its spirit. Josie had her passion for dresses to fulfill her.

Last night, Josie had pulled the vintage 1950s dress from the garment bag. She'd fallen asleep imagining the alterations she'd make to transform the gown into something worthy of Adriana Taylor. Now Adriana wanted to put on the dress. And Josie wanted to share her ideas. "Let me get it."

"I'm not interrupting your evening plans, am I?" Adriana followed Josie.

"I have an appointment in an hour then I'll be back here to work into the night." Josie took the garment bag from her workroom and hung the gown on the oversize bronze hook inside the dressing room. "I have plenty of time for this fitting."

"I just want to see it on. My grandmother would've liked that. Theo will hate it." Adriana shook her head and laughed. Yet there was a wistful note in her voice. "Although Grandma Pearl probably would've told me it has lost its luster."

"Yet she kept it all those years. Now it's a piece of your family history." Josie always wanted to know her history—something as simple as her grandmother's name or a good family memory.

All she had was a birth certificate that listed her birth mother's name, Josephine Elizabeth Beck, and her birth father's name—blank. Her birth mother had signed over parental rights to the state on the day of Josie's birth. She'd learned that fact from one of her foster brothers who was adept at locating and translating the paperwork inside every foster child's folder. The only connection Josie wanted with her birth mother had ended with their shared full name. Josie hadn't needed to learn anything more.

"Grandma Pearl always told me 'Addy, honey, love brings you to the altar. But marriage is longer than any vow recital. Marriage is a lifetime.'" Adriana touched one of the tiers of ribbon-trimmed ruffled white lace on the gown. "Then she'd wink and tell me 'Addy, you best start that journey wearing an eye-catching dress that dazzles your new husband all the way to his toes.'"

Josie was certain the elder Taylor had stunned in her full lace, rosette-adorned wedding dress. Josie undid the self-covered buttons that trailed in a straight line down the back of the gown. "I wish I'd met her."

"She was my favorite." Adriana hung her coat on the empty hook and slipped off her boots. "I want her to be a part of my wedding. I want a dress that dazzles just like my grandmother's."

Josie wanted that for Adriana, too.

The shop's bells chimed, startling her. "I didn't think Mia was coming back tonight. She's working at the Christmas Town gingerbread-house reveal this evening. Let me see if she needs anything."

Josie eased out of the dressing room and froze. Behind her, she yanked the thick velvet curtains closed. Her words came out in an abrupt shout. "Hello, Theo!"

Theo nodded his head at her. A smile tipped the edges of his mouth. "Do you always yell a greeting at your customers?"

"Only when they arrive after-hours and scare me." Josie latched onto a bare body form and rolled it closer to guard the dressing-room entrance.

"You should lock your front door." Theo frowned toward the storefront, as if concerned about her safety.

"Adriana and I were just finishing up." Josie tugged the measuring tape off the body form and rolled it into her hands, pretending she'd been holding it the whole time. She kept her voice pitched an octave higher than normal to include Adriana in the conversation. "Then we were leaving."

"Adriana?" Theo glanced around the boutique.

Josie pointed at the dressing room. "We were discussing changes to the prototypes and taking measurements."

"You have the prototypes already?" Surprise lifted Theo's eyebrows.

"We worked through ideas for both gowns," Josie hedged. That was the start of her stretching the truth. Just close enough that she tiptoed near the border of the outright fibbing zone. They hadn't looked at the designs, let alone discussed changes. But Josie had shared her ideas on Adriana's voice mail.

Josie stepped into her workroom and pushed another body form, covered in the muslin template for Adriana's second gown, toward the platform. With luck, she'd distract Theo.

She knew that Theo would not be pleased to learn both women had been more interested in Grandma Pearl's gown. The last body form Josie retrieved was draped in the Helen-inspired gown. "After speaking to Adriana, this first gown appeals to her aesthetic more than the second."

"Appealing or not, we requested two *original* gowns." He emphasized the word *original*. His voice was inflexible and weighty, as if he'd highlighted the word in bold, neon yellow.

"That you'll have by Sunday," Josie promised, stopping herself from revealing there could likely be three gowns if Adriana liked her grandmother's dress.

"If you can't fulfill my requests, tell me now." Theo ignored the dress forms and stared at Josie.

Tell him she'd failed. Never. Josie eyed him, unable to find the weakness in his impassive face. The kindness that would convince her Theo didn't want her to fail. Didn't expect her to fail. "I've already scheduled a fitting with Adriana for tomorrow afternoon."

She had an opening in the late afternoon. Josie left out the specifics, like Adriana needed to accept the spot. And their grandmother's dress would be included in the fittings.

"So soon?" Theo asked.

Clearly not soon enough for stuffy, single-minded Mr. Taylor. "Custom gowns require custom measurements, Mr. Taylor."

"I've never been a part of the process of making women's clothes." The crack in his smile slanted his stiff tone toward amused rather than apologetic.

"Why are you now?" Josie rearranged the body forms and secured her internal filter. Outbursts were not her style. Except with Theo. He made her want to challenge him. To push past his reserve.

He didn't censure her. Only arched one eyebrow in what was a more charming look than a surprised one. "Why wouldn't I be involved? It's my only sister's wedding."

Charm never affected Josie. At least not before Theo. Josie argued, "But it's her wedding dress."

The same as it was Josie's heart. If she chose not to let her heart flip, then it wouldn't. Her heart skipping now was only her fear that Theo almost caught his sister in his grandmother's gown.

"Do you have siblings, Ms. Beck?" The formality returned to his stance and voice.

"I do not." *Fortunately.* Traversing the foster system by herself had been difficult enough. If she'd been separated from a brother or sister, it would've been devastating. But with a sibling, she would've been less alone. Josie shook her head, stomping down that old sadness back beside her Christmas spirit. Grieving something she never had was a distraction. She didn't need another one. Theo was more than enough.

"I promised to look out for Adriana." The edges of his eyes flinched, which disturbed his poise, as if he'd stumbled over a memory. "I intend to keep my word."

His voice dropped off, as if his words tumbled over a cliff. Josie studied Theo. "A foster mom once told me 'You can't be angry at the past if you want to enjoy the present.'"

Those had been Mimi's first words to Josie. Then she'd embraced a scared and lonesome ten-year-old girl and instructed Josie to leave her shoes and her bitterness on the front porch. Inside Mimi's hug, Josie had let go, then cherished every moment they had spent together.

"Sounds like a fortune-cookie quote." Theo touched a jeweled headband and frowned. "With its empty promises and simplistic insight."

"And you sound angry." At himself or someone else, Josie couldn't decide. For the slightest moment, she considered embracing him. Holding on until his anger eased, just like when Mimi had held her. That wasn't her place. And it was beyond unprofessional. Business arrangements required boundaries.

His half smile barely creased his face. "Not angry, only determined."

Josie was determined, too. To keep her word on their business agreement and deliver finished gowns to Theo on Sunday. To stick to her to-do list that included blind stitches to complete, appliqués to apply and buttonholes to finish. Getting to know Theo better—embracing him—wasn't on any to-do list of hers.

Adriana stepped out of the dressing room and tugged at the curtains, clearly annoyed. "Really, Theo? Were you following me or checking up on Josie?"

"I was in the neighborhood and decided to stop in." Theo's grin appeared in his slate eyes. "Is there something wrong with that?"

Josie rolled an undressed body form toward her workroom and yanked the curtain on the dressing room completely closed. "Now that you've checked on my progress, is there anything else I can do for you, Mr. Taylor?"

Theo stepped to the Jin-inspired gown on the other body form and touched the white feathers Josie had tacked on the shoulder. He said, "I'm surprised you prefer this first gown, Adriana. Given your distaste for feathers and faux fur."

"Yes, well, Josie convinced me to step out of my comfort zone." Adriana touched her cheek, then her throat, finally letting her hand flutter like a falling feather. Her hands were as restless as her voice. "The feathers add a certain degree of whimsy."

"You've told me repeatedly you want a refined and elegant theme." He crossed his arms over his chest. His gaze shifted toward the dressing room—one brief pass—before he scowled at his sister.

Josie wanted to shove Theo away from her creation. Or perhaps tip several bags of feathers over him and dare him to remain indifferent, covered in all that white fluffiness. "The feathers keep the dress from dipping into the staid and uptight." *Like you.*

"What about the chin-length veil?" Theo's hand brushed against the feathers. "I forget the style name."

Would Theo's touch be as soft against her own skin? Josie scratched the back of her neck and pulled her gaze from Theo's hand. "Birdcage."

"Right." Theo watched his sister and Josie over the body forms, as if he were trying to figure out a puzzle. "Adriana, what did you call the birdcage veil that arrived from that New York fashion house? A lunch lady's hairnet, or was it a visor?"

Adriana touched her chin as if catching her faltering smile.

"I never showed Adriana that birdcage veil." Josie walked to her design book and flipped quickly through the loose pages before finally, she located the matching sketch she'd drawn at Helen's house. The sweet woman's voice circled through her. *Keep your chin up, Josie.* "I changed the design after I left our lunch. We added a full mantle veil instead."

Adriana took the design and traced her finger over the drawing. "This is quite stunning, isn't it? Even with the feathers accenting the hem of the sheer cape. And the sparkles are a lovely touch."

"That's the beading." Josie shrugged. "It's all in the details."

Adriana glanced up, her eyes wide. "The details that we discussed earlier, of course." She shoved the design at her brother and glanced at her wrist. "I need to go. I'm meeting Ryan for dinner. Now."

"Don't forget about tomorrow's fitting," Josie added.

"Right." Adriana hugged Josie and whispered, "Please don't give Grandma Pearl's wedding dress to Theo." Then she spun around to face her brother. "It would be a good time to apologize since you're in the neighborhood."

Theo watched his sister, tracking her hasty departure. Josie watched him.

She clapped her palms together and drew Theo's focus to her. Not her best idea, given his full attention on her was like standing under direct sunlight: mood-boosting and energizing. But then even with sunscreen, her skin always burned too quickly. "I should be going, too."

He checked his watch. "If you're closing up, I'll walk you home."

"How do you know where I live?" Josie set her hands on her hips. She never invited anyone to her apartment. *Ever.*

"I do my research," he said. "I don't work with just anyone."

"Neither do I, Mr. Taylor." Josie tugged the design from his grip. "I researched you, as well."

He grinned at her. "You know my home address?"

"No," she muttered. She slid the design back into her book, making a mental note to nix the birdcage veil and up the sparkle.

"If it makes you feel any better, I know people." He stepped closer to her.

Clearly, she needed to know different people. Especially if standing within less than a yard of Theo made her want to reach for that sunlight and linger longer. "I know people, too. I prefer to trust my gut instinct rather than the internet."

"Have your instincts ever been wrong?" he asked.

His voice brushed across her cheek, soft like that feather. Warmth seeped through her, melting her heart. Her instincts were obviously very wrong now. "Definitely. My divorce papers prove as much."

"You were married?" His words came slowly, as if he thought he might've misheard her.

"Four years."

"What happened?"

"Our styles were too different." Much like Theo and her. Worlds apart. Except right now, she felt… "My style was better suited for charity than boardrooms and partner lunches."

"Are you always so honest?" he asked.

No. If she was honest, she'd give him his grandmother's gown. But she'd promised Adriana. If she was honest, she'd admit she wanted to move even closer and dare to test that attraction she felt whenever she was around him. "Pretending to be what you aren't can be exhausting."

A shadow of a smile passed over his face. "Then, tell me, who is Josie Beck?"

"A woman determined to succeed on her own." Josie locked her gaze on his. "I don't want handouts or help from anyone who feels sorry for me. I want to know I earned what I have."

"Sounds like more fortune-cookie references." A low roll of humor swiveled around his words. But the admiration—that was there in his steady gaze.

Her own smile spread through her, unrestrained. "Fortune cookies sound more like this—'The lazy only ever accomplish one thing—nothing.'"

"So, Josie Beck is dedicated and hardworking." He reached up and tucked a curl behind her ear. "Anything else?"

Her pulse accelerated, tripped her heart into the express lane. Josie focused on the wall clock, seeking something stable to regain her balance. She read the time and latched onto the detour. "I'm late for an appointment."

And much too late to start listening to her heart.

Josie picked up her travel sewing bag and purse. Lights turned off, she stepped outside. Theo waited within confessing distance. She locked the door and bolted down her daydreamer of a heart.

"Where's your appointment?" he asked.

"Penny's Place." Josie searched the street and frowned. No cabs waited in either direction. If she hadn't been sidetracked by Theo, she'd have already ordered a ride on her phone app.

"I can drive you," he offered.

"That's kind, but not necessary." Josie walked to the street corner. Surely she could find a cab. And a taxi driver who couldn't see inside her. One who couldn't reveal the painful things she wanted to hide.

"My sister believes I owe you an apology for the other day at our offices," he said.

Josie turned toward him. "What do you believe?"

"That I was merely expressing my opinion about my grandmother's old dress." He shrugged. "However unpopular it was."

Josie waited.

Theo's shoulders lowered and he added, "Apparently I should've used different wording."

Josie studied him. "What would you have said instead?"

"I would have said, 'I prefer my sister never finds my grandmother's wedding dress.'"

She shook her head. She'd been right. Theo wouldn't understand Adriana's connection to their grandmother's gown. Such a shame. But it wasn't Josie's job to educate him. "You must not have liked your grandmother very much."

He stepped closer to her, blocking her view of the street. "I loved my grandmother. She passed when I was young, and I still miss her every single day."

Josie's mouth dropped open. Sincerity echoed in his voice. There was pain, too—in his gaze and tense jaw—and that confused Josie. Theo Taylor was a complicated man—one she'd like to figure out. Mimi had taught Josie to sew and had introduced her to puzzles. Who knew that hobby would get her in trouble one day? "Why not celebrate your grandmother's memory then?"

"My sister's wedding is the start of her new life. She should begin her journey unhampered by the past," he said. "It's the foundation for good memories to be built on."

How was Josie supposed to argue with that?

She'd believed the same thing with her marriage, but it all proved to be false. Not that Adriana's marriage would end like hers. It was clear why Josie wanted to avoid her past. But why did Theo?

Yet she couldn't start to like Theo, to connect with him—that would only make Sunday all the worse if she didn't measure up. She stepped around him and her curiosity, then pointed. "Oh, look. There's an available cab."

"My car is right across the street." Theo hit the unlock button on his key fob. The brake lights on a four-door sedan flashed and the interior lights lit up the inside. "And besides, this ride is free."

Josie crossed the street next to Theo, wondering how much this one free ride would cost her.

CHAPTER NINE

"YOU DON'T NEED to walk me to the entrance." Josie held onto the passenger door of Theo's car as if she intended to use it to block him.

Theo parked in the private alley behind Penny's Place. The three-story house was a mismatch of styles, additions having been completed and redesigned in each new decade. Even the detached garage hadn't been spared from the architectural chaos—it was now shrouded in contractor's netting and caution tape, and looked to be undergoing another transformation.

"It's the polite thing to do." Theo cut the engine, opened his door and gestured at the backseat. "Do you want me to get your bag?"

Josie scrambled out of the car and grabbed her sewing bag like a doctor running to a medical emergency. "I'm sure you have things you need to be doing."

He was sure he did, too. Only right now, the thing he wanted to do was stay beside Josie. He couldn't quite figure her out. He wanted to know for certain who she was before talking to her about the opportunity to be featured on TV. "This is my chance to see inside Penny's Place and learn how the house works. Perhaps meet some of the residents and learn their stories."

Josie rushed along the gravel walkway leading to the front of the house. "Any reason you want to do that now?"

You. Theo lengthened his stride and opened the black iron gate for her. He spent his days surrounded by contracts, spreadsheets and employees paid to follow his instructions and his vision, down to the very last detail. Josie had her own vision—one he wanted to see through her eyes. Then maybe he'd understand her, even if he didn't agree with her.

Warm light glowed from the twin porch sconces, layering a soft welcome across the etched-glass front door. A thick door swung open to reveal an even more welcoming petite woman with her arms spread wide as if to embrace the world. There was resilience in her dimples that hadn't surrendered to time. And her sweet gaze only reflected acceptance. Theo had been fortunate to meet Penny Joyce at several charity events over the years and every time he encountered Penny, he liked her even more.

The security cameras above the entryway were only a portion of the system he'd paid to have installed around the perimeter of the house. Given Penny's quick response to their arrival, he knew she was using the system.

Penny enclosed Josie's hand between hers. "Could it be that you've finally brought a date to introduce to me?"

Finally? How long had Penny been waiting for this occasion? Josie was single. He liked that, but wanted to know why she wasn't dating. And what it might take to change her mind. If he was interested in changing her mind, which he wasn't. After all, distractions like Josie Beck weren't good for business. And Theo lived for his business.

"Theo drove me here. That's all." Josie pulled her hand free and waved at Theo as if shooing him away.

"Then I escorted you to the door," Theo added. Josie's frown deepened and made his smile go wider. He nudged Josie aside enough to lean down and hug Penny.

Penny squeezed him and held on. "Theo, it's wonderful to finally welcome you here."

Josie stared at him. "You've been invited before?"

Theo shrugged.

"More than a dozen times, at least. Always claimed a lack of time was keeping him away." Penny adjusted Theo's collar and patted his arm. "I've been wanting to show Theo how his support has improved the house."

"Then I'll leave you to the tour." Josie stepped into the wide entryway and glanced from the curved staircase to the hallway as if plotting her quickest escape route. From him. She said, "I'm trying to catch Shanna for a few measurements. She told me that she'd be here between work shifts."

"Though Shanna moved out over a month ago, she still spends most of her free time here. Right now, she's in the kitchen, teaching Tansy how to bake peppermint brownies." Penny shut the door and linked her arm with Theo's. "Just follow the scent."

"It smells divine." Josie turned left and headed through the dining room.

Penny shook her head. "That dear girl needs to sit down, put her feet up and enjoy life."

Did Josie enjoy her life? No doubt a profitable business plan for her boutique would make her life more enjoyable. Would Josie agree?

"When was the last time you put your feet up, Penny?" Theo walked beside Penny down a long hallway. The deep scuffs and scratches in the hardwood floors were reminders that life wasn't always gentle or kind, yet the resilient survived. And with the support of Penny and her home, they learned to thrive.

"My feet are just fine. Haven't worn holes in my socks yet." Penny pointed at her shearling-lined boots. "Besides, what kind of example would I be to these women if I sat around all day?"

"If you won't sit during the day, perhaps in

the evening when no one is watching," Theo suggested.

"Someone is always watching. Even if it's just the world passing by outside our windows." Penny leaned into Theo, not as if she required support, but as if to encourage him.

He rarely rested. Rarely sat to watch the world pass by. He preferred to be out in front.

Penny continued, "I tell the residents here that they can't learn to live with their feet propped up. Have to touch the ground to take even the smallest step."

"Good thing my feet are always on the ground." That was the only way to stay in the lead. The only way to capture success. Success was all that mattered.

Penny looked up at him, concern on her face. "But are you living, Theo?"

He paused and his gaze landed on the framed paintings lining the hallway. Watercolors, fruit bowls, abstracts, animals. Every different skill level was represented. Every possible paint color and color combination illustrated. A collision of personalities and styles, yet Theo recognized the story. Felt the connection. Understood the hope in the tears of the weeping woman. The fear in the dark gaze of the tiger. The sadness in the bruised apple outside the fruit bowl. The women in Penny's Place lived. Could Theo say the same? "I like to think so."

He had no personal dream. Surely that wasn't a requirement for living. Yet when he'd stood inside Josie's boutique, her blue eyes inviting, her face fragile and honest, she could've been his dream.

"Working all the time isn't living." Penny squeezed his arm as she scolded him.

But there was nothing productive about dwelling in emotions—feelings only interfered. Weakened a person. "You work every day, Penny, from what I hear."

"This house. These women." Penny drew a deep breath and straightened one of the paintings, her fingers lingering on the frame as if she touched the painter's cheek instead. "This isn't work. Never that. This is my passion. The way I make a difference in my corner of the world. This is my calling."

Theo had been called. Called by his father after his college graduation to take over the family business. Despite the job offers from international companies answering Theo's dream to explore the world. As for passion, what did he know about that? Other than earning a profit was what fueled him. "Few people have that."

"I'm blessed," Penny said. "Josie has passion, too."

But it took more than desire to build a profitable business. It took dedication and hard decisions. Sacrifice. It took withstanding accusations of being emotionally unavailable, indifferent, cold. It required detachment. Josie had warmth. Too much empathy. "She's talented."

Penny stopped in an open archway and met Theo's gaze. "You don't know what she's done here, do you?"

"I know she's designing a wedding gown for Shanna." *For free*. Despite the negative impact to her bottom line. Ignoring the bottom line ruined businesses, bankrupted owners.

"That's one dress among many." Penny tapped her fingers, counting off Josie's accomplishments. "Josie also tailors, hems and creates clothes for all the women in the house. Clothes for job interviews, for first days at work. For anything the women need."

"How long has she been doing that?" No wonder the exterior of her shop was worn down and the interior dated. She'd invested in her charity work, not her business. He wanted to fault her. Wanted to save her.

"She started soon after she was married." Penny stepped into a room and flipped on the light switch.

Theo stood in the hallway and blinked, letting his eyes adjust and thoughts clear. Josie had mentioned that her ex-husband and she had different styles. But she'd meant that her design style wasn't worthy of boardrooms and partner lunches.

"After the divorce, Josie never stopped." Penny walked farther into the large space and turned on more overhead lights. "Despite working two jobs and saving to open the boutique."

Josie was certainly dedicated. He had to give her that much.

"Everyone here adores her," Penny admitted. "I think the feeling is mutual. She's like another mother to them—protective and nurturing."

All the things he'd wanted his mother to be. Theo blinked again. Considered shielding his eyes, but it wasn't the glare of the overheads that startled him. Josie never had a mother of her own to guide her. Still she was kindhearted. Compassionate.

"You're a sly one, Theo. The quiet, attentive type who a woman can spill her secrets to." Penny shook her finger at him. "But this lady has rambled on enough. You'll get nothing more from me."

"Are you sure?" Theo persisted.

"Quite." Penny pulled two French doors closed, blocking the evening air from coming inside.

"What if I wanted to help Josie?" Theo asked.

"I don't recall asking for help." Josie stood behind Theo, a measuring tape around her neck, suspicion in her cool, direct gaze.

Pride pulled her shoulders back. And Theo knew—Josie would never ask for help. In fact, she'd probably resent his help—claim that he only felt sorry for her. "What if you needed it?"

"I run a decent business that I love. I solve my own problems. I may not earn the same money or run in the same lucrative circles as you, but I'm not weak and defenseless. Don't think you can treat me like that."

Theo held up his hands and backed away. Yet he really wanted to pull her into his arms and reassure her that he didn't think of her like that. "Accepting help doesn't make you weak."

She adjusted her sewing bag in front of her, deflecting his words and returning his judgment. "Have you ever asked anyone for help?"

No one. He'd been relying on himself since his school days. This wasn't about him. He had a very good plan for her boutique. She needed him. He just had to prove it to her. "I could help you with your business."

"I'm not asking," she repeated.

Her blue eyes were fixed on him, fiercely unwavering, just as they'd been earlier when he was at her shop. He held up his hands. "I guess I'm not offering."

"You might not be asking, dear, but I certainly

am." Penny patted an outdated desktop computer on an oak desk in the far corner. The behemoth desk looked sturdy enough to survive any natural disaster or the wrath of a woman determined to make it on her own. "Theo, I need to get these details posted on our website before our art class. It starts in an hour. Can you help me?"

"When did you start teaching art, Penny?" *Why didn't he know about this?*

Josie stepped around Theo in a wide arc and set her sewing bag on the first of several folding tables.

"I haven't." Penny grimaced. "Iris went to Florida to paint and redecorate her parents' new home in time for the holidays. They've retired down there."

"Iris Quinn teaches art to the residents." Josie pointed at the collection of framed paintings covering one wall. Her tone was pleasant, but her irritation at him still churned in her blue eyes.

She hadn't forgiven him quite yet. But he could be patient when required. He'd respect her boundaries and wait her out.

Josie continued, "Iris teaches everything from painting to ceramics to jewelry making."

"And anything else she considers art." Penny laughed, but then interrupted her cheer with a firm slap against the ancient computer monitor.

Theo dropped into the chair behind the desk.

He wasn't as tech-savvy as his IT team at Coast to Coast. Fortunately, his same IT team had taught him a few things over the years. Because he'd asked to learn. He'd asked for help. Josie was wrong about him. He could ask for help when he wanted to.

An hour later, the computer refused to boot past its blank screen and blinking cursor. Theo made a note on his phone app to order Penny a new computer setup and have her DSL service updated.

Meanwhile, Josie guided a group of four women in a basic sewing lesson. The women wanted to surprise Shanna with wedding favors on her big day. Josie explained how to create and decorate the lavender-filled sachets for Shanna's wedding. She'd given the women scrap pieces of fabric to learn on, then promised to bring the real materials the following day. The lavender filling was added to Penny's to-do list after she claimed to know the perfect place to find it.

Laughter and several ouches from needle pricks in the finger infused Josie's hands-on lesson. Along with her encouragement and praise—that never stopped. Contentment curled through Theo. He rose, rapped his shin on the hardwood desk and paced toward the French doors, breaking his connection with the moment. Severing his awareness of Josie. Whatever he felt was completely wrong. Contentment had never been his calling. Or his objective. He knew better than to fall into contentment's trap.

Finally, the details of the surprise endeavor were worked out and Josie concluded the practice lesson. The women headed to the kitchen to sample Tansy's brownies. Theo and Josie returned to his car.

Josie buckled her seat belt. "Could you take me to the Silver Monarch Hotel?"

"You're not going home?"

"Not yet." She settled into the seat and glanced out her window as if watching the traffic. Except there wasn't any traffic, cars or pedestrians on the quiet street.

"Meeting a date in the hotel bar?" he teased and pulled out of the parking space.

She shook her head. "Definitely not that."

"You don't like to date?" he pressed. Not because he wanted to ask her. He rolled his eyes.

"I don't have the time," she said.

But if she was inclined to date, would she make the time? Not that it mattered. Theo had neither the time nor inclination. And knew even if he was inclined, he wouldn't make the time. *There's no satisfaction in contentment, Theo. You can always be more. Be better, Theo.* "Then what's at the hotel?"

"It's silly." She kept her attention on the window.

"It's also several miles from your apartment." He kept the car idling in the alleyway.

"It's the first night of the Christmas Town gingerbread-house reveal." She shifted and faced him, sounding full of earnest enthusiasm. "I go every year on opening night. I haven't missed one since high school."

He noticed the warmth and vulnerability in her eyes. She expected him to make fun of her.

"There are over a hundred unique gingerbread houses on display at the Silver Monarch," she said slowly, as if her eagerness had blurred her words.

He'd heard her fine both times. Excitement infused every part of her face. Her single-sided smile hovered just shy of a squeal. He wanted to touch her cheek, capture the feeling for himself.

"You've never heard of it, have you?" Surprise filtered through her delight.

He rubbed his chin and shrugged. "Gingerbread houses aren't really my thing."

"You sell custom gingerbread kits in your stores." She set her hands on the center console and leaned toward him. "From single houses to small gingerbread villages. New this year is Santa's workshop and sleigh."

He concentrated on keeping his hands at a ten-and-two position on the steering wheel rather than grasping her hand and her charm. "So you shop in our store?"

"Everyone does."

But he was interested in only one person. Josie liked his stores. Shopped there. His send of pride soared. "Have you purchased one of our gingerbread kits?"

"I've never built my own gingerbread house." The indifference in her tone dimmed her happiness.

Yet she went to see one of the largest gingerbread-house displays in the city every year. Theo wanted to know why—what drew her to the hotel? What kept her returning every Christmas?

The series of green lights on the one-way street leading to the hotel seemed like a sign. As was the lack of traffic. He pressed on the gas, catching every light, then discovered a parking space at the corner across from the hotel. If that wasn't a sign he was meant to visit the gingerbread houses, too, Theo didn't know what was. He parallel-parked, guiding the car into the space, and turned off the engine.

Josie never moved in her seat. "What are you doing?"

"Joining you for the reveal of this gingerbread house community." He released his seat belt, then unfastened hers.

"Why?" She touched his arm, a simple brush of her fingers.

Nothing that lingered. Nothing that demanded.

But something about her simple touch generated a warm glow inside him.

She added, "Don't make fun of it."

He wondered if she'd meant to say "don't make fun of me." "Why would I do that?"

"It's… Never mind." Her voice cracked, her gaze slid away.

A crease dented the skin between her eyebrows. The pain on her face, like she'd stared into a bad memory, splintered through Theo, fragmenting his thoughts. He reached toward her, wanting to comfort her. She turned away, opened her door. His fingers brushed against the seat, supporting nothing more than the air.

She'd climbed out of the car.

Theo met Josie on the sidewalk and escorted her to the hotel. Just as he recognized shifting market trends and fading social fads, he knew that for Josie this visit was bigger than a gingerbread-house display. More important to her than a simple gingerbread kit. That kept him at her side.

Yet his sudden urge to protect her—that kept him within hand-holding distance.

CHAPTER TEN

JOSIE QUICKENED HER PACE, wanting it to match her racing heart so that she could flee her mortification. She'd made a huge silly deal about a gingerbread display. Worse, she couldn't have been more transparent or vulnerable in front of Theo.

Now Theo walked beside her. But she didn't want his pity. Not on this night—the one night she looked forward to all year.

"After you." Theo opened the hotel's heavy brass door off to the side. A revolving glass door rotated slowly in the center of the entrance. "I get stuck in those spinning doors. Hate them. And I can't believe I just admitted that out loud."

She took in his easy grin and the laughter in his gaze. If he pitied her, he wasn't revealing it. Her pulse settled into a slow jog. "Good thing there's more than one way into a building."

Just as there was more to Theo. Her fickle heart kicked up. She stepped into the lobby and looked at the massive crystal chandelier and away from Theo's all-too-compelling gaze.

She knew all she needed to know about Theo. He wanted to help her.

But that really meant he wanted to change

her, like so many before him. Except Mimi. The patient woman had pulled the best from Josie, highlighting Josie's strengths while accepting the rest of her. Mimi had never apologized for who she was and had never expected Josie to apologize, either.

"I always forget how impressive this hotel is on the inside." Awe widened Theo's gaze, as if his senses raced to take in every decoration inside the gold-infused lobby from the floor to the fresco dome ceiling.

"It's inspiring." Josie ran her hand over the gold wall. "I have thread that is an exact match."

"What are you making with it?" He walked beside her through the lobby filled with an array of Christmas trees in every size, past the silver-bell-and-garland-adorned registration area.

"An ivory wedding dress with gold appliqués." Floor-length. Sweetheart neckline. Strapless. Full skirt. Chapel-length train. Whimsical, elegant, magical, bold—everything she'd experienced inside the hotel lobby that very first night she'd walked in. Mimi had gripped her hand tight, instructed her not to let go so they wouldn't lose each other. Then Josie had lost herself in the enchanting experience.

Theo's voice bumped into her musings. "Why isn't that dress on display in your boutique?"

Josie yanked her hand away from a gold

phoenix statue as if it had burned her. Or perhaps it was Theo's veiled criticism. "It's not finished." Or rather, not started. The dress sketched in her design book waited for its season to be revealed. Josie waited for a sign—anything to convince her it was the right time.

"How long did it take you to find that gold thread?" he asked.

"Several seasons." Each Christmas, she'd bring spools of gold thread to the hotel. Set each against the wall, discard it. Continue her search. "There are more nuances in gold than you can imagine."

"If you dedicated that much time to locating the perfect thread, it only seems right to show it off in your gown." Theo bumped his shoulder into hers. "Otherwise, you'll give the gold thread a complex and make it feel unworthy."

Her laughter relaxed her. Apparently, there were more nuances to Theo, as well. Perhaps he would understand the appeal of the gingerbread town. Maybe he'd even understand her. But all she wanted from Theo was his acceptance of her designs and his payment for her dressmaking services, didn't she?

The back of Josie's hand brushed Theo's arm. Her pulse jump-started. If he took her hand, would he promise not to lose her?

But she wasn't lost. She'd simply been around

too many head-over-heels-in-love brides recently.

Josie kick-started her tour-guide voice and rambled off facts. "The tearoom is one of the few original spaces. Much of the hotel was damaged in the 1906 fires. The tearoom connects to an intimate glass ballroom with views from bridge to bridge. Both spaces are transformed for the gingerbread display."

A woman outfitted in full Victorian yuletide garments from her lace-and-plaid-trimmed bonnet to her flocked velvet dress, faux-fur capelet and lace-up boots sashayed in the tearoom entrance, greeting guests. Josie took the holiday brochure from the woman, grateful to have something to hold onto. Something that wasn't Theo's hand.

Theo paused beside her, a broad grin on his face. "This is incredibly overwhelming. And quite spectacular." He plucked the brochure from her grip and opened it to the map. "Where should we start? Holly Hills Historic District, Santa's Neighborhood or Christmas Town Central?"

Josie took in his boyish delight. "You pick. It's your first time."

He lowered the map and eyed her. "But this is your place. You know its secrets…like the best viewing spots."

"Santa's Neighborhood is the most crowded. The working carousel is always a big draw." She'd stood there the longest on her first visit, Mimi beside her. They'd invented story after story about how the elves and reindeer spent their days. For every toy built, they earned one turn on the carousel. For every gown Josie up-scaled, she earned the reward of an overjoyed customer.

"I need to see the carousel." Theo straight-ened and scanned the crowd. "My grandmother took me to the fair one summer. I rode on a fly-ing lion for hours. It was all I wanted to do." He closed his mouth and blinked at her as if he hadn't recognized his own voice. Or his own admission.

"I always preferred the unicorn." Mimi had taken Josie to a fair, too. Cotton candy, kettle corn and sunshine had filled that summer after-noon. "Let's head to Holly Hills first."

"What's there?" Theo watched her as if noth-ing could surpass a flying lion.

"It's the place where all the Christmas Town gingerbread people live."

He arched one eyebrow, clearly unimpressed.

"Come on. You have to see it. You'll want to live there, too." She grabbed his hand, daring him to pull it away. The warmth of his touch unforgettable. "I promise."

Josie wanted to stay there. Right there. And make a different kind of promise.

He stared at their joined hands. Slowly his fingers curved around hers. His grip tightened, locking her hand fully within the safety of his.

Please don't lose me.

"Let's go to Holly Hills." Coarse wool scratched less than the rasp in his voice.

He never released her. Simply guided Josie closer to his side. Together they debated their favorite house: the Victorian mansion with sunroom versus the festive Tudor versus the stone cottage with cotton-candy chimney smoke, red pickup truck and frozen pond in the backyard. After agreeing not to judge each other's ice-skating skills, they chose the stone cottage. In Christmas Town Central, they disputed the best location for their Victorian shop—near the town's center or closer to the train station? They finally decided two storefronts would be more than appropriate.

All the while, Josie's hand remained tucked inside Theo's as if meant to be there. As if she belonged beside him. Like this.

"Hey, there's Mia." Theo leaned toward Josie, his focus aimed over the crowd weaving toward Santa's carousel. "She wants us to head over there."

Mia lowered her camera and smiled at them.

"Josie, you made it and brought company. We could've double-dated."

Date. This wasn't... Josie released Theo's hand.

"We were working." Josie pinched her lips together, then tried again. "I was working. Theo drove me."

Mia eyed her. Her keen gaze trailed over Josie's face as if she had too many questions and needed to put them in order first. Josie tried to remain impassive.

Theo interrupted the friends' standoff. "Where's Wyatt?"

Mia pointed to a seating area away from the bar. Her new husband sat on the edge of a tall-backed leather chair and leaned over a round cocktail table. "Wyatt is taking notes for the family gingerbread contest that Helen and my mom have planned. He thinks he's going to win this year."

A family gingerbread contest was exactly the kind of holiday tradition Josie longed for. The kind Mimi had wanted for them. Josie wanted to reach for Theo as if he shared her same interests. Wanted the same things like holiday traditions and boisterous family meals.

Theo nudged Mia. "He looks quite serious. You should be worried."

"He's not going to win because I have a master plan this year to take first place." Mia lifted her camera and laughed. The sound was more evil villain than good-natured.

"You're going to copy one of the gingerbread houses on display." Theo nodded as if appreciating her strategy.

"Something like that." Mia straightened the camera strap around her neck.

"Isn't that cheating, though?" Theo chuckled. "Shouldn't you create your own gingerbread work of art?"

"It's more like visual notetaking," Mia countered.

"Copying is a form of flattery," Josie added.

Mia nodded and pointed at Josie, then at Theo. That clever glint was back in her gaze, as if she'd just answered her own questions without Josie's assistance. "You two should take notes. You're both invited to the party. This year, I'm not accepting any excuses."

They were both invited. Could attend together. Her pulse accelerated, swerving her heart back in the lead.

Theo stepped back as if Mia had poked him. "I was opening our new retail location in Chicago last year."

Josie retreated, too, bumping into Theo's shoulder. Delight bounced through Mia's gaze. Josie argued, "I had to deliver costumes for

Somerset Playhouse's Christmas extravaganza that night."

She'd skipped Mia's holiday party. Josie preferred strangers. Strangers never lingered long enough to ask the difficult-to-answer personal questions. Strangers never expected more from Josie than she could give. The guests at Mia's gathering weren't quite strangers. Still not ready to return to the quiet in her apartment that evening, Josie had lingered at the theater and watched the performance from an empty seat on the side of the stage. For a few hours among so many strangers, she'd pretended the magic of the season had included her.

Her gaze settled on Theo's profile. If he was beside her, perhaps…

Perhaps if you stepped out of the library, you would make friends. If you stopped drawing in your notebook, you could talk to the kids around you. Engage in the world. It has to be lonely inside your head all the time. That can't be good for a kid your age.

She'd also been safe inside the library and inside her head growing up. Putting herself out there hurt. Loneliness was better than being heartbroken. Yet she never moved away from Theo's side.

"This year I've already checked everyone's calendar." Mia aimed her camera at them and clicked. "Theo, you have no travel plans scheduled, according to Fran. And Josie, Somerset's play is the prior weekend this year."

"Looks like we better check on Wyatt and take some notes." Theo set his hand on Josie's back.

There was nothing pretend about Theo's touch on her lower back. Or the flicker of awareness curving around her spine, tapping between her ribs. Or the way his touch steadied her.

"Just don't copy off Wyatt," Mia warned. "He's brilliant in the ER, but his gingerbread house never stands straight and the roof always slides off."

Theo and Wyatt interspersed greetings into their conversation about proper gingerbread construction. Josie shook her head. Mia was correct. Wyatt's talents were not in finessing gingerbread. Neither were Theo's, given he supported Wyatt's suggestion for basic icing dyed red to hold the walls together. The true secret, according to Mimi, was melting gummy bears, caramel and marshmallows together for the wall cement.

Wyatt and Theo fist-bumped, impressed by their creativity. Josie covered her mouth to hide her laugh. She hadn't built a gingerbread house, yet she'd designed quite a few on paper. For the first time since Mimi's passing, Josie was tempted to build one. To test Mimi's theories on proper gingerbread construction against whatever Theo and Wyatt would cook up.

She was ready to join in. Wanted to risk.

Josie swayed, off balance again. This time Theo's grip wasn't there to steady her. She dropped into the chair on the other side of the small table and was thankful Wyatt and Theo's debate over pretzels or ice cream cones for trees consumed them. Certain her sudden stillness and rapid blinking would alert them to the shift in her world.

"I'm finished." Mia set her camera on the table, sat beside Josie and nodded toward the grand piano in the alcove beside the bar. "Josie, isn't that your more-bling-is-better client?"

Josie concentrated on her client like a gleaming beacon in dense fog. Marissa Delaney wore a sequined sapphire sweater and dark denim jeans embellished with rhinestones. More crystals adorned her upswept hair and ears. Josie waved to the woman. "Marissa likes to shimmer and sparkle, claims it makes her shine on the inside, too."

"That's quite a lot of sparkle." Theo rubbed his chin.

"She should be glowing from the inside out." Wyatt nodded and stood up. "I see one of the pastry chefs lingering near the gingerbread candy store in Central Town. I'm off to learn how to get my windows to glow the same way on my gingerbread house."

"They're gingerbread architects," Mia said, correcting her husband. Then she wished him good luck.

Josie watched Theo track Marissa's movement toward the bar. Her client always stood out. Always captured the notice of everyone around her. More importantly, Marissa held onto that attention. Josie never wanted to stand out. Only ever wanted to blend in. As for holding Theo's attention, that temptation would lead to certain heartbreak. After all, she'd have to keep his interest. Then she'd falter and stumble over the truth—she'd never been worth keeping.

But what if? What if one time she was wrong?

What if one time she was worth…?

Mia picked up her camera and scrolled through her photographs. "Did Marissa like the subtle and tasteful shimmer you added to her ball gown?"

"She liked the second jeweled belt I attached." Josie cringed. Marissa had slipped on the gown in Josie's dressing room, posed at every possible angle in the floor-length mirror. Then uttered the most appalling three words ever: *it's not enough*.

But Marissa had very specific ideas on how to improve her gown. On how to make sure the gown was enough. Josie had apologized to the dress every other stitch.

Mia lowered the camera. Horror strained her words into a tight whisper. "You added another belt? More bling?"

"It was what she requested," Josie argued. If only Josie had the courage to request Marissa not mention Josie had done the alterations. That wasn't exactly the style of work she wanted tied to her name. If only it wasn't exactly the kind of custom alterations that helped pay her bills.

Dismay lifted Mia's eyebrows upward.

Josie was supposed to stand behind her work. Except picturing those twin crystal-and-rhinestone belts made her shudder. Acknowledging her reluctance eroded her optimism. "Marissa was delighted."

Mia frowned at her.

"Sometimes you have to stand up for your design style. Too much compromise dilutes what you're worth." Theo shifted his full focus to her. The criticism in his tone deflated the lightness in his voice.

Now Josie wanted to kick Theo under the table, not loiter under his blunt, albeit charming gaze. She pushed her words past her gritted teeth. "Marissa paid well over full price for the alterations."

He arched one eyebrow before he nodded.

Not that she needed his endorsement. But she required his approval. If she intended to take her business and Mia's to the next level, his family had to want her custom gowns.

"But you had other ideas," Theo pressed.

"It wasn't my dress." Josie shrugged. It was her business. Her brand. One that required money to sustain itself.

"You have other dresses." Theo leaned toward her, not letting Josie avoid him. He tapped his finger on the gold inlay inside the marble tabletop.

The same gold that matched her thread.

"Wait." Mia scooted closer to Josie. "You have original Josie Beck clothes that I haven't seen. Ever."

Josie nodded. She'd sewn a dress for attending *The Phantom of the Opera*. A sundress for a sunset walk on the beach. A skirt and blouse for a picnic in a vineyard. More for a ride in a horse-drawn carriage. A visit to the botanical gardens. A candlelit dinner. Formal events. Informal date nights. Places she dreamed about visiting. Special occasions she wanted to experience.

The invitations never came. Even during her marriage, her ex had preferred the company of his business associates and laptop. So she'd filled her closet with dreams, like Mimi had taught her to do.

"How did I not know this?" Mia glanced from Josie to Theo and back. "How many are there?"

Theo shrugged. "I haven't seen them yet."

Mia rubbed her hands together. The firmness in her tone suggested she was going to double down on locating Josie's custom dresses. "I'm betting on dozens."

Theo considered Josie, surprise in his voice. "You have a collection."

"I have a hobby." Josie rubbed her hands over her legs recalling her ex-husband's words. *If you wore these name-brand clothes rather than your own, you'd fit in with the partners' wives. Did you know your clothes look handmade? Is that really the image we want to put out there?* "I make clothes."

She made clothes when she was sad. To fight the loneliness. To fill her sleepless nights. To pretend she had places to go. Mimi had given a ten-year-old Josie the chance to imagine a different life for herself and create that world in clothes. She'd continued the tradition even now.

"Why wouldn't you display your work at your store?" The confusion in Theo's voice pulled Josie's gaze to him.

Josie stared at him. He wasn't pretending. Wasn't passing judgment. His eyebrows pulled together. He watched her as though she'd just admitted she lived a double life, and was an astronaut. Josie gave him the same response as before. "They aren't ready." *I'm not ready.*

"What you have is a stubborn streak." Affection and kindness swirled through Mia's voice. She recognized her own stubbornness and appreciated Josie's, or so she liked to inform Josie.

Perhaps. But that stubbornness protected her.

"Tell her, Theo." Mia waved at Theo as if he was the voice of reason. "Tell Josie she's being selfish keeping her designs tucked away and not sharing them with the world."

Theo drummed his fingers on the arm of the leather chair, his face thoughtful. There was a reflective tone in his words. "At the very least, you should have guided Marissa in the direction you believed was best."

"He agrees with me." Mia jumped up, triumph in her voice. "My work here is done. Now I'm off to rescue these gingerbread experts from my husband."

But would Marissa have been upset and refused to pay her? If Josie changed Theo's grandmother's gown, would Theo approve? Would he have faith she could transform that wedding dress into something exceptional and fitting for his sister? Josie swallowed, too afraid to ask. The same way she feared revealing her so-called collection to the world. Some things were better left undiscovered. Better left unjudged.

She looked at Theo. “What do you think about the gingerbread Christmas Town?”

“It’s quite an experience.” He leaned back in his chair, as if allowing the obvious change in subject to pass by him.

“For me, it’s about the memory.” Josie smiled. Mia and Wyatt both hugged an amused pastry chef, then slipped outside onto the patio together.

Theo rose and moved to the chair closest to Josie. “How many memories of this place do you have?”

“One.” Josie squeezed her eyes closed. Only a moment. What was it about Theo that made her open up? She hated being exposed. Hated revealing herself. She willed herself to stop talking.

“Must be an extraordinary memory to keep you coming back year after year.” His quiet voice surrounded her.

She stared at her empty hands. She’d been coming back every Christmas for more than a decade. How strange that she didn’t have more than one memory to hold onto. “It was supposed to be our tradition.”

“You and your ex’s tradition?” he asked.

She wasn’t certain if it was the idea or his

question that startled her. She looked at Theo and shook her head. "My ex-husband never came here." To be fair, she'd never invited him.

"He wasn't into traditions." Theo angled toward her, holding her gaze.

"Not holiday traditions." She grimaced. "Those interfere with business."

"In defense of business traditions, our back-office employees have the week between Christmas and New Year's off every year." His grin, small and quick, signaled his triumph. He knew he'd surprised her and redirected her traipsing too deep into her past. He added, "It's a very popular tradition among the staff."

"What do you do on that week off?" Josie leaned toward him, bracing her elbow on the armrest.

He shrugged. "Work."

Now he'd strayed back into her ex-husband's category. Suddenly, she didn't like Theo being there. She'd sensed there was more than profit margins and eighty-hour work weeks to him. Wanted to believe she hadn't been wrong. Then perhaps she could prove to him she was more, too.

"Would you stop scowling at me if I told you it's one my most productive weeks every year?" He watched her. His expression was full of hope. He smiled.

Josie laughed. "As long as you tell me you take a real vacation each year."

"Define 'real vacation,'" he said.

"Not a staycation. Not a work-on-the-beach trip. Or work-in-the-ski-lodge weekend."

His smile faded beneath his pensive tone. "It's been too long since I've taken a real vacation."

"You could start a new tradition," she suggested.

"Like coming here is yours."

"I come back to remember." Josie heard the laughter from her very first visit like bursts of starlight all around her. Saw the joy in the families gathered around the massive display. Pictured the gingerbread town—half the size than it was now, yet no less enchanting that afternoon. Noted the same wonder she'd seen on the faces of the girls and boys straining to see inside each window and past each door. "I come back to remind myself to dream."

"I was taught dreams were a waste of time." Theo stretched out his legs, unconcerned by his confession.

Josie gaped at him. "Who told you that?" And why? She'd have given up long ago without her dreams.

"My teachers." He folded his hands together on his lap. His tone offhand. His voice indifferent. "The school counselors, even our headmaster. The Copper Cove Academy activates its students' academic and emotional potential to ensure success throughout every stage of life. Through proper character formation, a student's full academic capacity will be reached."

And Josie considered her childhood rough. Character formation sounded like some medieval-style punishment. "Sounds strict."

"The Copper Cove Academy raises men to thrive in the world, not boys who collapse under pressure." Theo lifted his hands and made finger quotes. "That was a favorite of several high-school professors and the varsity coaches."

"I thought parents raised their children," she said.

"I was enrolled in Copper Cove Academy from first grade until I graduated high school. In third grade, after my grandmother passed, I was sent to board there full-time." His voice was remote, as if he'd deleted himself from the memories. As if he'd detached his feelings from the situation. "Then I went to college."

"What about your parents?" She searched his face, then curled her fingers into her palms rather than touch his cheek and chase away the cool indifference.

His fingers flexed on the armrests, as if he was bracing himself. "They were busy building my inheritance."

"But who gave you a snack after school? Who hugged you when you had a fight?" She'd seen the photographs of the Taylor family all together. Before and after his father's death. The similar smiles. The linked arms. The easy affection. It appeared in every snapshot. Over and over again. An ideal American family. There was nothing ideal in his rigid posture. Or the isolation he'd wrapped himself in.

Her voice snagged on the emptiness in his hooded gaze. "Who…?"

She stopped asking because she knew the answer. *No one.*

She ached for him. Everywhere. His pain leaked inside her chest, joining with her own.

"You never read that in any article about me." He rubbed the back of his neck, as if removing the past, and glanced around the tearoom.

He'd spent more time in a boarding school than with his own family. The same as she'd spent more time in the school libraries than at her foster homes. Should she share how much and how well she understood him? Would he reach for her this time or turn away? Unsure what she wanted, she asked, "Why did you tell me?"

He lowered his arm and faced her. His gaze locked on hers, open and candid. He was no longer detached. He was present in this moment. With her.

"I told you because I've never built a gingerbread house, either."

Josie exhaled and tested the stability of the common ground between them. "When I was ten, my foster mom brought me here to see the gingerbread-town display for the first time."

His smile was swift and fleeting.

She worried she'd gone too far. *Too late.* "We couldn't afford the tea service here at the hotel. Mimi brought her own blend, tucked inside her sewing basket. She carried a basket like most women carry a purse." A small, bittersweet laugh flowed through her at the forgotten detail.

Josie picked up her own tote bag—but unlike Mimi's straw one, hers was leather. Yet like Mimi, she stuffed the bag with her own sewing supplies and Mimi's favorite thimble. Grief needled through her. Even the metal thimble lacked the strength to push back the loss inside her. Her voice wobbled. "It's silly, I know. But I still carry the exact tea flavor in my purse."

"So each year, you sit here, drink your tea and toast your foster mom." He nodded as if he appreciated the sentiment.

Josie shook her head and caught the stray tear that tumbled free. "I've only passed through the display. Never sat and really remembered." *Until tonight. With you.*

Theo ran his hands over the leather armrests

and pushed himself out of the chair. He studied her, his face impassive. He opened his mouth, closed it, then turned and walked away.

Josie sat back in her chair and closed her eyes. *I'm fine. This is fine. Everything is fine.* Except…

Something rattled beside her head. Josie popped open her eyes. Theo stepped around the chairs, carrying a teacup on a saucer and a pot of hot water. Uncertainty seeped through his voice. "There's no pressure. But if you want to sip your tea and take yourself back, it's here."

And he was there. Beside her. For the moment in the Silver Monarch Hotel, Josie felt safe again. Like that evening with Mimi so long ago. *Collect the happy moments, Josie, and your life will be full.* Mimi had taken Josie's hand and walked out of the hotel, content that she'd collected another happy moment. Josie blinked until the tears cleared slightly. She picked up the teapot and filled the cup. "Thank you."

Theo nodded, pulled his chair closer to Josie and sat down.

"Mimi and I sat on the velvet benches near the windows until past my bedtime and designed every inch of our own gingerbread house." Josie opened the tea bag and set it into the hot water. Inhaled the spicy scent and the sweeter pieces of the past. The ones that coated the sorrow.

"Pretzel Christmas trees and melted hard candies for windows and candy-cane pillars on the front porch."

"What did you plan for the roof and chimney?" he asked. "Santa needs a chimney to deliver the gifts."

"Stacked caramels for the chimney and frosted-wheat cereal for the roof," she replied. His frown drew laughter out of her. Wyatt and he had planned differently. Still, she appreciated him guiding her away from the pain and into the good parts of this particular memory.

"I suppose that's both creative and sturdy," he finally acknowledged.

"There wasn't a detail we'd missed that night." But so many she'd misplaced. Until now.

"Sounds like a magical time."

"The best I can remember." She sipped the cinnamon-orange tea, warmed by the hot liquid, her memories and Theo's presence.

"Why not build that gingerbread house now?" he asked.

"It wouldn't be the same." She curved her hands around the teacup and skimmed her gaze over the families and couples strolling through the display. "The joy and magic are in creating and building something together. As a family. Mimi always said that was the secret to the perfect gingerbread house."

"Mimi is your fortune-cookie muse." Affection gentled his voice, mellowing his tone. "What else did Mimi tell you? She sounds like my Grandmother Pearl—always brimming with life advice or a quick, witty quip, as she called them."

"She often told me 'Josie, bleeding is going to happen and sometimes it's going to be all your fault.'" Josie laughed at the look of horror on Theo's face as his jaw dropped open. "She taught me to sew. 'The needles are quite sharp, and our fingers sometimes get in the way.'"

Theo's face cleared. "She sounds like a talented woman."

"She was that and so much more." Josie added water to her cup, extending the moment, clutching the fond memories that she so seldom revisited.

"Where is she now?" he asked.

"She passed away the following spring." Grief burned where the tea had soothed. Josie exchanged Mimi's cottage for one foster family after another. All the while Josie had continued to sew and learn her craft. Every stitch, every finished garment had helped her feel closer to Mimi. Helped her remember Mimi's love.

"I'm sorry." The low timbre in his voice was as warm and soothing as a hug.

Sometimes it was the simplest things—the

smallest words—that righted someone's world. Josie curled into the chair with her teacup and relaxed.

Theo spread hotel cocktail napkins across the table and asked a passing waitress for a pen. He grinned at Josie. "Now we plan."

"What?"

"Our gingerbread houses, of course." He accepted the pen from the waitress and wrote Josie's name on top of a napkin and his name on another.

An hour later, Josie walked out of the hotel next to Theo. Their gingerbread napkins folded and stuffed in her coat pocket. The happy moment collected.

CHAPTER ELEVEN

JOSIE SET HER hands on her hips and stepped back to study Adriana in the first of the prototype gowns. Adriana had piled her dark hair into an intricate updo, then added a single red rose from the dozen Ryan had sent her that morning for no particular reason. Other than he was a man in love.

Ryan adored Adriana openly and honestly, as if Adriana gave his world meaning. Josie might've envied the woman if she was looking for someone to share her life with, which she wasn't. Despite the moment she'd collected last night with Theo.

Small branches of baby's breath burst from Adriana's hair like tiny clouds. Her upswept hair complemented the illusion sleeves on the Helen-inspired dress and the fitted shape exposed her elegant figure.

"It's impeccably crafted." Adriana twisted to take in the plunging back of the gown. "Well-constructed. Lovely."

Josie lifted her gaze to Adriana's face, pursed her lips and arrived at one conclusion: a garbage bag would look fashionable on Adriana Taylor. It was the woman's gift. In this instance though, more of a curse, at least for Josie. She was proud of her work and considered the gown lovely herself. Adriana was so striking, however, the gown became super flattering and beautiful on her. Hovering above nice.

Josie followed Adriana into the dressing room and helped her out of the dress. There was still the Jin-inspired gown. Still a chance for Josie to get it right.

"I'm sorry for putting you in an awkward position with my brother." Adriana slid her arms into the silk robe left for clients and faced Josie. "I'm sorry I forced you into stretching the truth."

Josie had given Theo the full truth last night at the Silver Monarch Hotel. Shared parts of her past she hadn't told anyone. As if the gingerbread town was a safe zone. Theo her protector. That was only her heart confusing the past and the present. Mimi had been her support. Now the only safe zone was inside herself. As for her heart, she had to stop listening to its whispered lies.

Josie gathered the gown to drape it back over the body form. Her curiosity was harder to gather. "Why do they call you a bridezilla?"

"I suppose I can be," Adriana confessed. She rearranged several branches of baby's breath in her hair and met Josie's gaze in the mirror. "But the truth is… My brother is the impossible one."

He hadn't been impossible last evening. He'd been thoughtful and considerate. Her teacup had gone dry yet he'd stayed beside her. He'd drawn one gingerbread house after another, making her believe he'd have stayed there all night if she'd asked, as if content to let her end the moment on her terms. In her own time. As if he'd known she'd needed exactly that. Josie hugged the gown to her chest to muffle the sigh in her heart.

"The papers have it wrong about us." Adriana fiddled with the silk sash on the robe.

"Why don't you correct them?" Josie asked.

"Theo always looked out for me growing up." Adriana smiled. "I want to do the same now. For him."

Loyalty—such a rare gift. And Theo and Adriana shared it. She slipped outside, lifted the gown from the body form and left her envy on the floor. *Find your own blessings, Josie, even if you have to search harder than others.*

Theo would laugh at the fortune-cookie adage. Tell Josie to go out and make her own.

"Theo was the one who turned away all those designer dresses." Adriana lifted her foot to step into the Jin-inspired dress. "One after another. Claiming that none were special enough for me."

That, Josie imagined, was what a big brother should do—watch over his sister. Care about her. Like he'd watched over Josie last night. Except he hadn't looked at Josie like a sister. Josie concentrated on buttoning the dress and sealing away her own reaction to Theo. Besides, what did her damaged heart know about loyalty and lasting love? She knew she wanted…

Josie yanked open the velvet curtains of the dressing room. Scanned the consignment gowns, the accessory wall, Mia's photographs. All she wanted was right there in front of her: her business. And success for herself and her friend. There was too much pain in wishing for anything more.

Adriana stepped outside the dressing room and onto the riser. "None of the designs worked until the Linden Topher gown."

"You have a wedding dress from Linden Topher?" Josie tripped on the platform step. Her chest clenched like a bodice cinched tight enough to crack a rib.

Linden Topher was an A-league fashion designer. Josie wasn't even qualified for the minors. She adjusted the skirt of the gown—the satin fabric suddenly felt more like a school craft project. A nice, valiant effort against one of the premier designers in the industry. Cinderella after the clock struck twelve.

"The Linden Topher is not the dress now." Adriana's hands curled at her waist. She shook her head. The motion wasn't enough to hide the tremor in her words.

Josie clipped the cape-style veil on Adriana. Fluffed the ends to drape as she wanted and slowed her words to conceal her own dread and sudden curiosity. "What happened?"

"Another bride." The crisp tone in Adriana's voice only emphasized the sadness in her gaze.

"Surely that was an exclusive gown for you." Exclusives were exclusives for a reason. There were unspoken rules. Linden Topher understood those rules—he had to.

"It's complicated." Adriana brushed her fingers over her eyebrows, as if clearing away the conversation and any lingering distress. "It doesn't matter now. Thanks to Mia, Theo found you."

Every pin Josie placed in the fabric of the Jin-inspired gown jabbed a tiny hole of uncertainty inside her. How was she supposed to compete with Linden Topher?

He'd trained in Paris and Milan. She'd practiced on Mimi's front porch. He owned a design houses in Paris and New York. His designs walked the runway at New York Fashion Week. Josie walked four blocks to her little boutique.

Her custom designs hung in her apartment closet.

Josie set the last pin on the hem and stepped back. The fitted gown accentuated Adriana's graceful stature. The cape draped over her shoulders, flowing perfectly around her.

"It's simply stunning." Adriana's fingers strayed to the white feathers trimming the edges of the veil. "It's exactly like the drawing."

But the drawing had more animation than Adriana's voice. The sketched figure had more connection to the hand-drawn gown than Adriana.

"The details are exquisite." Adriana's fingers stilled on the feathers. Her voice was quiet, yet there was nothing tranquil in her tone. "But it's..."

"Not Linden Topher," Josie said, finishing for her, her shoulders sagging. Josie wanted to take the dress off Adriana, run to her apartment and stuff it into the closet beside the others.

"No. But you don't want to imitate him." Adriana met Josie's gaze in the mirror. "I want..."

So did Josie. She wanted Adriana to wear one of her dresses and glow from the inside like Shanna. She wanted Adriana's love for her fiancé to shine and sparkle through the dress, just as it radiated from her face whenever she spoke his name. That was the magic—the feeling Adriana searched for and couldn't describe.

Josie worked the gown off Adriana. She never lit from the inside in the second gown. Stunning wasn't enough. Neither was well-crafted. Theo would dislike them if his sister failed to shine. And she hadn't. Josie draped the second gown over a body form, her mind racing on changes and alterations to make it worthy of Adriana. To make Adriana glow from the inside out. "I have work to do."

Adriana clasped her hands together, excitement swirling around her. "Can I try on Grandmother's dress now?"

Josie was out of options. And unable to deny the bead of anticipation inside her. Josie rolled the body forms away from the platform and retrieved Grandma Pearl's gown from the workroom. In minutes, Josie fastened the last self-covered button on the bodice. She fluffed the skirt, letting the train fall over the platform.

"It's something of a lace mess, isn't it?" Adriana touched one of the taffeta rosettes at her waist.

"It's vintage and was the height of fashion when your grandmother married." More than a dozen rosettes settled into the many tiers of lace ruffles on the sides and back of the dress. Easily removed. The floral pattern in the white lace could be stunning if edited. Josie worked her gaze over the gown, ideas churning through her. Some she discarded, some she held onto.

"It fits as if it was tailored for me." The wonder in Adriana's voice tugged Josie's focus away from the gown and back to the woman.

"Your mother was correct." Josie studied Adriana's face. Was that a flicker of a glow? "You and your grandmother were built very much alike."

Adriana touched the lace reverently. "That's lovely to know. I always wanted to be like her—kind and free with her hugs. I was quite young when she passed and yet I lost a piece of something inside me after she was gone."

Josie rubbed her chest in solidarity over lost beloved maternal figures.

"I never considered myself sentimental until I put on her dress." Adriana wiped at her eyes. Love, however, strengthened her wobbly smile. "You're going to talk me out of wearing her dress, aren't you?"

In its current state: yes. But not the gown Josie envisioned this one becoming. "Your brother thinks you should be in an original, exclusive dress."

Although Josie wanted to change his mind. Wanted him to see that sometimes the past wasn't something to shun. But she was a divorced foster kid with a past better ignored. Why would he believe her?

"My brother is paying for the entire wedding." Adriana touched the scalloped neckline. "I shouldn't complain."

"He wants the best for you," Josie said. And he expected the best from Josie. But the two custom gowns she'd come up with lacked that spark. Adriana looked stoic and too composed in those gowns. But she smiled and cried in her modified grandmother's dress—she connected to that one. Josie could imagine Adriana walking down the aisle in her grandmother's dress. But Josie's gut instinct and her imagination wouldn't pay the rent or the electric bill or fix the leaking faucet in the restroom.

"Can I have a moment?" Adriana asked.

"Take all the time you need." Josie stepped off the platform and walked toward her workroom, ready to sketch her ideas in her design book. "You're my last client for the day."

Ten minutes later, Josie looked up from her sketchbook to find Adriana in the workroom doorway, still wearing her grandmother's gown.

Adriana's eyes were rimmed in red. Her cheeks dappled. "I need help with the buttons so I can take it off."

Josie pulled several tissues from a box on

her worktable and pressed them into Adriana's hand. "What's your favorite part of the gown?"

"All of it." Adriana wiped her eyes. A small laugh burst free. "And none of it."

Josie nodded and kept her alteration ideas to herself. This wasn't the gown Theo wanted or the one he wanted to pay for. Josie helped Adriana out of the dress, carried it back to her workroom and secured it inside the garment bag.

Adriana returned and picked up Josie's design book. "This is Grandma Pearl's dress. Only it isn't."

"That's nothing." Josie zipped the garment bag closed. "Just scribbles."

"You need to show this to Theo," Adriana urged her.

Josie shook her head. He'd recognize Grandma Pearl's gown. Even though she'd assured him he wouldn't know where the old finished and the new began.

"You could convince him that Grandma Pearl's gown is the one." Hope and confidence merged into her upbeat tone.

"What makes you think that?" Josie closed her design book.

"You convinced Theo to go to the gingerbread display last night." Adriana followed her into the storefront.

"That was nothing." *Nothing*. Josie straightened the prototype gowns on the body forms and rolled them to the side of the platform. "He was being nice and offered to give me a ride."

"My brother isn't nice." Adriana picked up her jacket and purse from the couch. "He's charitable. Benevolent. Protective. But not really nice."

Josie stepped behind her checkout counter and laughed. "Then why did he offer me a ride home?"

Adriana leaned her elbows on the counter and grinned at Josie. "That's what I'm trying to figure out. Maybe he likes you."

Josie's heart bounced. She opened her mouth, ready to tell her heart to stand down and set Adriana straight.

Adriana patted her hands on the countertop like a drum roll. The sound suspended Josie's words.

"Hear me out," Adriana implored her. "This is good. If he likes you, he'll listen to you. He'll believe you when you tell him about our grandmother's dress."

"You should talk to him," Josie suggested. "Tell him how you feel." As for Josie, she had nothing to tell him except to thank him. *Thank you for giving me the chance to design a wedding gown. Thank you for urging me to focus on the best parts of her gingerbread memory. Thank you for holding my hand.*

Adriana ran her palms over the counter. "I wish it was that simple."

"It is. He's your brother," Josie said. "He wants the best for you."

"Are you certain you won't talk to him instead?" Adriana's eyebrows lifted in a plea.

"Only if you speak to him first." Josie locked her cash-register drawer.

Adriana pushed away from the counter and eyed Josie. "Are you busy now?"

It was one hour until the official end of the afternoon and start of her Saturday evening. Alterations waited in the workroom. Final details needed to be added to the costumes for the children's program. And two prototypes waited to be transformed into something spectacular. "I have work I should complete."

"Could you spare an hour?" Adriana asked.

"What do you have in mind?"

"A quick visit to the chapel and the reception venue." Adriana buttoned her coat. "If you saw the settings, then you could tell me if my grandmother's dress is wrong or not for the event."

The only wrong in a wedding gown came from within the bride herself. But Adriana's request, earnest and genuine, nudged Josie. Adriana wanted her opinion and her insight. Josie wanted to help her. “Let me finish locking up.”

“Are you up for a walk?” Adriana opened the front door.

“It’s my first time out of the boutique today—I’d prefer the walk.” Josie locked the door, dropped her keys in her bag and matched Adriana’s pace.

Four blocks into their walk, Adriana stopped at a busy corner and scowled. “That cannot be her. Not there.”

Josie searched the busy intersection, scanning for whomever riled Adriana. “What happened?”

“My mother happened.” Adriana marched across the intersection and swung right at the corner, anger stiffening her movements.

Josie finally located Lilian Rose, standing beneath the wide awning of Bouquets by Baylee Flower Shop, surrounded by a variety of Christmas plants and seasonal floral arrangements. Lilian Rose was in front of the poinsettia table, her face tilted toward the bright yellow and pink potted flowers, her mouth moving as if she was whispering advice to the plants.

Josie stood next to Adriana, who’d stopped within listening distance yet never interrupted her mother.

Lilian Rose finished her one-sided conversation about dull-versus-daring dating choices.

Adriana stepped forward and tapped her mother's shoulder. "Mother, why are you talking to a table of flowers about preferring a gentleman who is more daring and makes bold choices like champagne roses and an artichoke stalk in the same arrangement?"

Lilian Rose brushed her fingers into her hair, as if Adriana's voice had startled the upswept strands loose. "Why are you and Josie… It's Josie, isn't it?" The accusation in her voice matched the cunning narrowing of her eyes. "Why are you two together?"

Adriana ran her fingertip over a pale pink poinsettia petal. "Josie and I are working on a special project."

Lilian Rose's eyebrows dipped, her gaze sharpened into shrewdness. "Is Theo aware of this special project?"

"It was his idea." Adriana leaned around her mother and lifted her arm in a half-hearted wave. "Who is that gentleman with his nose buried in a handkerchief rushing down the sidewalk? He keeps glancing back here."

Josie shifted and winced. The man in question slammed a white handkerchief against his face as his whole body jerked. Onlookers moved to the outer edge of the sidewalk to pass around him. Another sneeze seized the poor man.

"That's Samuel. It's not going to work between us." Lilian Rose linked her arm with Josie's and adjusted her stance until Josie faced the poinsettia table. "Remember, Josie, not every date is going to be perfect. Matchmaking takes time and patience."

Josie scanned the sidewalk on the other side of the thin table, certain Lilian Rose wanted to position herself for the best vantage point. Except the foot traffic was quite light for early Saturday evening. And Lilian Rose never acknowledged any sidewalk shoppers. Once again, she spoke to the potted plants. Josie scooted to the left, but Lilian Rose tugged her back the other way, anchoring Josie against her side.

Finally, Josie discovered the cell phone—propped up, with the screen lit up—tucked in between two bright yellow poinsettias. A red record button flashed on the bottom of the screen.

Adriana leaned her hip against the table and considered her mother. "Did you make your date cry?"

Josie blinked at Adriana. She'd said "cry" as if her mother always made people cry, the same way a balloon artist always made kids smile. As if it was not only normal, but also expected from Lilian Rose. Adriana shared her mother's outer elegance. Yet there was a defiance in the slant of Adriana's head and the way her arms crossed over her chest.

"Indirectly." Lilian Rose's tone was matter-of-fact, not apologetic or remorseful. She touched a pine branch of a miniature potted tree nestled among the flowers. She addressed the table of potted plants and her concealed phone, rather than her daughter. "It's always best to know flaws early in any relationship. After all, are you willing to give up the beauty and calmness of live flowers inside your house for the rest of your life?"

Josie wasn't certain allergies could be considered a flaw. She peeked at the cell phone, wondering if Lilian Rose's viewers agreed. That was assuming she had viewers. Otherwise why was she recording herself at a flower shop, of all places?

"Did he ask you to give up flowers for the rest of your life?" Adriana pulled away from the table. A weariness saturated her words. "You refused and upset him."

"We never ventured much past first names." Lilian Rose smoothed a hair behind her ear and twisted away from Adriana to face the flower table. "I would think severe allergies should be listed on each candidate's application. Leaving out pertinent information could be a sign of future deceit. Something to keep in mind, Josie."

Theo had boundaries, had she breeched them? Had Theo left out pertinent information? Josie leaned back out of the camera's recording area. "Maybe he wanted to share more of that kind of information with you in person."

"I joined a matchmaking service precisely to avoid such a thing. I want those details known to move the relationship along quickly." Lilian Rose ignored Josie's comment as if Josie's words carried no more weight than the pollen from spring daisies. "Had it been listed on Samuel's résumé, I'd not have wasted the past few hours getting ready."

Josie watched Lilian Rose speak to her phone, her voice casual, friendly and informative, like Josie's favorite sewing vlogger. She glanced at Adriana. Her fingers tapped an irritated beat against her folded arms. The corners of her mouth pulled down, stopping shy of a full scowl. Lilian Rose's indifference to her daughter's presence no doubt frustrated Adriana. Yet Josie sensed from the way Adriana pulled herself inward from her shoulders to waist that her frustration with her mother ran deeper than video recordings.

Suspicion sliced through Adriana's tone. "Why did you pick my florist for a first date?"

Tension descended like a thick curtain on a Broadway stage. Adriana straightened her shoulders. This was not the quaint family gathering Josie assumed the Taylors always experienced. Both women seemed to be circling around each other, withholding from each other. It wasn't the mother-daughter relationship she'd expected.

"I chose to meet Samuel here. It's a perfectly suitable place. Public and open." Lilian Rose never flinched beneath her expertly applied makeup. "Now that you're here, we can discuss the flowers you've chosen for your wedding." She turned and leaned toward the poinsettias and her phone. "This is called pivoting in the moment to make the most of your situation. It's also important to know when to pivot to take advantage of an opportunity. More on that later."

Josie examined the cell phone, propped at the perfect angle for maximum coverage. She'd helped Mia enough on photo shoots to recognize the correct placement for optimal lightning and ideal selfies. Now Lilian Rose had imparted another life lesson in less than ten minutes. She was definitely speaking to an audience. Definitely recording for more than her own vanity.

"The flower arrangements have already been chosen, Mother." Adriana adjusted her purse on her shoulder and glanced down the sidewalk. "Josie and I were heading to Rustic Grill."

Josie blinked. Rustic Grill hadn't been their destination. Josie would learn nothing about Adriana's wedding venues at a bar and grill.

Unless Adriana booked an after-hours private room to continue the celebration after the formal reception. That hardly seemed like Adriana's style, let alone Theo's.

"But I haven't seen your floral choices." Lilian Rose pivoted, added one quick glance and smirk at her cell phone. "And the wait time at Rustic Grill can be unbearable at this hour on Saturday evening. What's a few minutes' delay?"

A woman wearing a snowman-print apron and name tag that read Baylee stepped out of the floral shop and greeted Adriana. "I thought that was you. The Casablanca lilies that you called about last week came in earlier than I expected. I'd love to show them to you."

"That's perfect timing." Lilian Rose snatched her phone from the table and opened the floral-shop door. "Shall we?"

The florist walked inside, answering Lilian Rose's question about the lilies' scent.

Adriana moved beside Josie and whispered, "Remember that other bride I mentioned?"

Josie nodded.

"It's my mother," Adriana whispered, her tone brittle.

That was complicated. Josie rubbed her forehead, as if that would sort the truth into something she could understand. What happened to the mother-daughter duo she'd seen in the photographs? Josie pointed at the entrance to the floral shop. "Wasn't Lilian Rose just on a first date?"

"She's not exactly doing things in order." Adriana's cheeks had reddened. "Would you mind joining us? I could use a buffer."

The Taylor family wasn't so perfect, after all. Josie was oddly fascinated, not that she should be. Yet for Josie, this brought the Taylors into the approachable, ordinary category. This brought the Taylors into a category Josie could relate to. Made Theo's world not so different from her own. She held open the door for Adriana.

Lilian Rose sniffed a bouquet of red roses and asked Baylee, "Would it be a problem to double the order of white roses?"

Adriana lifted her hands and shook her head. "I don't need that many roses."

Her mother seemed taken aback. "What am I supposed to put on my tables?"

"You don't have tables." Adriana's face hardened into impassiveness. A harshness scuffed her low-pitched voice. "Or a reception venue."

"I will soon," her mother assured her. "And I'll need flowers, too."

"You can't choose the same flowers." There was nothing flexible about Adriana, from her low voice to her rigid posture.

"Why not?" Lilian Rose cradled an arrangement of winter blooms as if she'd just made the finals in a beauty pageant. "Copying is the highest form of flattery. Not to mention I've always adored white roses and Casablanca lilies."

"Pick something else to like," Adriana challenged.

"Perhaps you should change your choices." Lilian Rose stuck the roses back into the bucket of water and spun around holding a miniature pine tree. "Pine branches and eucalyptus could be quite nice together." Lilian Rose waved to Baylee and asked for sample.

Josie wanted to ask for a cease-and-desist between mother and daughter.

"I already chose my bouquet and centerpieces. There's no need for changes." Adriana returned the volley with another swift hit. "Besides, I've always disliked eucalyptus."

Josie disliked family discord. Ariana should be enjoying planning her wedding, not competing with her mother to be "first one down the aisle." Josie typed a text to Theo: You need to come to Bouquets by Baylee now.

His reply came swiftly: In a meeting.

Josie glared at her phone and typed: Leave.

No.

"You need to open yourself to change and not be so uncompromising." Lilian Rose handed

Adriana a branch of eucalyptus. "Otherwise you'll stop growing. And no one wants that."

Adriana paced away from her mother, then spun around. "You're not getting married, Mother."

"I intend to." Lilian Rose snapped a leaf off the branch.

"Why?" Adriana asked.

"It's past time." Lilian Rose frowned at the flower arrangement. "You and your brother don't need me. You're all grown up now."

"We never needed you." Adriana fired a verbal shot with the skill of a pro. "You made sure of that."

Lilian Rose blanched.

That couldn't be good. It was also never good to order someone around. Still, Josie continued texting. Yes. Now. Otherwise your mother and sister might start a bridal war in the floral shop right now.

What?

Now she had his full attention. Josie typed: Your mother wants the same flowers as your sister.

On my way. Keep them separated.

Lilian Rose recovered and swiped clear lip gloss over her lips, sealing that first crack in her polished veneer. She looked at Josie, her voice imploring Josie to take her side. "It's not as if Adriana chose unique flowers. Pinecones, holly berries and lilies are hardly rare and uncommon. They're the staple vanilla choice of every winter bride from here to the Midwest."

Josie retreated, dodging Lilian Rose's unkind words.

"My choices are not bland or ordinary." Adriana's voice eased, her expression brightened. "Ryan and I chose our flowers together as a couple. That's what real couples do. Real couples make the big decisions together."

"Real couples are also strong enough individuals that trust their partner will make the best decision for them both."

Adriana curled her fingers around a glass globe filled with petite stemmed roses and baby's breath. "You aren't suggesting that Ryan and I aren't a real couple, are you?"

"I wouldn't dream of it." Lilian Rose's smile barely moved her cheeks. "Just as you wouldn't dream of being so cruel as to tell your own mother that she was never needed."

Adriana lifted her arm with the glass vase. Josie intercepted, eased the vase from her grip and guided Adriana across the small space.

This was not the Taylor family depicted online or in the Coast to Coast Living brand. Josie searched for a way to defuse the situation. Was there ever a dispute-resolution section in the *Coast to Coast Living* magazine? If she left the floral shop intact and undamaged, she was going to insist *Coast to Coast Living*'s advice columnist do a year-long series on dysfunctional family dynamics.

In the meantime, Josie sought a distraction.

CHAPTER TWELVE

THEO GRABBED THE door to Bouquets by Baylee.

A man shouted, "Wait!"

Theo spun around and scowled. The film crew—Barry and his two sidekicks, Timmy and Nolan—rushed toward him. To collect rough footage for the TV series, the trio had followed Theo around the Coast to Coast Living offices the entire day, filming him and interviewing any staff who'd made the mistake of working on a Saturday. "What are you doing here?" he asked them.

Timmy lifted the camera. "Same as we've been doing all day."

"This isn't the offices." Theo turned his back on the floral shop.

"Your mic is still turned on." Nolan pointed to Theo's shirt collar.

Theo winced. He'd forgotten about the wireless mic. He wasn't even certain if there was a power button or where it even was. He'd let Fran know where he was going, then told her to go and enjoy what was left of her Saturday.

"Foster and Caitlyn, aka Cat Woman, really want more footage of the entire Taylor family together doing family stuff. Less of the business side." Barry rolled forward onto the balls of his feet and peered inside the floral-shop window. "This could be our only opportunity."

He surveyed the crew. They were quiet and inconspicuous, despite the camera, and good at their jobs. They'd finagle their way into another opportunity. "I need to make sure my mother and sister are agreeable right now." And not arguing over bridal bouquets. "I'd also like to request permission from Baylee Russo, the owner of the floral shop, to film inside."

Nolan held up his phone. "I took care of that on the way over. Baylee gave both verbal and written consent to film on her premises."

"You're quite thorough." Theo's frown reinforced his bland tone.

"It's my job." Nolan opened the door and urged everyone inside. The kid's good-natured charm and polite manners were impossible to ignore. Nolan grinned. "I also have consent from your mother and sister on file. Those agreements were signed early last month and remain valid through the filming of the entire first season."

Thorough, diligent and professional. Theo wanted to fault the young man. But he'd rather hire him. Those were admirable qualities in any employee.

"Shall we go smell some roses?" Barry lifted his bushy eyebrows and followed Theo.

Theo scanned the quaint flower shop. His gaze landed first on Josie. Strands of blond hair slipped from her bun, the curls resting against her neck as if exhausted. Her owlish eyes peeled wider, beseeching him to intervene. His gaze to his mother and sister—standoff positions firmly staked on either side of a square table. His mother sat ramrod-straight in a chair. Adriana stood, looming on the opposite side of the table. Everything about the scenario alarmed Theo. Josie resembled a rose surrounded by two very thorny branches.

One more rose prick and Barry and his sidekicks would have the very footage Theo never wanted them to record. Verbal collisions and outbursts and incessant drama. Talk about a reality TV show.

Josie escaped from her referee position between his family members and moved to stand beside Theo. "What are you going to do?"

His mother was collecting greenery and different branches from the pile on the table as if she was a guide on a nature hike. Adriana never reacted, remained motionless and focused on their mother. Tension spiked through the fragrant air. Theo glanced over his shoulder.

Nolan nudged his bony elbow into Timmy's ribs. Barry snapped his fingers and inclined his head toward Adriana and his mother. His mother added two stalks of berries to her arrangement and presented the horizontal bouquet to Adriana. "Garden roses and jasmine vine will finish it off rather nicely."

Adriana never flinched. "What is that?"

"It's an olive branch." His mother clasped the arrangement as if guarding it from Adriana's censure. "And proof that I can be useful. In minutes I designed a less bland and more eye-catching bouquet for you. It's intentionally asymmetrical for added visual interest."

"I don't want you to create a new bouquet for me." Dry leaves crinkled less than the crackle in Adriana's voice.

"I'm your mother. I should be involved." His mother rose, cradled the bouquet and slid her cunning gaze to the production trio. "I should help my only daughter. You only get married once."

"Or twice," Adriana challenged.

"I'm fortunate." His mother lifted her arm, giving an offhand flick of her wrist. "Would you like to practice carrying your bouquet? You'll want to hold it differently down the aisle, after the ceremony and during pictures."

His mother curved one jeweled finger at Nolan. No way would Theo allow her to enlist the aid of the production crew for her practice session.

Theo clutched Josie's elbow and spun her around to face the trio, impeding Nolan's access to his mother. "Gentleman, this is Josie Beck. The proprietor of Rose Petal Boutique."

The men glanced at each other and grinned, recognizing Josie's name from their prior meetings with Theo. He'd put off an official meet-and-greet between Josie and the TV producers. He'd wanted to wait until he'd talked to Josie first. Unfortunately, preserving his family's name now garnered priority.

"Josie, I'd like you to meet some colleagues of mine—Barry, Timmy and Nolan." Theo tossed Josie into the fray swiftly and decisively.

"Seems like the entire Taylor family is into filming." Josie tipped her chin toward Barry and his two assistants. Timmy switched his grip on the camera and brightened his smile.

Josie continued, "Do you have a large internet following, Theo, or is this camera crew for something else?"

"The company maintains a prominent social-media presence." Theo altered his stance to block his sister and mother. "We're in the very early stages of a Coast to Coast Living TV show. They're gathering preliminary footage to make a teaser reel for the network."

"Are you its star?" Curiosity and caution merged in Josie's tone.

"No." Theo raised his voice over his mother

and sister's bouquet quarrel. "It's about the company, not the Taylors."

Barry drew his fingers through his goatee. His steely gaze tracked Theo's movements. One of his bushy eyebrows notched as if he noted Theo's reluctance to move too far from Josie. Speculation lifted one corner of his mouth. "Josie, would you mind answering a few questions for us about the Coast to Coast Living brand?"

Josie shifted toward Theo.

Barry's eyebrow and the corner of his mouth hitched higher.

Josie almost tucked herself into Theo's side. Almost made him reconsider his decision to use her to divert the attention away from his family.

Theo tucked his hands in his pockets rather than around Josie's waist. Barry's gaze sharpened. Behind him, the argument escalated. His mother's shrill demand for more specific flowers and sprigs of leaves clawed against Theo's back. Baylee scurried into her back room.

Josie crossed her arms over her chest. "Who will be viewing this film?"

"This footage will be used for internal purposes." Nolan's grin released twin dimples.

"It allows us to get a feel for what we'd like to highlight on the show and who." Barry tilted his head as if watching Josie through a camera lens and searching for the best angle.

"They've been filming me all day." Theo used his most casual tone and avoided his guilt. He achieved two goals at once: protected his family and introduced Josie to the producers. "I'm sure they'd appreciate a different viewpoint. And a more pleasing subject."

Josie freed her hair around her shoulders, but then twisted it back on top of her head. "If you're certain you want my opinion, I can give it."

The trio surrounded Josie. Theo moved to the table between his mother and sister. "Adriana. Mother. Perhaps we could take this conversation off-line." Or end it completely.

Theo glanced over his shoulder at the film crew. Josie spoke to the camera, her hands moving in time to her words. The sidekicks grinned and laughed. Barry, normally a reserved spectator, gave Theo two thumbs-up. They hadn't been that animated all day. Theo credited Josie.

He'd believed Josie would fit his TV show. Barry validated his theory. Theo focused on his family and blamed them for his lack of triumph. "We're in public. It's not the place for this kind of spotlight. Otherwise the production team is going to take more than Coast to Coast Living live."

"We aren't putting on a show, Theo." His mother extended the bouquet toward Adriana, held the greenery like a sacred, unreturnable offering and held herself still until Adriana accepted it. “We’re practicing for our weddings.”

Adriana bristled and thrust the bouquet into Theo’s chest, her exasperation clearly aimed at him. “I cannot do this.”

Theo caught the bouquet before it fell on the floor. Adriana yanked open the door and walked out. Cold air and annoyance washed over Theo. Couldn’t his family cooperate? A nice, sedate departure wouldn’t have given the trio much fodder. A nice, sedate departure would’ve been expected from the well-mannered Taylors.

Josie stepped beside him and whispered, “I think my interview went much better than this.”

Her light tone undid the lingering tension inside Theo. He passed the bouquet to Josie.

“The colors in the greenery complement you, Josie.” His mother leaned her hip on the corner of the table and eyed her. “Have you ever considered a winter wedding?”

Josie fumbled with the bouquet.

Theo never wanted to consider weddings again. But as he looked at Josie, her clutching the bouquet, he could imagine the very event. A gold-and-ivory gown. Rustic flowers. A long aisle. A Windsor-knotted tie. Exhilaration and affection. Impulsive and foolish. Endearing and lasting.

Theo rubbed his neck, stretched his shoulders. Nothing helped. Obviously the wedding madness had infected him, too.

Nolan stepped between Theo and Josie. The assistant unclipped the mic from Theo's collar and beamed. "We have what we need."

"More than enough." Barry's gaze shifted from Theo to Josie to his mother, as if he'd discovered the Bermuda Triangle. He bounced again, rocking onto the balls of his feet and back down. "We're going to review the footage at the office and then call it day."

The trio filed out of the floral shop, discussing angles and voice-overs. More animated than ever. Theo felt deflated. His hasty dash to the flower shop only increased their interest in his family.

"Why haven't I been interviewed privately yet?" His mother picked up several forgotten white and red roses on the table. "I'm part of the Taylor family, too."

"They were here for the business side." To help promote the Coast to Coast Living brand. Not expose the Taylor family discord.

His mother stuck the long-stem roses into Josie's bouquet, adjusted the leaves and Josie's hold. "We are a family business, are we not?"

"Always." Until the company stepped into the open market and went public. Then he'd carve out another rung on the success ladder, ensuring his family stayed together. His father would have approved.

"I know Josie is part of your secret project. No doubt why she earned an interview over your own mother." His mother picked up her purse and cell phone. She stepped close and leveled her shrewd stare on him. "If interviews are required to be considered for a role on the TV show, I expect Fran to schedule me an appointment. She knows my availability."

She notched her chin just shy of superior and walked to the door. She called a cheerful goodbye to Baylee and added, "Thank you for your patience. Theo intends to pay for the bouquet."

Final words and instructions issued, his mother stepped outside, disappearing down the sidewalk. Theo paid Baylee for the flowers and added a generous tip. Baylee took the bouquet into the back to wrap it in cellophane.

"That was unexpected." Josie rearranged a selection of potted pine trees on the counter. "And a bit surreal."

"That's my family." Theo shoved his hands in his pant pockets and paced the small retail space.

"Your mother is quite passionate about getting remarried." Josie straightened a red bow on the top of a small tree.

"My mother is quite passionate about anything that puts her at the center of attention." Theo leaned against the counter and watched the world pass by outside the flower shop's window. "The growth of our company has allowed my mother a rather large platform to work from."

"Maybe she is lonely and wants to share her life with someone." Josie never looked at him.

The sentiment was exactly something the kindhearted Josie would want to believe, but Theo dwelled in facts. He needed Josie to understand. The confession at the gingerbread house was an isolated incident. His professional career consumed him. That left no place for sentiment or sticky emotions. "My parents wanted me home when they realized I could improve the family fortune. Or rather, when they realized I could make a fortune for the family."

"How did they know you could do that?" she asked.

"*Fortune* 500 companies wanted to hire me. International corporations offered me positions out of the country." Theo had packed his bags. Already booked flights. The world opened its doors and Theo wanted to run through every single one. "I was so excited I shared the details with my father."

"Your father didn't want you to move farther away, did he?" Josie looked at him.

"He expected me to focus on family as if

we'd always been a real family." But his father had started talking to Theo only after Theo had started winning. Once he finally came in first: top of his class. Top on the rowing team. When Theo stood out among his peers, then his father showed an interest in him. "My father claimed he hadn't sent me away to boarding school so I could abandon my family."

"So you came home instead." Her quiet voice blew the dust off his forgotten sentiments.

"I wanted to make it real." Theo focused on Josie, as if she anchored him. "But..."

"Home wasn't perfect." She gripped his arm and squeezed. "Like you always wished for."

Wishes weren't for the serious and dedicated. Wishes weren't for the experienced and informed like Theo. Wishes never garnered results. Still, he stared at Josie's hand on his arm and found himself wishing. "Have you ever taken Mimi's advice about collecting moments?"

"I have." Josie accepted the bouquet from one of Baylee's assistants. "Though not nearly enough."

"Let's do that now." Theo waved good-bye to the floral staff and his common sense.

"What?"

"Listen to Mimi." Theo held open the door for Josie. "Do something we consider a moment. Something we could collect to look back on."

"I have work to finish." Her voice dipped as if she'd spilled her certainty like a dropped ice-cream cone.

"As do I." More work than one person should handle. Maybe he'd inhaled too much pollen inside Baylee's place. Whatever it was, nothing interested him more than spending a little more time with Josie. "We'll take an hour. Then it's back to work and reality." Back to results. Back to focus on the things that mattered. Back to no more wishing.

She grinned at him. "What do you have in mind?"

"We visited the gingerbread-house display." Theo ran his hand through his hair. Impromptu had never blended well into his life. He was a planner. A scheduler. "What about another Christmas field trip?"

"There's the tree in the square." Her smile grew in degrees, spreading up into her gaze.

"I've walked by that tree and ice rink countless times on my way to meetings." Unsure that was the moment he wanted.

"But have you seen it lit up. At night." Josie pointed at his phone, which he clutched in his hand. "While not on a conference call."

"Good point." Theo tucked his phone into his pocket. "Taxi or walk?"

Josie adjusted her grip on the bouquet and indicated her boots. "Walk if you're up for it."

Theo held out his arm to Josie. "Let's go visit a Christmas tree."

"It's not just any Christmas tree." Josie's grip flexed on his arm. "It stands over eighty feet tall and features more than thirty-two thousand lights. And it's reusable."

"That's rather specific." Theo folded her arm into his side, easing Josie closer to him. Where he wanted her.

"The square was featured on the news the other night." Josie shrugged. "I wish the tree stood outside my apartment. Every night, its lights would fill the inside of my place with Christmas cheer. It's instant decorations without the work."

"You find the holidays to be work?" he asked. Not sure he liked the idea for Josie. He'd seen her at the gingerbread display, her face lit up brighter than most of the mesmerized children there. When she'd described the people who lived in the Holly Hills Historic District homes, those same children had crowded around her, enthralled and captivated.

"Don't you?" she asked.

"It's one of our most profitable quarters."

Her elbow nudged into his side. She shook her head. "That's not what I meant."

"I never really considered it work. I also never skipped out on a meeting before today, either." And he'd never envisioned himself standing at an altar, waiting for his bride.

She paused at the street corner and glanced at him. The surprise on her face lengthened the one word. "Never?"

Theo shook his head. "Work comes first."

"Well, let's consider it a day of firsts." Josie waved the bundle of greenery. "I've never held a bridal bouquet."

No doubt another oversight by her ex-husband. "Haven't you caught the bouquet at the bridal toss at a wedding reception?"

"I've always managed to skip that portion of the reception." Josie touched one rose petal, then another. Yet her fingers moved as if tracing an image. A secret smile curved across her face.

Theo wanted in. He tapped his elbow against her arm. "What are you thinking?"

"I'd tie gold, deep purple and white silk ribbons around this arrangement." She curved her free hand around the flowers as if straightening the silk ribbons. "Then add a vintage locket with the couple's initials and wedding date engraved on the inside."

"You should include that kind of display at your store. Then you could negotiate a mutual referral agreement with Baylee." Theo motioned to the flower shop. He hadn't considered that angle. Perhaps those vendors could be featured on the TV show after Josie. He twisted, assessed the floral shop behind them, noted several obvious exterior upgrades. Made a note on his phone to check Baylee's background and financials. "I can arrange a meeting with Baylee if you'd like."

"Another time." Josie peered down the street. "She has customers. Likely, she needs a break from us."

Theo walked along beside her. "Weddings come at a cost, even ones with a small budget. You should take advantage of that."

"Why do dreams have to be done according to a budget?" Frustration blew through her voice. "I believe every bride should experience their own fairy tale regardless of their budget."

He could offer Josie her own fairy tale. But he'd never lived in either dreams or fairy tales. He survived in the corporate setting. Thrived among balance sheets, responsible fiscal year-end budgets and sustainable profit margins, not enchanted gardens, storybook romance or make-believe.

What he could give Josie—what mattered—encompassed a solid return on investments, retirement plans and financial stability. "Just don't discount the power of the up-sale. It's like every time a fast-food worker asks 'do you want fries with that?'"

"I never can resist the French fries." Josie nodded.

They turned the corner and paused. Across the street, the eighty-foot tree reached toward the sky. Its lights sparkled against the dark business towers and high-rises. Christmas carols and the scent of hot chocolate infused the evening breeze. Tourists and locals mingled, gliding across the ice rink and lingering around the Christmas tree.

Theo guided Josie across the street, heading toward the massive tree. "I think we can agree on one thing."

"What's that?" Josie tilted back her head, revealing her wide smile.

"We definitely wouldn't need to decorate if this tree was right outside our apartment windows." Theo rubbed his chin. "I'm thinking even its shadow would sparkle."

"We actually only need one branch." Josie bumped into him. "Do you think they'd notice if we borrowed one?"

Theo forgot about the tree. The sparkle in Josie's gaze captured him. And those wishes became whispers.

CHAPTER THIRTEEN

Code red. Times a million. Josie shoved her hair out of her face as she sat up in bed and read the text again. Code red. Times a million. Her phone chimed for a new text.

Seriously. Code red. Times a billion. Josie jumped from her bed. Mia's texts were not exactly the soothing morning alarm she'd expected to ease her into another Sunday—and another workday for Josie. The hour Theo and she had planned to spend at the holiday square had turned into several. She'd pushed her evening work on Adriana's prototypes late into the night. At least she hadn't reached for Theo's hand, despite wanting to last evening, as if they'd been on a date and it was the natural thing to do.

You need to be at the store now. Josie tossed her phone on the bed. She tugged on her fleece-lined leggings, added a wooly sweater and one of her hand-knit scarves, not bothering to check the mirror or her color combinations.

The store was her world. All she had. What had happened? A fire? She would've heard the sirens.

Her hairbrush remained on the bathroom

counter. Her fingers shook too much to hold it. A chill skimmed over her. She tangled her fingers in her hair and wound the strands into a bun, secured it with a long scrap of fabric lying on her couch.

Earthquake? She hadn't felt anything. Still she scrolled through the news feed on her phone and rushed out of her third-floor apartment.

Robbery. Broken water pipe. Gas leak. The chill descended into her bones. Panic bumped against her, pushing her down the stairs. She stumbled once, gripped the handrail and hurried on.

Outside, Josie ran the four blocks, yanked open the door to the boutique and stumbled inside. "Mia. There's no fire truck outside. No smoke. No rush of water."

Mia shouted a greeting from the back of the store.

Movement near the checkout counter caught Josie's eye. Her gaze landed on a familiar blond-haired man leaning against her desk. The run left her breathless. The man smiling at her made her throat close. Bending over and bracing her hands on her knees wouldn't refill her lungs. There wasn't enough air in the boutique. Her one word was a coarse gasp. "Mitch."

"Josie. You look good." Her ex-husband

pushed away from the checkout counter and stepped toward her. "How long has it been?"

"Over two years, I think." If she didn't count the evening Mitch had dinner at the restaurant where she'd waitressed after their divorce. She'd switched tables with another server that night. Mitch still wore the same slim eyeglasses that softened his astute gaze. Still dressed as if every outing was a business occasion.

Voices drifted from the back, breaking into the awkward silence. She recognized Mia, but not the other higher-pitched voice of a woman. A burst of laughter escaped and tumbled around them. Mitch glanced toward the back. A shy smile of amazement slipped across his face.

"Sorry for the intrusion, Josie. We were out for breakfast and saw the lights on inside your shop." He smoothed his palm over his button-down shirt.

A checked-pattern dress shirt with the top button opened. That was a radical change from the starched white shirts and reserved ties he'd always worn during their marriage. Josie tipped her head. Mitch had stepped out of his comfort zone—something she'd never convinced him to try. Josie caught a glimpse of herself in the mirror behind the counter. She looked like she'd tripped inside Christmas, courtesy of the red leggings and velvet hair tie, and landed on the other side of Easter, thanks to her pale orange scarf and lavender sweater.

"I should've called first." Mitch motioned toward the back. "But Krystal insisted we should talk in person."

She waited. Even with his wardrobe change, her ex remained as put-together as always. As in control as always. Standing near him only reminded her just how far she hadn't come, despite her promises to herself and the universe.

She wanted to blame Mia for not warning her. But an encounter with her ex-husband was inevitable. The reality check inescapable.

"Don't come back here, Mitch," the woman shouted. Her high-pitched voice reached into an octave above thrilled. "I found my wedding dress."

Josie looked to the back of the store then stared at her ex-husband.

"I'm engaged." His smile widened, his expression reflected sheer giddiness.

The siren finally roared through Josie. He'd moved on. He hadn't been pining for her. Not that she'd been pining for him, either. But couldn't someone miss her? Just one time. One time in her life. Couldn't someone find themselves torn up because Josie wasn't around?

"To be married," he added into the silent space between them.

"That's great. Wonderful." Josie grinned, knew her small smile hesitated and faltered. But she was happy for him. She didn't blame Mitch for not missing her. She just wasn't someone people missed. That siren faded. Her ears rang, her head hurt. She'd definitely exceeded her reality-check limit for the day. Perhaps even the month.

"Krystal and I wanted to tell you together." He ran his hand through his hair as if he was nervous and not actually helping her realize facts about herself she hadn't want to face.

"Why?"

"Krystal insisted that we have your blessing." His words knocked together.

And disbelief knocked through her. Her words came slowly, like she'd pried them from deep inside her. She repeated, "My blessing."

"This is awkward. I want her to be happy. You, too." His hands waved around him as if he struggled to unscramble incorrect budget calculations. "I'd introduce you. She's better at this. But I can't go back there."

Josie set her purse on the stool behind the counter and paused to regain her balance. She walked into the back to meet her ex-husband's fiancée and end the bizarre morning.

A tall, thin woman stood on the riser, her back to Josie. The platinum blonde standing on the riser didn't cause Josie's breath to disappear. That the woman wore the Jin-inspired dress created for Adriana—that stole Josie's gasp.

"It needs to be taken in here." The woman pinched the fabric under her arm, tightening the bodice. "Maybe extra beading near the waistline. And it definitely needs more feathers."

Josie moved to the riser, lifted her gaze to the woman's face and stumbled. That spark—the one she'd wanted from Adriana—glowed from this stranger. This stranger wearing the wrong dress.

Josie picked up a mantle veil from the other body form and stepped up onto the platform. She clipped the veil around the woman's neck. "If you wear this veil, you wouldn't need more feathers on the gown."

That glow sparked into a flame.

Mia clasped her hands under chin. "I'm going to cry. Seriously start weeping."

The woman pressed her palms against her cheeks, catching her tears. "You're Josie. I'm Krystal Keller. And I imposed. I put on this stunning dress without permission."

Mia dabbed a tissue to her eyes.

"It's my big feet." The woman's face held her mortification. "I'm always overstepping."

Josie scooped up the box of tissues from the small table and handed them to Mitch's fiancée.

Despite her swollen eyes and the chagrin in her tone, Krystal's glow was genuine. So was her smile each time she caught a glimpse of herself in the mirror. Josie finally understood Mimi's advice about thinking beyond the pattern. Finally, she'd created magic.

Josie stepped in front of Krystal. "Where would you put that extra beading?"

"Here." Krystal described the changes.

Josie nodded, accepted her design book from Mia and made notes on a blank page.

"I've cursed my height all my life." Krystal turned and looked over her shoulder, studying the back of the dress in the mirror. "And my mother, too. But this dress."

"It was constructed specifically for a woman with your height." Josie eyed the gown, added more notes.

"How much is it?" Krystal asked.

"It's—" Josie began.

Mia blurted, "It's four thousand dollars."

The tip of Josie's pencil snapped off, along with her voice.

Mia added, "Without the veil."

"Let me talk to Josie," Mitch called. "Krystal, you need to change. We have to meet the wedding coordinator in thirty minutes at the hotel."

Mia released the mantle veil and handed it to Josie. "I'll help you change, Miss Kellar."

Krystal glanced at herself one last time, wiped at her eyes and stepped off the platform. Mia gave Josie a double thumbs-up.

Josie secured the veil on the body form and walked back to the checkout counter.

"How does this work?" Mitch pulled out his wallet. "Do I put down a deposit or pay in full?"

"It's not..."

Her ex-husband stepped forward, held up his hand. "We didn't work, Josie. You always lost yourself in the creativity. And my mind belonged to my business. I can't take back the hurt, but I can support your store." He picked up a pen, wrote on a notepad and handed it to Josie. "That's my offer for the wedding dress and the veil."

Josie stared at the number. He'd more than doubled Mia's price. She'd preached only yesterday about exclusive designs and unwritten rules in the fashion industry. She tried to follow the rules. "You and Krystal have my blessing and a wedding dress."

Krystal rushed forward and embraced Josie, rambling her thanks. Josie waited, her arms stiff against her sides, while her ex-husband peeled away his new fiancée. Josie had never quite gotten used to spontaneous embraces. She kept her personal space well-protected. Krystal harbored no such qualms. And Josie knew then that Krystal was responsible for the changes in her ex-husband. Love suited the pair. She picked up a business card and told Krystal to call to schedule another private fitting.

Josie headed to the dressing room. Mia had already draped the gown back over the body form.

"That was awkward, surprising and terrifying." Mia dropped onto the couch. "I'm sorry, I couldn't stop Krystal once she saw that dress. That was an original from your closet, wasn't it?"

"I just made rent for the next few months." Josie sank onto the cushion next to her friend. Krystal's hug still clung to her like static, although she was oddly calm.

"Congratulations." Mia tipped her head toward Josie. "You just sold a Josie Beck original."

"I just sold Adriana Taylor's exclusive gown." To the highest bidder.

Mia covered her mouth. Her shock and horror evident. "What can I do? This is my fault."

"I sold out for money." Josie dropped her head back. "This is all on me."

"Call Mitch. Tell him that he can't have it," Mia said. "Make up something about not being able to do the alterations in time."

Josie shook her head. "I already ran his credit card."

And trimmed Adriana's choices down to two: her grandmother's and the other exclusive—the one that neither Taylor sibling liked.

"What now?" Mia asked.

Josie stood up. "I get to work."

Most specifically on her persuasion skills. First, she had to convince Adriana to cancel her afternoon fitting. Josie needed to stall until later in the week and a promise to talk to Theo about their grandmother's wedding dress should be enough for Adriana to agree. That part was easy.

The real problem: she had no idea how she was going to convince Theo to embrace his past.

CHAPTER FOURTEEN

"We really like the idea of revamping both Josie Beck and her boutique, The Rose Petal, on the TV show." Foster tweaked his candy-cane-striped bow tie.

"We conducted a deep background check—foster child. No siblings. No parents to file claims for royalty rights." Barry pulled out a thick folder. "Josie checks quite a few boxes as an audience favorite."

"I secret-shopped the boutique this morning." Caitlyn spread both hands out in the air. "We'd like to stretch Josie's segment out over the entire first season."

"Her original work will need to be put away." Foster smoothed his palm over the projected financials like a magician improving the already generous profit line. "And then the dresses can be revealed at the end of the season."

"One of the gowns has been sold." Their assistant's voice was mousy, her flared glasses less obvious, making her look like Cat Woman's younger sibling.

Theo nodded, assuming that was one of Adriana's gowns. Gowns he'd yet to view after his sister had canceled the fitting yesterday. The minister wanted to meet with Ryan and Adriana. His sister informed him that the church took precedence. After all, without the minister, there would be no vow exchange or blessing of the marriage. The fitting had been rescheduled. Theo added, “Josie doesn’t display her original work at her shop.”

“Then the few gowns that we saw can be easily removed.” Caitlyn grinned. “None of her original creations can be sold or worn until after the first season airs.” Caitlyn swirled her chair toward her admin, instructing her to add that stipulation to Josie’s contract.

Once Josie signed the contract, Adriana could not wear one of Josie’s gowns. That ended one deal. But the TV show was a far better option for Josie. The upside was limitless. The money too good to turn away from. He stilled. “What about her upscaled consignment gowns?”

“Again, those can be sold, but not worn until after the season airs.” Caitlyn nodded to her assistant. “We want the most impact on the TV show. A reveal too soon lessens that, even if it occurs off-camera.”

If Josie signed the contract, Shanna lost her wedding gown. He wasn’t even certain how many other women might lose consignment gowns, too. A dull thud knocked against the back of Theo's eyes. He slipped on his reading glasses as if his poor vision was the problem.

"There's much to be gained from this particular segment, particularly with Josie," Foster said. "We'll showcase her transformation from a seamstress to a fashion designer in the first season."

"Did I mention Josie lived in more than six foster homes?" Barry emphasized. "Having the used-gown seller grow into an original fashionista on camera will play well to the viewers. It's a success story."

Theo held up his hand, silencing Barry from revealing more of Josie's personal history to the entire room. A room of strangers. Why wasn't the quietest one in the conference room keeping quiet? "I think we all agree Josie Beck is an ideal candidate for the show."

Theo usually appreciated all the information his team collected. Prided himself on having the most information in any business transaction. It put him in a position of power. Informed was forearmed.

But Josie… He'd invaded her privacy. He wanted her to share with him. To trust him enough to reveal the full truth.

That thud slammed into a throb. Theo slipped his fingers under his glasses and squeezed the bridge of his nose.

"We have a preliminary filming schedule. We'll shoot at Adriana's wedding venue, then again at the reception hall." Caitlyn clicked on a slide. "This will showcase the launch of Coast to Coast Living's new products for the premiere episode."

And prove to Theo's potential shareholders that Coast to Coast Living could compete in the wedding business. Theo had positioned the company to become publicly traded. Yet only Theo and his legal team knew that information. The potential shareholders wanted Coast to Coast Living to have a foothold inside several key markets in the retail sector. The wedding had to be perfect. The deal depended on a flawless reveal. Once Coast to Coast Living went public, the company could reach a new level of success. That would ensure his family's happiness and well-being. And Theo would have nothing to regret.

"We'd like to start filming inside Rose Petal before Christmas." Caitlyn advanced to another slide. "We'll finalize the contract and have it to you by the end of the week."

Theo just had to confirm Josie's consent before then. "Josie will want to review the contract with her lawyer."

"She doesn't currently have one on retainer."

Barry tapped Josie's personal file. "Or the funds to hire one."

Theo could remedy that.

"The contract will have been vetted by our legal team," Foster said. "She'll want to sign quickly. We're two weeks until Christmas day."

Theo had to act quickly, too, and get Josie to agree.

"I'll assume copies of all contracts will be forwarded to my legal team, as well." Theo made a mental note to have Fran follow up on the contracts. He stood, shook hands with the producers and left the building.

Outside, he inhaled. The bite in the air only prodded that insistent throbbing in his head. His phone vibrated. Thirty new emails had arrived during his meeting with the producers. A series of texts and several missed phone calls. Josie's name wasn't on the call list or unopened texts. And she was the one he wanted to talk to. The one he wanted to see.

His phone vibrated again. He didn't recognize the caller, so he sent the call to voice mail and turned off his phone.

Of course, he wanted to see Josie. He wanted to share the good news about her impending celebrity on the TV series. And it *was* good news. She had to recognize that. Theo strode down the block, heading toward the boutique. Everyone wanted more status and more notoriety. Then more doors opened. Bigger opportunities came along. Business rose. There wasn't a downside.

Theo quickened his pace but couldn't quite dodge his doubt.

Shanna and perhaps a few others would suffer setbacks. Surely new gowns could be purchased from another bridal salon in the city. Theo would pay—he'd offer no limit on their dress budgets. Who wouldn't want a brand-new wedding gown?

But that tiny voice of opposition barreled into him. *Josie*.

It always came back to Josie.

Theo turned the corner, saw her and smiled. Simple as that. Uncomplicated as that.

Josie Beck made him smile.

She stood outside her shop, fumbling with a bag and yanking on her door. One more point in the upside column: a complete renovation to include the exterior and a new working door.

One last tug and Josie yanked the door closed before Theo reached her. She locked the boutique's door and turned toward him, skipping past a greeting. "Where's your car?"

Theo glanced into the boutique and back at Josie. "I walked."

Josie checked her phone. "The nearest car is eleven minutes out." She eyed the street up and down quickly, then glanced at his shoes. "We can walk faster."

"Walk where?"

"Sugar Beat Bakery."

He crossed his arms over his chest and watched her. What had he missed? She typed frantically on her phone. "What are you doing?" he asked.

"Pulling up the address on my map." Her tone was twitchy and curt.

"It's on Gate Street, across from Roadside Burgers," he said.

"Perfect." Josie stuffed her phone in her tote bag and took off down the sidewalk. "Let's go."

Theo shook his head and jogged after her. This was not how he'd pictured this meeting unfolding. "Why are we running there?"

"Didn't you get your sister's texts and voice mail?" Josie huffed.

Adriana was standing in for Theo at the Children's Hospital. He'd had to take a call from his lawyers and capital-firm advisors. Then met with the producers. Adriana was presenting a large donation check to the hospital and staying for the press conference—a task she excelled at. There shouldn't have been any problems. "My phone is off."

Josie stopped and set her hands on her knees.

Winded from the run or his revelation, he couldn't be sure.

Her words came out in a pant. "You turned off your phone?"

"It's no big deal." Theo started across the street. "I needed… I'm fine."

"You're not fine," Josie called out and joined him at the corner. "But we have to get back to you later. I promised Adriana first."

"Promised what?" Now he was starting to get agitated. He'd clearly missed several steps during his walk. He pulled out his phone and pressed the power button.

"To stop your mother, although I don't know how to exactly." She shrugged, then considered him. "But you're here now, so you can handle it."

"My mother!" He clutched his phone. Stopped smiling completely.

"You would know all this if your phone was on." Josie flung her arms wide. The twitchiness turned to full distress. "Your mother and her current date are at Sugar Beat sampling Adriana's cake choices and making new suggestions."

Theo shoved his phone in his pocket and ran. He stopped once for a red light. And slowed only to avoid a collision with a dog walker and baby stroller. Theo yanked open the door to

Sugar Beat Bakery, motioned Josie ahead of him and wrestled to regain his breath.

Josie stepped to the side counter, filled two paper cups with water and handed him one. Theo scanned the bakery and choked on his lemon-infused water. His mother sat at a small table in the back corner, cake samples and menus spread out before her. Two plates. Two glasses. Twin forks filled the rest of the square table. She'd been there a while.

Theo crushed the paper cup and gathered his courage.

Trudy Riggs, the owner of Sugar Beat Bakery, stepped through the swinging door, her gaze harried. Her gray hair stood out beneath her cap like broken straw. Trudy's focus landed on Theo. The poor woman almost dropped the plate of cake samples she carried. She righted herself and lifted the platter. Theo shook his head. His mother had had more than enough sweets for one afternoon. Trudy danced back behind the swinging door, a smile flitting across her weathered face.

Theo started toward his mother's table.

Josie set her hand on his arm and stalled him. "Don't be too hard on her. I think she means well."

"If meddling is well-meaning, then she excels at it." Still, Theo couldn't quite catch his sigh.

One that Josie heard, too, if her grin of victory was any indication.

Theo stepped up to the table, greeted his mother and nodded toward the box of tissue. "Have you developed a food allergy?"

"Those are for Marshall." His mother shook her head, her voice forlorn. "Unfortunately, he's not quite over his divorce."

"Where is Marshall?" Theo glanced around the bakery. A mother and her child ate chocolate cupcakes at a nearby table.

"Restroom." His mother waved her hand over her shoulder then smiled at Josie. "Josie, remind me to tell Daphne to add a date range for widowers and divorcées. You don't want to choose any potential matches under the one-year mark. Most aren't over things yet."

"I'm not—" Josie said.

"You're right," his mother interrupted. "It's best to keep to the ones without too much backstory. Unfortunately, at my age, we all have backstory. But you're still young enough. Here's Marshall now."

A silver-haired gentleman in dress slacks and a button-down shirt took Josie's hand. Marshall covered their joined hands with his free one. Then he surpassed good manners, holding onto Josie entirely too long. Theo scowled. His mother quirked an eyebrow at Marshall.

"Just because your ex-wife went younger, you don't need to follow." His mother tapped Marshall's arm until he released Josie. "We discussed this earlier. Desperation never looks good on anyone at any age."

"Can we talk about why you have Adriana's dessert arrangement on the table?" Theo wiped the sweat off his forehead with a paper napkin. He wasn't interested in Marshall's divorce history or hearing the word *desperation* come from his mother. Although he was desperate to get the conversation back on track. The camera on his mother's phone captured his focus. "Why are you recording?"

"Never mind that." His mother picked up her phone and stashed it in her purse. She then waved at the two empty chairs on the other side of her table. "Marshall and I have suggestions for the wedding-cake table."

"The deconstructed wedding cake is quite inventive." Marshall sat in his chair, picked up his fork and pointed between two plates. "We weren't convinced almond cake with salted caramel, and the pink champagne cake were complementary flavors on the table."

"It's not your dessert table." More sweat tracked down the back of Theo's dress shirt, kicking his annoyance to another level. Business attire was not workout attire. His mother's preferences—and Marshall's, for that matter—weren't Adriana's.

Josie nudged aside Theo and pulled out a chair to sit down. "I believe the idea is to offer the most variety of flavors to accommodate all the guests."

"Dark chocolate with expresso mousse and cinnamon spice with maple buttercream would speak to more guests' palates." His mother nodded at Marshall. "It certainly did to us."

Theo tugged out the other chair far enough to sit down. He pinched the dessert menu titled *Adriana Taylor*. If only that pinched his patience back into place. "Surely you and Marshall had other plans for the evening than to debate wedding-cake flavors."

"It's been quite entertaining." Marshall's barrel laugh bounced around the bakery. "Unconventional, but that seems to be your mother's style."

"It's nice to be appreciated." His mother dabbed a corner of her napkin against her mouth and offered her date a tender smile.

"Shall we venture to the Fog City Hotel for a predinner drink?" Marshall asked.

"And appetizers. They have a divine seafood platter." His mother stood and slipped on her wool jacket. "We're dipping back into the conventional. Satisfied now?"

He'd be satisfied when his mother gave up her quest for a Christmas wedding.

His mother turned toward Josie and said, "Daphne has openings in her schedule. You only need to tell me a day."

Theo resisted the urge to crumple the dessert sketch and launch it at his mother. Why did she insist Josie join her on her matchmaking endeavors, too? Josie could be more than content being single. Theo was more than content to see Josie remain single. His mother needed to stop interfering.

Josie rearranged the clean silverware setting in front of her. "My weeks are rather full with appointments right now."

And Theo would fill up any free time Josie might have, if it kept her from meeting with Daphne Holland.

"Just remember you don't need to be so traditional on your dates, either. Changing things up adds a certain amount of fun and spice to what could be a rather intimidating process." His mother tugged on Marshall's hand. "Remember that advice. I need to write it down. It'll be useful for later."

"Already logged it." Marshall tapped his forehead, then held out his arm for Theo's mother. "You two enjoy your evening. We certainly plan to."

Marshall and his mother stepped outside to continue their date.

Theo scanned Adriana's menu for her dessert-bar. He picked up the pencil his mother had left on the table and crossed off her cursive handwriting. Then nixed several of Adriana's original choices, replacing the desserts with his own selections.

Josie leaned toward him and grabbed the pencil. "Tell me you aren't changing Adriana's dessert bar, too?"

"It's not a big deal." Theo reached for the pencil. Josie raised her arm above her head and out of his reach. If he leaned any closer, he'd find himself within Josie's personal space. And close enough to kiss her.

His gaze lowered to her mouth. One second. Enough to spark his interest. And spread a deep awareness through him. He wanted to…

"You just told your mother it was Adriana's wedding," Josie accused.

"Red velvet is universally loved." And would look exceptionally delicious on the new Coast to Coast Living dessert plates being showcased for the first time ever at the wedding reception. There, he'd just proven he could focus on something other than kissing Josie.

"I don't like it." Josie curled her fingers around the pencil and stared at him.

"Have you ever tried it?" *Have you ever thought about kissing me?*

"I don't really like cake." She bit into her lower lip.

"How can you not like cake?" *How can you not like the idea of sharing one kiss?* Nothing more than that. Because that would imply…

He forced his gaze away from her mouth. "You must have had cake at your wedding? What flavor did you choose?"

She lowered her arm and gripped the pencil like she wanted to snap it in half. "We were married at the courthouse."

"What about the reception?" he asked.

She shook her head. Her posture remained stiff, her voice composed. "We were married at the courthouse because my ex wanted to spare my feelings. I couldn't fill my side of the church. He hadn't wanted me to feel bad, as his side would've certainly overflowed with family and friends."

"And you would've been alone at the reception, too," Theo mused. He wanted to talk to her ex, sit the man down and explain that he wouldn't tolerate Josie being hurt. Theo pressed his fingers into his temples. He sounded seriously close to man in a relationship. And he hadn't even kissed Josie. *Yet.*

He motioned to one of the bakery staff and

ordered a large slice of red velvet cake. He'd have to sort out his protective streak concerning Josie later. Right now, he'd eat like any regular guy who wasn't on a date.

"I like it. A lot." Josie swiped the last bite of red velvet cake from the plate and pointed her fork at Theo. "Although it still isn't right to change Adriana's choices."

Theo wiped a napkin over his mouth and considered ordering another slice of cake. His sister would understand once everything was revealed. Just like Josie would understand once he told her about the TV series. He just had to tell her. He pointed at the dessert-bar menu. "Pick one."

"What?" She lowered her fork.

"Pick any one of Adriana's choices that I crossed out." He ran his finger over four of the removed flavors. "We'll taste it together. If we both like it, I put it back on the dessert table."

Josie took the menu and studied it. Her grin was playful, her voice spirited. "Confetti."

"That's a kids' birthday cake." Theo leaned toward her and scanned the list again. "Are you sure?"

"I always wanted a Confetti birthday cake growing up," she admitted.

"Why didn't you have one?" The words escaped and he tensed. On the insensitivity chart, he just launched himself to the top. This was the part where Josie told him she'd never had a birthday cake growing up.

He glanced behind the counter, searching for the staff, wanting to right his wrong. He was prepared to order a slice of every flavor of cake in the bakery. They'd sample each one until she discovered her favorite. Until she picked her favorite birthday cake.

"I was too afraid to ask." Josie tore the corner off her paper napkin, then crumpled it. Her voice was bold, as if she crushed the melancholy from her tone. "I had vanilla cupcakes one time. Chocolate-chip cookies and brownies. It was more than enough."

But it was her birthday—the one day everyone deserved to be special, according to Grandma Pearl. His grandmother made sure his birthdays were full-size celebrations: party games, balloons, four-layer cakes and candles. At boarding school, his own mother had mailed birthday packages that had always included his favorite things. In college, the packages had continued to arrive every year on his birthday. His mother still singled him out on his birthday—still made the day important. He should thank her for that.

He went to the counter and returned to their

table carrying a large slice of confetti cake and two clean forks. "Let the tasting begin."

Josie rubbed her hands together and took the fork he handed to her. "We taste at the same time so we can't be swayed by the other's reaction."

"You're taking this quite seriously." Theo adjusted his chair and picked up a fork.

"Absolutely," she said. "I'm fighting for Adriana."

Would she fight for him? This was about cake. Nothing more significant than that. He loaded a bite onto his fork and looked at Josie. She toasted him with her forkful of cake. They tasted the concoction at the same time. Only Theo forgot to taste his sample. He forgot everything except Josie. Delight radiated across her face like the sun streaming through a window. Theo wanted to scoot closer. He set down his fork, held himself in place and pushed the plate closer to her. "Well?"

"It was so much better than I thought it would be." She scooped another bite onto her fork. "What about you? Did you like it?"

I like it because you like it. I like it because I like you. "It was better than I expected."

She eyed him, her fork balanced over the cake. "But does it make it back onto the dessert table?"

How could he disappoint her now? He wasn't giving in, either. He liked the cake, too. Not nearly as much as he liked Josie. Theo picked up the pencil and erased the line he'd drawn through *Confetti* on the dessert-bar sketch. His unplanned feelings proved harder to erase.

Josie cheered. "This is going to be the first cake finished that night. Mark my words."

"Care to make a bet?" he asked. "The confetti against the red velvet. First one finished is the winner."

"What do I win?" Her grin raced up into her sky-blue eyes.

"Winner gets to choose what we do on New Year's Eve." He blinked, slow and measured. The sprinkles in the cake clearly gave him more than a sugar rush. His suggestion hung suspended between them.

Josie never balked. Interest drifted into her voice. Uncertainty shifted into her gaze. "We're doing something together on New Year's?"

Theo rubbed his palms on his pants. It was a bad idea. One he should take back. Change out with something simple, like winner gets twenty dollars. Or a cake of their choice from Sugar Beat. Perhaps he was suffering a sugar crash instead. "Seems like the right thing to do. I figure by Christmas we'll have exhausted the Christmas events around the city, and we'll need to move to the next holiday."

Josie swirled her fork in the cream-cheese frosting and considered him. "Do you usually go out on New Year's Eve?"

He shook his head. He hadn't wanted to, not in a while. Until now. Until Josie. "How about you?"

"I haven't for a long time." She took another bite of cake and held out her hand. "Challenge accepted."

The bet sealed, Josie finished the confetti cake. Theo turned over the list for the dessert bar and rewrote the requested cake flavors. On the bottom, he made a note to change the table-linen colors, adding dark purple napkins and champagne accents.

Josie finished the last bite of cake and leaned toward him. "Adriana mentioned a winter white theme."

"She'll have that with a few accent colors." Theo wrote "gold flatware" in the margin. He'd viewed and approved the new flatware collection in his first meeting that morning. "Besides, deep purple is regal. How could someone not like it?" And dark purple paired well with the gold-trimmed plates—also approved to be part of the new collection.

Josie tugged the paper from Theo and read

his new notes. "This feels more like something from the *Coast to Coast Living* magazine."

"Isn't that the point?" He sat back and crossed his arms over his chest.

Josie countered, "I thought the point was to celebrate Adriana and Ryan."

"I'm doing that, too." Theo drummed his fingers against his arm. He needed to add a note to check on the design of the chair coverings—another Coast to Coast original product.

"You could celebrate Adriana in your grandmother's wedding dress," Josie suggested. "Redesigned, of course."

"Tell me Adriana didn't find my grandmother's dress." He tipped his head at Josie. It was for the best that neither his sister nor Josie become attached to the idea of Grandma Pearl's gown. "Tell me Adriana didn't try on that dress, too."

"Would it matter if she did try it on?" Josie toyed with the folds of her scarf.

Yes. Very much. Beyond the fact that Adriana should be in an exclusive gown to maintain the new, fresh and innovative direction Coast to Coast Living was taking. There was also Josie's contract for the TV show. Once she signed, Adriana couldn't wear Josie's gowns, including an updated version of Grandma Pearl's dress. There was a plan for Josie mapped out—a new direction for her, too. She just had to follow it and abide by the contract terms. He just had to tell her those terms: no more consignment gowns. No more theater costumes. Original bridal only. "I'm not certain Adriana has spoken to our mother about wearing Grandmother's gown."

"I don't think she needs to." Josie stacked the empty plates and brushed the crumbs onto the top plate. "Your mother didn't speak to Adriana before trying on the Linden Topher gown. Then she'd decided to keep it for her own wedding without talking to Adriana."

"Adriana told you about that?" Theo ran his hand over his face.

"It came out during her first fitting, then later at Bouquets by Baylee."

That wasn't exactly the kind of family incident he'd wanted shared. Perhaps now, Josie would understand why she was better suited for the TV series than his own family. "My mother..." What could he say about Lilian Rose Taylor? How could he explain his own mother?

"Your mother wants to find her place," Josie said.

"She has one already in our family." Theo picked up his mother and her date's plates and tossed the stack in the trash can. He provided for his mother, like he'd promised his father he would. She had her own suite in his house, a private entrance and freedom to do as she pleased.

"I'm not sure she sees that." Josie followed him.

He was quite certain his mother saw things just fine—according to how she wanted to see them. There wasn't enough time left in the evening to debate his mother. And Theo was more interested in Josie. "What about you? Have you found your place with your boutique?"

"I've found a place." She cleaned off the table, tossed out the napkins and picked up her purse.

"But you want more." Of course she did. Everyone always wanted more. And he could give her more. So much more if she signed the contract.

"I want to make it on my own." She tugged on her coat and went to stand beside him. "And I want to make an impact."

The do-it-yourself sentiment was fine. But Theo opened doors and he'd yet to encounter someone unwilling to exploit the chance. The bigger impact would be made on the TV series. He held the door for her. "Do you have a plan?"

"I'm figuring it out." She glanced up at the evening sky as if figuring out how long the rain intended to hold off. "Do you always have a plan?"

"Always." He tucked his hands into his pants pockets and walked toward the plaza. "One-year. Five-year. And ten."

"That's impressive." She matched his pace. "Where will you be in five years?"

"Running Coast to Coast Living." By then, it would be a publicly traded company that he'd built. "Working to introduce the brand to an international customer base." Always seeking that next level of success. That next step that would ensure he wasn't someone's regret.

"Anything else?"

"The company is all-consuming."

"What about family?" She moved around a couple, dressed for running and using the sturdy trunk of a sidewalk tree for balance while they stretched. "What about marriage?"

Marriage? Marriage was for the content. He wasn't complacent. He had more to accomplish first. More to prove.

"That's not part of your five-year plan, is it?" She stopped at a corner for a red light and studied him. "What about the ten-year plan?"

He searched the street, looking for a taxicab and an interruption. He was supposed to be talking about Josie, not dissecting his future.

"You've only built plans for work," she accused.

"That's my life." He raised his arm, flagging a taxicab less than a block away. "Your ride home is coming."

She ignored the street and eyed him. "Don't you want more than work?"

Work provided satisfaction. That always fulfilled him. His gaze trailed over Josie's face, stopping on her pretty eyes. He had everything he wanted with his business. Everything, except… "Do you want more?"

"I'm still working on my one-year plan." She lifted her arm for the cab driver. "Can I get back to you?"

"Sure." *But don't wait too long. I'm not sure how much longer I can wait.* The taxi pulled next to the curb. Theo latched onto the door and opened it, welcoming the distraction.

"Want to share a ride?" she asked.

He wanted to share more than a ride. Josie tempted him to reveal parts of himself no one knew. Josie made him consider marriage and family—the kind he'd dreamed about while growing up. Josie made him consider a life of contentment.

He shook his head. "Going to walk off all that cake." And his wayward sentiments.

CHAPTER FIFTEEN

THEO HAD MANAGED one full workday without seeing Josie. He hadn't managed one hour without thinking about her. Not that he'd let her affect his work.

At least not until his two-o'clock meeting yesterday afternoon. His event director and staff had been finalizing the details for the Saturday-night annual holiday gala Coast to Coast Living hosted for its vendors, advertisers and suppliers, everyone who helped make the company a success. He'd okayed the menu: liked the heavy-appetizers option. Approved the addition of a carving station for beef tenderloin, smoked pork loin and seared tuna. Agreed that the cheese boards, pasta bar and salad station offered something for every taste bud in attendance.

Then the conversation had proceeded to the dessert station. Homemade gelato. Assorted truffles. White- and dark-chocolate-dipped strawberries. Fresh whipped cream and hot chocolate. And cake pops: peppermint-brownie, chocolate-toffee, pumpkin-spice, lemon and vanilla. Theo had paused, asked his director to read the cake-pop flavors again. Then he'd requested confetti for a cake-pop flavor.

His director had dropped the menu. Theo hadn't altered the menu in the six years they'd been hosting the gala. Not that it was problem…sort of. Only a surprise, as it was four days until the event. And confetti wasn't an option on the cake-pop menu. Theo's request had resulted in multiple calls to the hotel catering staff. During the phone-tag session, Fran had helpfully reminded the staff in his conference room that Theo's favorite cake was red velvet. Surely he'd rather have that. Theo had shaken his head. After all, Josie would rather have confetti. Finally, the executive pastry chef had been located. And twenty-three minutes into the next hour and into his next meeting, Theo's special request had been granted.

Meanwhile, his staff had left, curious about his sudden craving for confetti.

That morning, Adriana had stopped him in the hall between meetings to casually suggest that Theo take Josie out to dinner to thank her for coming to her rescue at the bakery the other evening. Adriana would've taken Josie herself, but Theo had pawned off several more social events for Adriana to attend as a representative from Coast to Coast Living.

His mother had overheard—she'd been coming from her office, Mia beside her. The two women had shared a knowing look before his mother offered several suggestions for restaurants to take Josie to. His mother had been coordinating a meeting between Josie and Daphne Holland.

Since Josie had already been on his mind. He'd used Adriana's thank-you as a motive.

But now, standing outside Rose Petal Boutique, Theo worked through the conversation he needed to have with Josie. The one about the TV series. The one about the contract arriving on Friday—only two days away. The one about filming schedules and the changes to her business and life.

His stomach knotted. Perhaps dinner hadn't been the wisest choice for this conversation.

Worse, he hesitated. He never hesitated in business. Especially in profitable situations. The TV series benefited Josie and his company. There was nothing to hesitate about.

Theo reached for the door handle of Rose Petal Boutique but answered his phone instead.

"I need your help, Theo." His mother bounced past a formal greeting. "They won't accept your credit card without you here."

Theo stepped into the thin alley beside the boutique and closed his eyes. "What are you doing with my credit card?

"That's not important right now." His mother's words tumbled through the phone. "I haven't ever had any problem using it before."

"Aren't you on a date?" Theo plugged one ear with his finger, blocking the noise of a garbage truck.

"Yes, with Kirk Townsend." His mother's excited sigh stretched into an earnest plea. "I want to appear independent, Theo. Not like I need a man to pay for my dinner. Besides, if he pays, then he might expect something from me."

Theo squeezed his forehead and sighed. "Where are you?"

"I'll text you the address." His mother rushed on. "Don't be long."

Theo walked inside the boutique and checked the time. He was early, thanks to an open parking spot outside Josie's shop. They had time to put out his mother's latest crisis and arrive at Savory Window Restaurant in time for their reservation.

Josie walked from the back, surrounded by six teenagers, each one vying for her attention. Their conversation swirled like an ice-cream twist dipped in sprinkles. A red-haired boy mentioned Leo's recent breakup. Several girls shook their heads in sympathy. Camille would take the lead on opening night. More head shakes, less sympathy. Nathaniel would return for the second act. That earned a collective groan. There was something about a knee that needed icing and elevation. Licorice-root tea being brewed. And a Friday-night cast-party invitation. Followed by quick hugs for Josie and a group departure.

Josie waved them out and flipped the sign in the window to Closed. She exhaled a long sigh. “Opening night is tomorrow evening. They’re really excited.”

And she looked really tired. Shadows settled under her eyes. “How are you?”

She pulled back and considered him, as if no one had really asked her in a while. Or waited around long enough for a real answer. “I’m good. Thanks.” She tucked her hair behind her ears, tugged stray threads off her sweater and nodded. Her words picked up speed. “I have three costumes to alter. One zipper replacement. Several hem adjustments now that the girls made tap-shoe changes. And two last-minute costume additions to complete before the curtain rises at seven tomorrow evening.”

Every item on her task list for the high-school play added more power to her voice. Her hands waved, but not to cover a yawn. He said, “Now you look recharged.”

“I am. It’s an adrenaline rush of sorts.” Josie locked the cash register and flipped the light switch for the back of the store. "The kids are so much fun. Energetic, interesting and appreciative. They're already discussing costume designs for the spring production of *Beauty and the Beast*."

Her contract prohibited costume designs. Theo ignored that knot in his stomach. "What if your wedding-dress-design business surges in the spring? You won't have time for high-school theater groups."

"I'll always make the time." Josie picked up her jacket and purse.

"Why?" he asked.

"It's important to them," Josie said. "That makes it important to me."

But he wanted to know why…and would it still be important if her business was moving in another direction, like into the bridal industry? "I thought you wanted to be a custom-wedding-dress designer?"

"I do. Very much." Josie wrapped a scarf around her neck. "There's just something inspiring and so uplifting about working with the high schoolers. It's hard to explain, except I'd hate knowing I let them down."

Surely there were other seamstresses in the city. Even talented amateurs who could handle the costumes for the high-school plays. "You need to set a focus for your business and work to that goal."

She set her hand on her stomach and grinned at him. "My focus right now is dinner and then we can talk about goals."

"Fair enough." He took her keys and locked the door for her.

"I'm teaching several of the high schoolers to sew." Josie laughed. "How crazy is that?"

"You're teaching more sewing lessons now, too?" Theo dug out his car keys. Why hadn't Barry discovered that in his thorough background check? Theo's appetite bottomed out.

"It's something new." Josie glanced at him over the top of his car. "As in last-week new. The kids convinced me it would be fun."

"Are they paying for these lessons?" He unlocked the car doors, trying to knock out the terse bite to his tone. He already knew the answer.

"No, I couldn't charge them. I've never taught before." She climbed into the passenger seat, grabbed the seat belt and paused to consider him. "I might be awful. What if I'm awful?"

"You won't be." She'd be terrific. Theo had seen her at Penny's Place teaching the women. They'd all responded to her. Even several of the children at the gingerbread displays had requested more of her stories that night. She'd obliged, been patient and accepting. Would she accept his offer and the strict terms? He asked, "When do these lessons start?"

"This weekend." Josie buckled her seat belt.

Theo cringed. He'd need to check with the producers about sewing lessons. Although teaching high schoolers a basic life skill like sewing could fit into the segment format. But that would require releases from the students and their parents. More contracts. More paperwork. More approval. "I'm surprised you'd want to take more on."

"That's just it." Wonder drifted through Josie's voice. "It's not work when I'm with them. It's my first year working with the theater groups and I wished I'd started sooner."

Theo wasn't certain he'd ever had a time when work wasn't work. When he wasn't working to maintain an image or the status quo. Or working on an improvement for his company or his family. Except with Josie. He started the car, disregarded those whispered wishes and pointed at the convenience store down the street. "We need to make one quick stop on the way to the restaurant. Would you like a snack to hold you over until dinner?"

Josie patted her purse. "I've got chocolate in here."

Theo checked the address his mother texted,

then grinned at Josie. "Are you willing to share?"

"I could be persuaded."

One chocolate bar and a stalled debate over the best chocolate combination later, and Theo had parked outside a four-story loft-style office building. The first-floor accountant and real-estate offices were dark and closed for the night. The same for the third and fourth floors, as if those businesses all adhered to the normal eight-to-five business hours.

Colorful Christmas lights outlined the second-floor windows. White light warmed the interior of the windows and made the rose gold lettering for Waltzing Along Dance Studio glow. Disquiet dripped through him. Josie's chocolate tasted more like burned charcoal, souring his stomach. As if his mother walking around with his credit card hadn't already given him enough unease.

Josie peered out the window. "Are you sure this is the right address?"

Theo read his mother's text out loud. Adriana had mentioned signing up for private dance lessons to practice their first dance as Ryan wanted to discover his natural rhythm. Theo couldn't recall Adriana ever mentioning this particular dance studio.

"This is the right place." Josie set her hand on the door handle. "Should we go in?"

Theo opened his door and adjusted the level of hope in his tone. "Perhaps there's a private lounge on the second floor, too."

Every step on the indoor staircase intensified the notes of the classical music drifting from the dance studio. Theo's hopes dwindled. His unease amplified.

At the landing, Josie looked from the elevator bay to the studio. "It's only the dance studio on this floor."

Theo eyed the oversized double glass doors, propped wide open in welcome. Classical music flowed through the archway like an invitation. A couple twirled by, swept up in the promise of the harmony.

"That looks like your mother." Delight looped from Josie's voice into the curve of her fingers around Theo's arm. She gave a playful tug, urging him into the archway. Then she stilled beside him as if afraid to intrude any farther.

Theo stilled, too, unwilling to jar his connection to Josie. Her touch grounded him. A bald gentleman supported his mother, guiding her in a wide circle around the grand ballroom. Laughter rippled, blending into the music, then swirling free. His mother glided across the dance floor, her head thrown back, her smile infectious, as if she was twenty and in the midst of her debut. Not a widow on a frenzied quest for a second husband.

He preferred his mother like this. There was no guessing about her feelings. No questioning her agenda. Where had that mother been when he was growing up? Why wasn't she around even more now? Now that they were all adults. All grown and their childhood hopes long forgotten. In the span of one turn, Theo realized he didn't really know his mother. In the span of the next rotation, he discovered an unexpected sense of loss. As for the blame, he considered that they might both be at fault.

"Theo. Josie." His mother twirled to a stop and dropped into a deep curtsy. Pleasure rushed through her breathless voice. "Come in. Join us."

"You've finally arrived." A lean gentleman, his brown hair cropped short against his head, clapped his hands together near the sound system. He descended on Theo and Josie. His cultured voice carried through in his refined movements. "Now the real dancing can commence."

Theo remained rooted in the doorway. Josie's fingers flexed around his arm.

"I'm Anton." The instructor embodied sophistication and style like Santa Claus embodied Christmas. "Don't fret. Your mother already told me you didn't inherit her agility. I'm here to help you release your inner swans on the dance floor."

Josie bumped into Theo. Her grip notched tighter, into a clamp.

Theo had no inner swan he wanted to release. He'd lingered, lulled by his mother's deception. And his own misplaced hopes. He should've known that wouldn't last. *Fooled again.* His mother lived according to her agendas. And it seemed he'd willingly walked into another one.

"It's not the time to be shy, my little porcupettes." Anton wedged himself between Josie and Theo, breaking their link. He hooked one arm around Theo's waist and one arm around Josie's, propelling them into the room. "This is where we practice until you shine."

"Practice?" Josie squeaked.

"You cannot step onto the ballroom floor at the wedding reception without practice." Anton positioned them in the middle of the floor. Placed Theo's right hand on Josie's left shoulder blade. Her left hand on Theo's shoulder. Then clasped their free hands together, raising their arms to the proper height. He stepped away, stiffened his arm into the frame he wanted them to mimic. "The Taylors have the ballroom reserved for the rest of the night. We have hours to locate those missing swans."

Josie swayed into Theo. "You planned this?"

"No." Theo braced his frame, preparing for the impact.

Josie caught herself, pulled back and set her frame to the proper distance approved by every strict chaperone at every high-school dance.

"I planned dinner at Savory Window." He stumbled. Josie looked down at their feet. Their bodies collided. His focus scattered. "This…"

The music stole his voice. Anton's instructions bounced around him. "Three-step sequence. Count it—one, two, three. It's a gradual rise and fall. Smooth. Land on the ball of your foot." Anton guided Josie closer. "This was once a forbidden dance. It corrupted or so they claimed."

"Eyes on each other." Anton touched their chins, lifting their gazes away from their feet. "It's the only way to lose yourself in the dance. To become a *we*."

Anton drifted away and demonstrated the steps, his partner imaginary. There was nothing imaginary about Josie. Nothing pretend about the feel of her in his embrace. Theo locked onto Josie's blue gaze. He wasn't interested in becoming a *we*. Business came first. He preferred his privacy and alone time. He preferred…

Josie stepped too soon. Her fingers squeezed his shoulder. His chest clenched.

"I don't know what I'm doing," Josie confessed.

Neither did he. Still, he guided Josie slightly closer and lost himself in her gaze. "That makes two of us."

"What happens if we make a run for it?" One corner of Josie's mouth eased up.

Take my hand and tell me where.

His mother and her partner spun in a slow circle around them. She smiled. "I'd like you to meet Kirk." Her partner spun her in a circle. "Isn't it a wonderful evening to learn to dance?"

Anton clapped his hands and announced, "Partner swap."

Kirk twirled Josie out of Theo's embrace, guiding her around the room. His mother settled into his arms. Theo lifted his elbows, locked his frame…and his wariness. "What about my credit card?"

"Later, dear." His mother patted his shoulder. "Tomorrow, even. Kirk arranged this evening for me. Isn't that the sweetest gesture? I won't ruin it with rude behavior."

His mother's date transferred Josie back to Theo and spun his mother away. Josie lost her balance. Theo curved his arm around her back and steadied her. "My mother would stop us if we made a run for it. It would be rude, and Taylors are never rude, Theo, dear." He lifted his voice an octave to mimic his mother, earned a smile from Josie for his effort.

"Then can we pause?" She curved her arms around his neck. "My head is spinning from all the turns."

He preferred this part of the lesson. Willed Anton to focus on turning his mother and her date into swans. "Did you look down? It throws off your balance."

"Kirk was kind, but he wasn't…" Her lips pressed together. Her cheeks reddened.

He traced the image of her like that into his memory. Then he pretended to overlook her breathless reaction and wistful voice. "We had to take dance classes my freshman year in high school."

Her gaze returned to his. Disbelief outlined her frown. "So you do know how to do this."

"It was one semester." Fifteen very long weeks. Theo shuddered. "I was the example of what not to do."

Josie laughed. "You're kidding?"

"I wish I was." He grinned. His height had been awkward on his frame. He'd been sweaty and, he was certain, stinky like every other freshman boy. "Every day, Mr. McCord made me repeat what I'd done in front of the whole class. Every day it was a new mistake."

"That's awful." Horror tinted her words. "Humiliating. That teacher shouldn't have been allowed to get away with that."

"No, I was really awful," he said. "Two left feet and no rhythm. I grew too fast. My brain had a hard time processing the balance issues and coordinating all my gangly body parts."

"But you were put on stage in front of everyone. Called out for being bad." She whispered, "For being different."

"We were all awkward and weird at that age." But that class had bonded and remained close friends until graduation. He hadn't thought about that group in a long while. Those friends had been his family and his support. "Several of the guys thanked me for taking the heat off them. Several others offered to teach me to dance."

"Did you learn quickly?" she asked.

"I purposely got even worse. Every day." He shook his head and laughed at her confused expression. "I helped several of the more clumsy ones survive the class. No one wants to be the worst. I'd already been given the title, so I made sure I kept it."

Her fingers brushed the back of his neck.

"That was kind and you told me you weren't kind."

"Seemed like the right thing to do." He shrugged. The wrong thing was to pull Josie even closer. Hold her tighter. The wrong thing was to believe this could be something more.

Anton floated toward them, twirling his imaginary partner. He wrapped his arms around them. "My little porcupettes, we came to become swans. This is not the way."

Josie rested her head on Theo's shoulder and giggled. "Are you sure?"

"Quite." Anton clapped his hands together. "I have a dance you two will love. Trust me?"

Theo peered at Josie. "Dinner or dance?"

"We have hors d'oeuvres arriving shortly." Anton beamed. "Delicious, I promise."

Theo linked his hands behind Josie's back, reluctant to end their impromptu dance. "Your choice."

Josie bit into her lip. Her blue eyes sparked. "Mimi would want us to dance."

Theo grinned. "Teach us, Anton."

His mother and her date nodded their approval. Anton gathered his class around him and the dance lesson began.

Two hours later, Anton declared the evening a success. Crowned Josie and Theo young swans and invited the group to return any time. His mother and Kirk stayed in the dance studio to enjoy a champagne toast with Anton. Josie and Theo stepped off the elevator and walked outside, leaning on each other.

"Thank you. I can't believe we learned to dance. Really dance." Josie flung herself into Theo's arms and wrapped him in an all-consuming hug. "That was one of the best moments."

It was the kind of full, warm embrace he'd always hoped for from his parents as a kid. The kind that now always took him by surprise. Such pure affection disconcerted him. He stopped wanting that years ago, hadn't he? Yet in Josie's embrace, he wanted even more. Felt even more.

Theo pulled away, tucked that one strand of her hair—the one that always swept across her cheek—behind her ear. He trailed his fingers across her cheek like he'd wanted to do since he'd first met her. His fingers tipped her chin up. "Josie."

Josie swayed forward. Theo leaned in.

But Josie paused and yelled, "Cab!" She jumped out of Theo's embrace and raced toward a taxi. "I need that cab."

Theo dropped his suddenly empty arms. Cleared his mind. Followed Josie.

She opened the cab door, climbed inside.

Theo reached for her.

"Shanna's fitting is tomorrow." Her gaze skipped from his eyes to his mouth and back. Her smile twitched, restless and nervous. So very flustered. "Come to the boutique around four if you want to see what vintage looks like new."

"Josie. Wait." *I want to kiss you. That wasn't a proper goodbye. You should know...*

Her car door shut. The cab pulled away. Its exhaust captured Theo's plea.

CHAPTER SIXTEEN

"MY HANDS ARE SHAKING." The bride-to-be, Shanna, clutched Josie's arm and followed her out of the dressing room.

"Deep inhales." Josie guided the woman up onto the platform and positioned her in front of the mirror. "Keep your eyes closed."

Theo wasn't closing his eyes. Not now. His gaze was fixed on Josie. A tint colored her cheeks. She stepped back, pressed both hands to her face. Then she shook her head, as if her amazement couldn't settle inside her.

Josie amazed him. She was invested in this moment as if it was her own wedding day. It was personal. Not a simple sales transaction. Not any other dress. Josie smoothed her hands down the curve-hugging gown.

"I'm so excited." Shanna's arms flailed at her sides as if she was afraid to touch anything. "I can't breathe."

Theo held his own breath for the woman, too. The transformation of the dress was incredible. No more obnoxious bows, puffy shoulders or bulky skirts. Only the deep open back remained to hint at what had been. Josie had added sleeves—she called them illusion for the sheer lace.

"Deep inhales. I'm almost ready." Josie attached the train at Shanna's trim waist, then she fluffed the material until it draped off the platform in a wash of embroidered silk.

Theo moved closer to see the detail on the gown, drawn to both Josie's work and the dressmaker herself.

"Open your eyes." Josie stepped back and faced Shanna. Her gaze shifted over Shanna's shoulder and collided with Theo's. "What do you think?"

The corner of Josie's bottom lip disappeared. That tint increased from a pale flush to scarlet. He thought Josie was breath-stealing. Incredible. Talented.

"I can't..." Shanna touched the beading on the scalloped collar, then tried again. "It's..."

Josie clutched her hands together and pressed them against her mouth. "I'm not supposed to have favorites. Our designs are like our children—each one precious and unique. But this one."

Theo had a favorite, too. A woman that wove dreams into fabric. He wanted to be by her side. Wanted to share in this moment that wasn't his. He had no place there. Except beside Josie—that was the place he wanted to be.

"I know." Shanna twisted, glimpsing the back of her gown.

Theo stepped onto the platform. Pride and satisfaction swirled through Josie's gaze.

Shanna turned and faced the mirror. Theo winced, taking the woman's former pain as his own. And then he understood. Understood Josie's insistence that Shanna should have her personal fairy tale. It wasn't the burn scars that flickered up Shanna's right cheek, damaging the skin on her neck, then disappearing beneath the neckline of the gown. Those proved Shanna was a survivor. No, it was the hope and courage buried inside Shanna's hazel gaze. Josie wanted Shanna to believe in herself the same way Josie believed in her.

Shanna lifted her hands to release her hair.

Josie reached out. Theo touched Josie's arm and shook his head at her. Confusion crossed over her face, yet she held herself back.

"Shanna. We haven't officially met. I'm Theo Taylor." Theo moved to stand in front of Shanna, blocking the woman's reflection in the mirror. "Josie has been kind enough to include me in the transformation of your gown. It's quite remarkable."

Shanna's hands stilled in her hair. "It's more than I ever imagined."

This woman was more than she imagined,

too. Josie had already known that from the first. Now, Theo knew, too. "Can I give you some unsolicited advice? You should leave your hair up for your wedding day."

Shanna's hand dropped to her neck, covering her scars. "They're…"

"A part of you." Theo's voice was gentle. Sincere. Heartfelt. He channeled everything Josie was. Everything he wanted to be. "You're perfect as you are. Don't hide anything."

"What about my fiancé?" Shanna whispered.

"He'll want to see you just as you are now." Theo reached out and took Shanna's hand. "You're going to take his breath away."

Josie moved behind him, walked to the couch and the tissue box. She pressed several tissues into Shanna's hand.

"I am, aren't I?" Shanna wiped the tears from her cheeks. Her tentative laughter gained strength and depth. Her chin tipped up, her shoulders tipped back. Confidence and happiness burst from her. "I'm getting married. I'm in love. Really, really in love. And I look hot."

Josie picked up a chin-length veil.

Shanna shook her head and grinned at Theo. "I don't think I want a veil."

Part of her story. That's what Josie wanted. To be a small part of her brides' stories. He understood the appeal. And the draw. The feeling was energizing. Addicting. How was he supposed to ask Josie to give that up? Did Josie even want nationwide reach and national exposure? Or was this fulfilling enough?

Josie smiled, set the veil back on the mannequin and lifted her arms toward the accessory wall. "We have crowns. Jeweled headbands. Hair clips."

"I have a picture on my phone." Shanna's focus returned to the mirror, as if she was surprised by her reflection.

Theo was surprised by the power in the moment. Surprised about his own reaction. Surprised that he wanted to linger and encounter the same empowering boost with another client.

"Let me get your phone." Josie returned from the dressing room and handed Shanna her phone.

Shanna tapped on the screen and gave the phone to Josie. Theo peered over her shoulder. The model's hair was upswept into thick braids that circled her head like a crown. Fresh flowers had been woven into the strands.

"Do you think that would work?" Shanna touched her head. "I've been growing out my hair."

But not to hide herself anymore. Josie had given her that gift…in one beautifully crafted *used* dress.

Josie gave Shanna her phone and smiled. "It will be perfect on you."

"I'd add in lavender," Theo suggested. "Josie would call it that surprising pop of color."

He liked Josie's pop of surprised laughter, too. Yes, he remembered the fresh lavender party favors Shanna's friends were making. He remembered everything that involved Josie.

Shanna requested Josie's help to change and cried on her way into the dressing room. The woman hugged Theo on her way out. And wiped away more tears on her way out the door. All the while, a smile remained on Shanna's face. A light shone in her gaze.

"That was the magic. The magic Mimi always told me about." Josie sat beside him on the velvet couch. Amazement radiated from her voice. "And I created it."

He set his phone on the couch and studied her. "The dress was truly breathtaking." *Like the woman who designed it.*

"Have you changed your mind about vintage then?"

"I'm starting to see the appeal." And he was starting to see a life that included Josie. He took her hand, curved his fingers around hers. Her head dropped onto his shoulder. But that life included compromise and change. And he had a dream to offer her first. "What if you had to choose? What if you could only upscale vintage gowns or only create originals?"

"I don't want to choose." Her grip tightened around his. She curled farther into his side. "I love vintage and bespoke gowns."

"Launching a custom bridal line takes effort and complete attention." He set their joined hands on his leg. He didn't want her pulling away. Didn't want her to have to choose. "Redesigning consignment gowns will become a distraction."

"You're talking like I'm already launching a custom bridal line." She lifted her head and looked at him. "Like I'm distracted now. I understand what's at stake. Adriana's wedding dress can put my name into the bridal world. But only if I concentrate on that goal."

"Adriana's gown isn't the only way to do that."

She shifted on the couch to face him. "What do you mean?"

"Barry and his assistants showed the footage of you to the producers of our TV show. They want to feature you on the show." Theo wanted to give Josie her dream. And a part of him—the selfish part—wanted her to stay just like this, holding his hand on a faded couch in a small boutique and altering one bride's world at a time.

Josie squeezed his hand. Her words came slow. "You want me to be a part of your TV show?"

"The producers believe you'll be an instant fan favorite." She was already his favorite.

"What do you think?"

"I think they're right." He knew they were right. It'd been his idea. But once he launched her career and helped fulfill her dream, she wouldn't need him anymore.

"What's in it for you?"

I lose you. He stared at their joined hands. Pumped positivity into his tone. "Your success makes the show a success. That builds Coast to Coast's brand."

"What's the catch?" Suspicion lowered her voice.

He liked that about her. She never took anything at face value. "You have to agree to several conditions. There would be a complete makeover of the interior and exterior of the boutique."

"Who covers that cost?"

"The show."

"Done." She grinned.

That was the easy part. "You have to be a wedding-dress designer exclusively."

"I'm not allowed to work on charitable events

or design costumes for the kids?" Disappointment pulled down the corners of her mouth.

Theo considered her. "That could be negotiated."

"That will be," she insisted. "I have over forty elf hats to deliver tonight to the Curtain Call Children's Theater group."

Elf hats she'd probably stayed up all night to make. He paused only to nod. His next condition was swift and succinct. "Your exclusives cannot be worn or seen until after the first season airs."

"The first season. They want me on your show for an entire season." She pulled her hand from his and ran her fingers through her hair. "Why me?"

"The producers want to showcase your transformation from a consignment dress shop to a bespoke bridal salon that competes with top designers."

"That's impressive." Her fingers stilled in her hair. Her gaze narrowed. Sarcasm had leaked into her tone. "Are the producers offering me a chance to show a collection at New York Fashion Week, too?"

"The particulars for Fashion Week are being discussed. There was mention of a sponsorship." And a possible relocation to New York. A better boutique. In a new neighborhood. On another coast. The small-time dressmaker reaching for her dream in a true fashion capital.

She dropped her hands to her lap. "You're serious?"

He nodded. He was granting her everything she'd ever dreamed. And ensuring the success of his own TV show. Why wasn't he happier? "Just to be clear—the reveal of your exclusive gowns needs to be timed appropriately and according to the airing of the season finale."

Maybe it was his awkward shifting on the couch. Or the sudden silence. Or her ability to read him. Understanding widened her gaze. "A finale will be months away. You're telling me that Adriana cannot wear my gown."

"No, she can't." His wince creased into the edges of his eyes. "But the national TV exposure would more than compensate. Adriana's wedding won't have that kind of reach."

"Can I think about it?" She stood and buttoned her knee-length sweater, as if guarding herself from any more of his conditions.

"The producers and I meet on Monday. You can put together your questions over the weekend."

"That's fast." She hurried into the workroom.

"They'd like to begin filming before the end of the month." He stopped in the doorway.

She picked up a plastic bin of elf hats and her travel sewing bag. "Is there anything else?"

"Exclusive includes your upscaled wedding gowns." He grabbed the plastic bin and looked at her over the top. "They cannot be worn, either."

"Until when?" She didn't release her grip.

Nothing released inside Theo. "Next fall."

She paled. "Shanna's wedding is in two weeks."

"We'd offer her an unlimited budget for an off-the-rack gown at any bridal store." The offer sounded hollow even to him. No off-the-rack gown could match what Josie had created. No gown would boost Shanna's spirit like Josie's had.

"She isn't my only bride on a limited budget. I have others waiting for their upscaled gowns." Josie stared at him. Dismay on her face, sadness in her voice. "You're asking me to take away their dreams."

"But you're reaching for your own dream," he said. "You matter, too, Josie." So very much.

"This is a lot to consider." She released the bin to him.

"You need time to think." He walked with her toward the front of the store. "And we need to deliver these colorful hats."

"You don't have to help me." Her voice came

out in a distracted whisper, as if he'd already helped enough. Or not at all. She flipped off the lights and locked the front door.

"I'm giving you an opportunity and I know there's a cost to it." He waited until she turned and looked at him. "I'd like to simply help now." *I simply want to be with you as long as I can. As long as you'll let me.*

Silence crowded between them like too many extra passengers as they drove to the theater. Inside the theater lobby, silence was hard to find. Off to the side, Santa sat in a large chair surrounded by Mrs. Claus, several high-school-age elves and a setting that looked right out of the North Pole. A long line of children waited to share their Christmas wish list and take a picture with Santa. Mia held her camera and directed another elf on the proper lighting angle.

Across the lobby, Mia's mother and new mother-in-law sat behind a long table and chatted with the parents passing by. Josie swerved and headed in their direction.

Helen rose, greeted them both and showed Theo where to place the bin. Then she grinned. "Now, you both need a picture with Santa."

Theo shook his head and looked at Josie. They'd been checking off holiday events in the city quite rapidly, but a picture with Santa hadn't been on either of their lists. "We're a bit old."

"Nonsense." Helen picked up a photograph. "Jin and I already took our picture."

Jin laughed. "We were the first ones."

Josie waved her hand. "We wouldn't want to cut in front of all those eager children."

Helen grabbed Josie's hand and Theo's. "Mia needs another test picture. She's not pleased with the lighting and I've surpassed my photo limit for the month."

Ten minutes and too many test photographs later, Mia finally released Josie and Theo and opened the line for the anxious children.

"For your patience, you get an ornament." Jin held up a wooden picture frame shaped like a wrapped Christmas present. Josie and Theo's Santa picture was inside the frame. "The widows club created these keepsake frames for the kids."

"They're adorable." Josie ran her finger over the collection of present boxes, painted in bright Christmas colors and decorated in glitter, bells and candy-cane stripes.

Helen attached a bright red ribbon to their frame and let it hang from her fingers. "And useful as an ornament. Now you can hang it on your Christmas tree."

Josie reached for the ornament. "I don't have a Christmas tree."

"You don't have a tree?" Helen cradled the

ornament as if Josie had spilled water on the photograph and marred the visit.

"It's twelve days until Christmas." Jin arranged the picture frames.

Theo studied her. "I thought you were going to get one after we visited the square."

Helen and Jin perked up. Their perceptive gazes shifted from Theo to Josie.

"I've been busy," Josie hedged.

"You can't be too busy for the holidays, dear, otherwise you'll miss out on the fun," Helen said. "It's the fun that gets you through the rest of the year."

"I have every special collection of Coast to Coast's annual ornaments for the past ten years." Jin nodded and grabbed Theo's hand. "Except for last year's collection. I was too busy moving and they sold out."

Helen cupped her cheek and shook her head, adding to her forlorn tone. "Now Jin has a rather large gap in her otherwise perfectly flocked and exquisitely decorated tree."

"I told myself I would make time later." Regret shifted across Jin's face. Her sadness was clear. "Then it was too late."

Theo raised his eyebrows. He wanted to know how many acting lessons the two endearing women had taken at the theater.

"I'm sure it's still quite wonderful," Josie said.

"But that hole reminds me of what I missed." Jin took Josie's hand and connected Josie's hand with Theo's. "If only I hadn't been so busy with things that didn't matter."

Josie glanced at their joined hands. "I'll make time to get one."

"That's the spirit, dear." Jin smiled.

Helen harrumphed at Theo and stared him down. Neither Wyatt nor Mia had mentioned what a force Helen Reid was. He liked and appreciated the woman all the more. And knew what she expected him to do. He pulled his phone from his pocket. "I need to step outside and take a call. I shouldn't be too long."

"If you like to stroll while you talk, there's a lovely tree park three blocks down. Turn left at the light." Helen unraveled more ribbon and snipped off a section. She failed to snip her knowing smile.

"Don't worry about us, dear." Jin urged Josie around the table to the working side. "We're going to need Josie for twice that long."

"Unless the two of you have plans this evening." Helen paused and shifted her measuring gaze to them.

"We certainly don't want to interfere with your night." Jin rubbed her hands together. "We'll work fast."

"There's no need to rush," Josie said.

"There's every need." Jin picked up a supply bin. "The lighted boat parade is tonight. It was on the list of must-do city holiday highlights that we discussed."

"You can't miss it, Josie," Helen insisted. "Theo, have you been to the lighted boat parade?"

"I have not." That was going to change quite soon. He couldn't say he was disappointed.

"Perfect." Helen smiled. "You can take Josie. Now you both have plans tonight."

"Simple as that." Jin sat in the chair as if her work was finished.

"Theo, take your call." Helen shooed Theo toward the door. "We need to get to work so that we can all head to the parade."

Theo slipped out of the lobby, slid his phone in his pocket and followed Helen's directions.

CHAPTER SEVENTEEN

"YOU GOT ME a Christmas tree." Josie stood outside the theater house and touched the pine needles on the tree strapped to the top of Theo's car. Inside, she melted at the gesture. "Why?"

"You needed one." His half grin softened one side of his mouth.

Josie found that entirely too appealing. He'd given her even more reasons to be grateful for him. The gift he'd given Shanna… Josie's breath had evaporated and dissolved into the hushed air around them. Her own hands had been shaking. It wasn't even Josie's wedding day.

Now if only she'd stop wanting to kiss him. And, worse, stop thinking about hand-holding, slow dancing and connections beyond business.

"I also brought you special ornaments." Theo lifted the Coast to Coast Living shopping bag. "They're the misfits."

She peered inside the large soft-sided bag. "What are those?"

"The ones that can't be sold on the store floor," he said. "The imperfect ones. The reindeer with one antler. A noseless snowman. The chipped star. Nutcracker that doesn't crack."

"You thought I'd like the broken ones?" She searched his gaze.

"I thought we could fix them together." He shifted the bag to his other hand. A hesitancy drew through his voice, lengthening his words. "Add a feather for a missing angel wing—that kind of thing."

Once again, Theo took Josie's breath away. Theo took the pieces of her broken heart and made her feel whole. "Make them our own."

"Yeah." His smile flared in his gaze and stretched across his mouth.

"I love it." *I love...* Josie wrapped her arms around his neck, held on and muted her heart.

What she felt for Theo was simple gratitude. He'd reopened her eyes to the joy of the holiday season. The past week, she'd collected moments. Found inspiration and discovered her laughter. Gratitude was not love.

His arms curved around her waist and he pulled her closer. Cars passed by. Children chased one another along the sidewalk. Families shouted goodbyes to each other. Josie's heart raced. Her pulse pounded. And still she held on to Theo.

He pulled away and grinned at her. "Ready to decorate?"

"Definitely." Josie took the shopping bag from Theo and climbed into the car.

An hour later, a line of injured ornaments and proposed treatments waiting on the kitchen counter, Theo stretched his arms over his head and walked across the living room. The Christmas tree filled the corner of her apartment, its branches brushing against the couch and the window as if it intended to embrace the entire small space. The tree lights faded in and out, and the star on the top sparkled. Josie slid glass beads onto a copper brass wire, creating a new tail for a wounded unicorn, then she glanced at Theo.

He added several more Christmas balls they'd rolled in glitter to the tree and examined his decorating skills. "Our misfit tree is pretty perfect."

Josie swiveled around the stool. "It's the best tree I've ever had."

Theo set his hands on his hips. "This can't be the only tree you've had."

"The first here," she admitted.

Theo scowled.

Josie laughed and held up her hand. "But all my foster families put up Christmas trees. Every year. Every tree was different. The decorations over-the-top or subtle. But I remember feeling that each tree and every decoration transformed their houses into homes."

"How are you feeling about your place?" Theo moved around the couch.

"Like it's happier." Josie picked up her wire cutters and concentrated on the unicorn. Theo made her happier. "That I'm a little more at home."

"Since you're feeling so relaxed, you won't mind if I look around." He stood inside her junior studio apartment, near her walk-in closet.

The three-quarter wall dividing the bedroom from the living area allowed for the *junior* designation. They both knew there wasn't much room to look around. Josie propped the unicorn against a teacup, her movements slow, cautious. "I know what you're doing."

"Trying to get one up on Mia." Humor and hope spiraled around his suggestion.

A grin twitched across her lips. She concentrated on the unicorn's tail, as if the crystal beads granted her a glimpse into the future. "Why do you want to see my designs?"

"Curiosity."

Perhaps. But it was more. Today Josie had proven to Theo the value of vintage. Proven to him that old could be new again. Old could be cutting-edge and breathtaking. With the proper adjustments, alterations and edits. But she hadn't convinced him that his Grandmother Pearl's dress was the one for his sister. She hadn't even tried.

He'd offered her a segment on his company's TV show—a show intent on transforming Josie and her business. She should be even more grateful for the opportunity. Their relationship would truly become colleague-to-colleague if she agreed. A strange sense of loss shifted over her. Business was supposed to be her only focus.

Gratitude was not love.

Now he wanted her to reveal another part of herself to him. He wanted her to trust him. She wasn't ready. Would she ever be ready?

"I spent my entire first day as the CEO of Coast to Coast Living in my office chair and watched the door. I was convinced someone was going to claim I was unqualified. And call me out for being a fraud."

She swiveled the stool toward him. "What did you do?"

"I called a meeting. Laid out the company's daily goals, then the one-year and five-year plans. Sweat soaked my dress shirt. I rambled on about mission statements and visions. All the while I waited for the inevitable vote of no confidence." He paused as if lost inside his first day again. "At the end of the meeting, no one spoke. No one questioned me. I think I'd stunned them into silence. Or convinced them I would bankrupt the company before year-end."

"No one believed in you?" she asked.

"No one admitted they didn't believe," he corrected her. "Nobody told me I couldn't do it. So I did."

"That's the difference." Josie ran her hands over her jeans, slid off the stool, paced into the kitchen and back out. "They told me I couldn't. Expected that I wouldn't make it."

He pointed at the closed closet, but his gaze locked on Josie. The insistence in his voice reinforced his words. "But you did it, anyway."

Was it that simple? Did a closet she'd filled with clothes she'd designed and sewn together between shifts, more often on sleepless nights, prove she'd succeeded? Prove the critics wrong? Prove she was good enough?

Theo rested his hand on the glass and brass handle of the closet door. He wanted to view Josie's collection. Wanted to see the clothes she hid from the world. And with the door closed, from herself. She had no real defense against him.

She walked to the closet, flipped on the outside light switch and opened the door.

Theo whistled. "You have several collections in here."

"Most of it isn't current," she said.

"But you could make it fashion-forward again, if you wanted." He pulled out a suit. "Where exactly did you plan to wear this?"

Josie grabbed at the hanger. "I didn't plan to wear it."

Theo stepped away from her. "But you designed it and sewed it. You had a vision for this particular garment."

"I had a silly game I played with Mimi." She crossed her arms over her chest. One she still indulged in. "Mimi showed me how to imagine a different life for myself. I created that world in clothes."

Theo walked into the closet, hung the pantsuit on the rack. He never turned around, kept his attention on her clothes. He sorted through the skirts and blouses. Touched the jackets and scarves. Skimmed a hand over the dresses and gowns. Every garment was a piece of herself. Part of her story. He seemed to recognize that. He was gentle, courteous, tactful.

Finally, he tugged on a hanger and freed a cream-colored dress from the others. "It's a sweater, but longer."

"It's intended to be worn as a dress with knee-high boots." Josie fixed the slouchy hood. She'd watched one too many winter romance movies and designed the dress late one night.

Theo held up the garment. "The hood makes it ideal to wear outside on a cold night."

"I let you see my clothes—aren't you satisfied now?" Josie walked into the living room.

She wouldn't allow him to belittle Mimi or their game. "It's for a ride in a horse-drawn carriage."

"I can't arrange a horse-drawn carriage," he said. "But I've been told there's a holiday boat parade that isn't to be missed."

Josie turned around. Theo stood within hand-holding distance. "What are you saying?"

"You have the perfect outfit." He handed her the dress. "And I have a promise to keep."

Josie curled her fingers around the hanger. "You want me to wear this to the boat parade?"

"Yeah." He tilted his head and watched her. "I want you to accept my invitation. I want you to wear your clothes in this world. With me."

With me. Her mouth opened and closed. He was asking her to stop hiding. Telling her he'd be by her side. *With me.*

"You should probably hurry." He tapped his watch. "The parade starts soon, and I have a feeling Jin and Helen will be on the lookout for us."

Josie walked into her bathroom, closed the door and gripped the bathroom counter. She envied Shanna's courage. Channeled Shanna's bravery. Josie created dresses for women to wear and discover their inner beauty, their confidence—whatever it was they thought they lacked. Now it was time to follow her own lessons. Apply the same theory to herself. She pushed off the porcelain counter. No more hiding.

Josie changed out of her clothes and slipped the sweater dress over her head. The merino wool lowered to her knees, fitted and comfortable. The hood dropped around her shoulders, as she'd envisioned. But she'd never envisioned wearing the dress into the city with Theo.

She tugged on her boots, trying to tug her pulse back to steadiness. *I'm grateful. Grateful to Theo. Nothing more.* A handful of steps brought her into the living room. Theo waited beside the tree.

His gaze drifted from her face to her boots and back. A slow smile of appreciation took over his features. "I'm glad you never took that carriage ride."

"You don't like horses?" she asked. Her fingers twitched, her legs, too. She wanted to pace. To hide.

"I don't like sharing." He moved closer to her. "And whoever took you on that carriage ride in this dress wouldn't have let you go."

Her heartbeat quickened. Her pulse crowded her throat. "It's just a plain and simple off-white sweater dress."

He reached out, touched her cheek. "There's nothing plain about you, Josie Beck."

And there was nothing simple about his caress. Nothing straightforward about how *so very* safe her name sounded in his mouth. Josie edged into his space and reached for him. Their lips met. And what was complicated became simple. And so right in his arms.

The kiss lasted seconds, minutes, hours. Josie wasn't certain. She lost herself in Theo's embrace. *Was* certain that only her heart would never be the same. And with Theo beside her, she never wanted to hide again. The kiss slowed. Her feet returned to the ground. Her breath streamed back into her chest.

"Should we take that stroll to the wharf?" Theo asked. The rasp in his voice hinted that his own breath hadn't quite returned. "We don't want to miss the parade."

Josie nodded and took Theo's hand, seeking balance. But that *we* lodged in her chest, squeezed and twisted.

There was no *we*. *We* implied there was more between them. *We* implied relationships and commitments. But she'd only ever committed to herself. Only wanted to commit to herself, didn't she?

CHAPTER EIGHTEEN

"MOVE TO THE LEFT, Theo," Josie scolded him and never turned around from her place on the balcony. "You're blocking the Christmas lights."

"How did you know it was me?" Theo walked across the outdoor patio of the city's oldest hotel…and current venue for Coast to Coast Living's annual holiday gala.

"You're one of the few tall enough to disrupt the light." Josie glanced at him. "You're also the only person I know who walks as if you don't want to disturb the air."

"That's rather specific." He frowned, unsure if he liked the description or not.

"But true." Josie leaned against the railing and grinned at him. "Were you a spy in a former life?"

"Only in the pages of my comic books." In those rare moments, he'd defeated evil, rescued the weak and obtained superhero status. But the comic books ended. Then he was the kid who'd spent Thanksgiving with his roommate's close-knit family of eight. They'd embraced him as one of their own. Theo had wanted to embrace back, but he'd never found the right moment. Never wanted to intrude.

Josie eyed him and nodded, as if she understood. Then she walked to him and stepped into his embrace. And once again, Theo discovered the right moment. With Josie.

He guided her hands into the dance hold Anton had taught them. He asked, "Shouldn't you be inside networking? The Coast to Coast Living gala prides itself on bringing together the best in business."

"I did mingle for a while. Even handed out a business card or two." Josie laughed. Her steps matched his, in perfect time. "But the city lights drew me out here. It's a good quiet night. I can hear my thoughts out on this balcony."

She'd drawn him outside. Away from vendors, customers and potential shareholders. He wanted to hear her voice. Share her laughter. For a moment, with Josie, he could just be Theo. Not the CEO. Not the man who made the final decisions. Not the one responsible for growth, profit margins and family accord. "Care to share any of your thoughts?"

"Not right now." She broke the proper dance formation and smoothed her hand over his lapel. "I want to just enjoy this."

He spun her in a circle, twirling free her laughter…and his own. He said, "I've been practicing at home."

"I think I might need more lessons to keep up," Josie said.

He spun her one last time and slowed the dance. The side door opened.

Fran peeked out and winced. "Sorry to interrupt, Theo. But you're needed."

Theo bowed to Josie. She dropped into a curtsy and said, "Until next time."

"You could join me." He offered her his arm.

"You go ahead." Josie leaned to the side. "I see Adriana. I wanted to talk to her."

Theo eyed her. "Fine. But if you linger out here much longer, I might have to come back for another dance."

"I'm counting on it." She drifted down the balcony toward his sister. Theo stepped inside and back into his corporate persona.

JOSIE PRESSED HER hands to her cheeks. She was hot and cold at the same time. In love and terrified. She called out to Theo's sister, "Do you have a moment to talk?"

Adriana released the door and turned to Josie. "I'd love to. It'll keep me from the idle conversations inside."

Josie jumped right in. "Theo offered me a segment on the Coast to Coast TV show."

"That's fabulous news." Adriana hugged Josie.

"We'll get to see even more of you. I know my brother will want that. I saw you two dancing."

Josie's cheeks heated again. "It's not all great news."

"Did Theo do something?" Adriana walked with Josie to a private area on the balcony.

If making her fall in love with him was *something*. Then, yes, he definitely did that. "No. It's not Theo. It's the terms and conditions in the contract for the show."

"I'm sure Theo can change those," Adriana said.

"I'm not certain he wants to." Josie gripped the balcony rail and looked out over the city. He'd liked her original sweater dress on her. He'd liked Shanna's upscaled wedding gown. But he hadn't liked anything enough for his sister. Or enough to change Josie's contract. She assumed he believed his show would make her better. Turn her into a popular dressmaker that was good enough.

Adriana touched Josie's arm. "Why don't you tell me what's in the contract?"

"None of my exclusive gowns can be worn until after the first season's finale." Josie shifted to face Adriana. "That includes my upscaled vintage gowns like your Grandmother Pearl's dress."

Adriana pulled back. "If you alter my grandmother's gown, I can't wear it next weekend? In my own wedding?"

Josie shook her head and stressed. "If I sign the contract. I haven't signed yet."

"Why would he ruin my wedding like this?" Adriana's eyebrows lowered.

"It's what the producers requested," Josie said.

"Theo has the final say," Adriana argued. "He could change their minds if he wanted to."

If Theo let the contract stand as it was, he wouldn't have to reject Josie's original gown or his grandmother's upscaled gown. Was that it? Had Theo been counting on Josie signing the contract this whole time. "Why wouldn't he change the contract for you?"

"Profit." Adriana scowled. "The company and profit always come before family."

What about Josie? Was she only good enough for the show because her story could be turned into a financial gain?

"Why are you two looking so serious?" Adriana's fiancé, Ryan, walked toward them, carrying two plates of appetizers. "This is supposed to be a fun evening."

Adriana brushed at her eyes.

Ryan slid the plates on a small table and took Adriana's hands. "What happened?"

"I don't have a wedding gown," Adriana

cried. "It's Theo's fault and the TV show. And Theo won't change it."

Ryan glanced at Josie, then Adriana. "Have you talked to your brother?"

"You know how he is," Adriana mumbled. "He won't listen."

"This is our wedding," Ryan argued. "It's your wedding gown. You should wear the gown you chose."

"You know it's more complicated than that." Adriana used a tissue to wipe away her tears.

Ryan set his hands on his hips. "Then let's elope. Forget the wedding madness and get married. Just the two of us in a private ceremony. The way we want."

Josie covered her mouth.

Adriana shook her head. "I can't do that to my family."

"But look what they're doing to you? First your mother. Now Theo." Anger slashed through Ryan's voice. "I'm tired of your meddling family, Adriana."

Adriana stilled. "What are you saying?"

"I can't compete with them anymore." Ryan scrubbed his hands over his face. "I can't do this."

"Do what?" Adriana whispered.

"Watch you be loyal to a family that isn't loyal to you." Ryan shook his head, misery weighting down his words. "I can't spend the rest of my life waiting for you to stand up to them."

Adriana threw her hands to her sides. "What do you expect me to do?"

"Defend us to your family." Ryan's mouth flattened. "Stand up for what we want. What we chose."

"They're only trying to help," Adriana said. Her voice lacked conviction.

Ryan nodded. Defeat slumped his shoulders. "I love you, Adriana, but I can't marry you. Not like this." He turned and walked away.

Adriana covered her face with her hands. "Tell me that didn't just happen?"

Josie hugged Adriana, guided her to a bench and promised everything would be fine. It would be fine once she found Theo. She'd make him fix this. He had to fix this. For his sister. For Ryan. For the rare love the two shared. Josie eased open the side door and waved to Fran. "I need to find Theo. Now. It's Adriana."

Worry passed over Fran's face. She straightened in her heels and scanned the crowd. "He's over there with his mother." She lifted her arms and waved in a big SOS signal.

Several groups of guests responded. Fran waved more. More guests turned to look.

Josie ignored the spectators and searched for Theo.

"He saw me." Finally, Fran lowered her arms. "He's coming."

Josie sighed. Then noticed the number of people trailing after Theo, including his mother.

Theo reached Josie first. "What's wrong?"

"Adriana and Ryan had a fight." Josie held open the door to the balcony. Where had all the guests come from?

"Where's Ryan?" Theo walked out onto the patio.

"He just left." Josie blanched. The guests hadn't remained inside. They trailed after them. Worse, Adriana ran down the balcony and disappeared through an exit door. Everywhere Josie looked, cameras were recording every second.

"Prewedding jitters, I'm sure." Lilian Rose waved her jeweled fingers in the air. "That's quite common."

"It's more than that." Josie grabbed Theo's arm, pulling his attention to her. "The wedding was called off."

Lilian Rose lost her indifference. She rounded on Josie, her voice rising. "What did you say to my daughter?"

Josie stumbled over her words, lost her voice at the venom in Lilian Rose's tone. Josie had hugged Adriana. Then lied, promising the poor woman everything would be all right. Suddenly, nothing seemed right anymore.

"Do you know what happened?" Theo reached for Josie.

"Obviously Josie told Adriana that she couldn't wear any of Josie's gowns on her wedding day." A snarl twisted across Lilian Rose's bloodred lips. "Now Adriana has no dress for her wedding in less than a week."

Theo asked, "Did you sign the contract, then tell Adriana?"

Josie answered with her own question. "Who added the upscaled consignment gowns to the exclusion clause in the contract?"

"I don't remember," Theo said. "Why does it matter?"

Because he would never accept a used gown. Even altered it would always be used, dated and imperfect in his eyes. He'd never accept Josie as she was, either. Nausea clawed up her throat, chewed at her insides. But this time, there was no yelling "bathroom." No outburst, calling for a fountain. There was no escape. "You weren't ever going to let Adriana wear one of my exclusive gowns, were you?"

Theo opened his mouth. The truth came out, unspoken and soundless.

But the weight barreled through Josie like a runaway carriage, its horses spooked.

"Of course, you were never going to be Adriana's wedding-dress designer." Lilian Rose marched forward. "Who do you think brought your name to the production team? My son is a very gifted strategist."

Josie looked at Theo. Her heart withered. Her body drooped, overloaded. He wanted to rescue the poor foster kid, the same as her ex-husband had wanted to, and like her ex, Theo intended to build his own name in the process. She'd been nothing more than a business deal. A part of his corporate task list. How could she have misread every moment so horribly wrong?

Lilian Rose launched another sarcastic barb. "Tell Josie that you *weren't* considering her for the TV series this entire time, Theo."

Again, that noiseless silence came from Theo. Josie wanted to scream. Scream at him to say something. Like she had wanted to scream at all those potential families that passed her by. But her scream only echoed inside her emptiness.

She already knew: she wasn't perfect for Theo. She was perfect for his makeover TV show. All those nights together he'd used to gain her backstory. And she'd shared herself. Shared her secrets.

"You've quite the backstory, my dear." Lilian Rose touched her diamond earring. "You must know it will play exceedingly well to a TV audience."

Josie covered her mouth, holding back her anguished gasp. It was her life. The one she'd lived through—not a backstory fabricated in a screenwriters' room. She'd never wanted to capitalize on her childhood. She'd only wanted to forget the pain and loneliness. She'd almost believed she'd moved on. Found a place where she wasn't alone. Someone who made her feel like she belonged. Like she was wanted. How many times did she have to live this nightmare? How many times did she have to slam face-first into the truth?

She never knew it was possible for a broken heart to hurt even more. An ache built from deep within her.

Lilian Rose continued her verbal assault. "It's too bad you're already in breach of your contract, dear."

"Excuse me," Josie said. She hadn't signed a contract *yet.* Surely Theo would correct his mother.

Theo's voice finally gained traction. A warning slid through his tone. "Mother."

"It's not about your tête-à-tête on the balcony earlier." Lilian Rose gave a small, hollow head shake. Pity shaded her eyes. "Although with my son, I suspect there was an angle to that, as well, for the bottom line. Romance plays well, even if it's invented for the show only."

Another warning rumbled from Theo. "Mother."

"Did I pass?" Josie raised her chin and leveled her gaze on Theo. "Am I good enough to be on your TV show?"

"Josie, it's—" Theo began.

Lilian Rose cut off her son. "Josie already sold one of her exclusive gowns meant for Adriana to the highest bidder. Pocketed the cash and played you, too, Theo."

"Did you sell one of the originals?" he asked.

Ironic that he discovered his voice when he became the prey. As if he'd somehow lost in all of this. Josie nodded.

"When?" he prodded.

"Last Sunday." She watched the betrayal appear on his face. She'd lied to him, too. *How did it feel?* "But that gown was never the one for Adriana. I knew it. And your sister did, too."

"That wasn't your call to make." He slid his hands into his pockets, pulled himself in.

"Your grandmother's gown is—" she said.

He interrupted, "You let Adriana put it on after I asked you not to."

"It doesn't matter now. It never mattered." Josie turned and walked away. Her chin didn't waver. Not until she reached the elevators.

CHAPTER NINETEEN

"JOSIE. WAIT!" Theo hurried toward the elevator bay. "You don't understand."

Josie's arm blocked the elevator door from closing. "What more could I need to know?"

Theo stopped on the other side of the elevator doors. "There's more at play here than just a wedding. It's business, but I can't discuss the details quite yet."

"It's always business, isn't it?" Tears pooled in her eyes. Her cheeks were damp.

He caused her pain. Made her cry. Hated himself for that.

"Is that why you turned your sister's wedding into a billboard for Coast to Coast Living?" Anger pooled in her voice, stilling her tears from falling. "Because business is more important than your sister's dream wedding."

"I was giving her a dream wedding," he argued.

"But not her dream wedding." Josie's fingers curled into a fist. Frustration hardened her words. "Did you really believe the little girl Adriana once was dreamed about product launches and business deals at her wedding?

That little girl dreamed of unicorns, princes and forever love."

Dreams. Forever love. Those wouldn't sustain a legacy. Those wouldn't give someone worth. Or value. "We all have to grow up sometime."

"Still, a wedding should be the one time to dream again. To celebrate that forever kind of love." Josie's free hand tugged on her gown. "A wedding is not just a reason to display Coast to Coast Living's new housewares."

"The flatware and dinner sets were inspired by Adriana and Ryan," Theo countered.

"Do they know that?" She never waited for his answer. "Of course not. The gesture might've been special if the focus was on the couple and not your corporation. Not the bottom line."

Why couldn't she understand? "There's more at stake."

"So you've said."

"Why is that wrong? This business was built for our family." By Theo. To prove to everyone that he hadn't turned his back on his family. To prove his worth. "As long as the business stays strong, the family stays strong."

"I would have thought it was the other way around." She rubbed her forehead as if searching for more of Mimi's fortune-cookie wisdom. "A strong family makes everything stronger. Everything better."

"I won't apologize."

"Can you at least tell me why you never stood up for me?"

"You never stood up for yourself," Theo countered. "You give your work away for free because you don't believe it's good enough. You leave your custom clothes stashed inside your closet because you don't believe in your talent or skill. You're walking away now for the same reasons."

"No one stepped on you on their way up the ladder." Josie flicked her hand and her disappointment at him. "You took the ladder out from under them and left. They had to climb the rest of the way on their own."

Theo crossed his arms over his chest and widened his stance, prepared to let her lash out. He'd hurt her.

"You don't risk your heart, either." She straightened, stiffened her arm and her voice. "You reject first so you never really have to open your heart."

He could take the accusations. But he wasn't discussing hearts or himself. "This was never about hearts."

"No, it's always been about business and the perfect look of success." Josie leaned out of the elevator. Her voice lifted above a harsh stage whisper. "But do you want to know something?

I didn't fall in love with you because you were good for my profit line."

A weight like a twenty-pound steel ball smashed into his chest. He blanched and resisted. "You don't love me."

"I don't want to love you," she snapped. But her chin quivered, and those tear pools swayed, almost overflowing. "You made me feel safe. Safe enough to let myself love. Really love again. For the first time since Mimi."

The fury in her voice rattled his own. How dare she love him? He'd never wanted her love. He didn't even know how to love. That steel ball crashed through him again. Now he lashed out. "That was your mistake."

"But it's your loss." Josie removed her hand from the elevator door. The doors started to close. Her last shot was a direct hit. "One you're going to regret."

CHAPTER TWENTY

BING-BONG. BING-BONG. Josie smashed her face in a pillow and groaned into the feathers. Her doorbell rang again. *Bing-bong.* Muffled voices followed.

Josie pushed off the couch, where she'd slept last night. She'd fled Theo's gala, stumbled into her apartment, traded her dress for fuzzy pants and an oversize sweatshirt. Grabbed a box of tissues and curled into a ball on the couch. She still wore the fuzzy pants and sweatshirt, and had added fuzzy socks. She padded to the door and opened it.

Mia grinned and looked at her two companions. "I told you she would be here."

"And I told you the wreath would fit perfectly." Helen beamed at the pinecone-and-berry wreath she'd attached to Josie's apartment door. She flipped a switch hidden among the pinecones and turned on a string of fairy lights woven through the wreath. "It's a good thing we don't abide by the silent treatment. And we listen to our gut instincts."

"What are you doing here?" Josie smoothed her hand over her hair, her eyelids felt too puffy on her face and she hadn't looked in the mirror yet.

"Mia told us about last night." Jin held up food carriers and Christmas presents. "We brought double-chocolate peppermint cheesecake and lasagna."

Mia held up a cloth shopping bag. "Along with whipped cream."

"I owe you an apology, Mia." Josie touched her puffy eyes, wanting to still the oncoming tears. She gazed at her friend. She'd let Mia down. Shame moored her words in her throat. Her voice scraped across her disappointment. "I didn't think you'd want to—"

"Eat?" Mia brushed her hand in the air and swept into the apartment. Helen and Jin tagged close behind her. "We're family. We always want to eat. And, you don't owe me anything."

"That was our chance to get to the next level." A chance Josie ruined for them both. A tremor skimmed over her knees. Josie closed the door and leaned against the thick wood.

The trio quickly took over her tiny apartment, making their own mark on her little world. Helen set out the food and dishes on Josie's small counter. Jin folded the blankets on Josie's couch and fluffed the pillows, humming "Jingle Bells."

"That was one chance." Mia set several bags

and wrapped gifts under the Christmas tree. Then plugged in the lights. "It wasn't our *only* opportunity."

That dull ache in Josie's chest spasmed. Was it only a few nights ago that she'd kissed Theo right where Mia stood? Was it only a few days ago she opened herself to love? Time was supposed to heal all wounds. Hadn't it been long enough? Josie rubbed her chest. She feared she was going to need more time than time could grant her to heal.

"Besides, there are more important things than business and next levels." Jin carried an extra blanket to the closet, peered inside and nodded. She disappeared behind the partial wall and returned without the fleece blanket.

There was nothing more important to Theo. Josie pulled her attention away from the tree and walked to the kitchen. "Had I focused on business I wouldn't hurt so much now."

"The deeper your pain, the greater your love." Helen encompassed Josie in a tight, generous hug. "I would take the pain for you, if I could."

Josie dropped her head on Helen's shoulder. Her tears escaped. There shouldn't be any more. She should be cried out. Emptiness—that was all she had left inside her. Nothing more. Josie lifted her head, swiped at her cheeks. "I'm sorry."

"No, dear. Never apologize for loving someone." Helen dried Josie's cheek. "Now, I brought you a Christmas cactus. It's been in my family for generations. It blooms in the winter. In the coldest and darkest months, it'll remind you to bloom too."

Josie touched the fuchsia flowers, promised herself she'd bloom again. In time.

"Of course, you hurt, Josie. Even the pieces of a broken heart can still love." Jin disappeared inside Josie's walk-in closet and returned holding a straight black skirt and deep purple jacket. "Now, can this skirt be lengthened to cover my knees?"

Josie blinked to clear the tears from her eyes and examined the skirt's hemline. A hemline she'd purposely left longer than usual, uncertain of the length she'd prefer. She nodded at Jin.

"Excellent. I'll take it." Her abrupt smile lit her face like the star on top of the tree. Jin aimed her pleasure at Mia and Helen then shrugged. "What? I needed an outfit for our party. Now I have one."

Mia frowned her displeasure at her mother. "We're here for Josie."

"I know that perfectly well." Jin shook out the skirt and hung the outfit on the outside of the closet door. "It's why I want to wear these garments. It'll remind Josie where her strengths lie. Concentrating on our strengths helps shield us from the pain."

Josie sank onto the stool. "I don't feel strong."

"That's why we're here." Helen removed the cover on the lasagna pan then unwrapped the garlic bread. "To remind you."

"And to be strong for you when you don't want to be." Mia gave Josie a quick hug then handed her a slice of garlic bread. "Helen makes it fresh. You'll never look at garlic bread the same ever again."

"We're also here to enjoy this delicious meal." Jin lifted one shoulder in another small shrug. "I skipped breakfast this morning. I wanted to be sure I had room for extra cheesecake."

"I always have room for an extra helping of dessert." Helen laughed and picked up the spatula to serve the lasagna. "Now, Josie, shall we discuss Theo or your boutique first?"

"Theo is only interested in business." Josie tore a chunk off her garlic bread slice. Bitterness seeped into her tone. "His business and making it bigger and better."

The women busied themselves preparing the plates. Helen on lasagna. Jin scooping out salad. Mia added bread to each plate. All the while, Josie sensed their hushed debate: keep talking about Theo or shift topics. Josie had little more to say about Theo. The conversation would be short.

Mia handed a plate to Josie and urged her over to the couch to sit beside her. "Let's talk about the boutique first."

"There's not much to say." Josie stabbed her fork into her pasta. "The TV show would've completely renovated the boutique and my career. But I would've hurt people on the way."

Now the hurt was deep and consuming. But her clients would have their gowns and their dream weddings. That mattered. There was solace in that knowledge. Except for one particular bride.

Jin nodded. "The price of fame."

"I don't want fame," Josie said.

"What do you want?" Helen asked.

Theo. A forever kind of love. "I want to create gowns like the ones for Shanna and Krystal. Both used and custom. Even more, I want to connect with each client." Josie chewed on her lasagna, swallowed the delicious bite and added, "I want both our worlds—mine and my clients—to be a little bit better for having met each other."

"You have that now." Mia swirled her garlic bread in her lasagna sauce.

"But I don't have money for rent and bills," Josie said.

"Then we must figure out how to get you that." Helen finished her salad, her posture self-assured. She was confident they would solve Josie's problems together.

"A business plan." Jin nodded and pointed her fork at Josie. "You can never underestimate the value of a good, solid business plan. I had one for my real-estate company in New York. Guided me every step of the way until I sold and moved here."

Josie would never again underestimate the value of these three good, solid women. Her friends.

One hour and a piece of peppermint cheesecake later, Josie had a strong business plan written and typed up. Vendor applications had been filled out and submitted online for several upcoming bridal expos. Emails had been sent to Mia's friends to find someone who could create a Rose Petal website for a reasonable fee. Mia planned to photograph Krystal and Shanna's dresses to showcase on the website. And the pain inside Josie was there, pulsing into a throb occasionally. But Josie appreciated the distraction. Appreciated the women—her friends—even more.

"Now what about Adriana Taylor's wedding dress?" Helen placed the leftover lasagna into a small container and set it in Josie's refrigerator.

"I'm not designing her gown." Josie swirled whipped cream on her dessert plate and dipped her finger in it. The lightness reminded her of the silk lace she'd planned to layer onto Adriana's gown.

"But you have her grandmother's dress." Mia grabbed the whipped-cream can and added more to her plate. Then glanced at Josie. "I saw it hanging in the workroom."

Josie rinsed the whipped cream off her plate. "Can you return it for me?"

"No." Mia lifted her chin and her gaze challenged Josie to argue.

Josie glared at her friend and washed her plate. "You're supposed to be helping me." That was the reason the trio had arrived unannounced on Josie's doorstep.

"I am helping you." Mia took a bite of her cheesecake and extended her grin. "That is the dress for Adriana. I talked to her last week."

"That was before last night." Before the wedding had been canceled. Before Theo shattered Josie's heart. Before Josie told him that she loved him.

"It's the right dress," Mia insisted. "You know it, too."

"Theo won't go along with it," Josie said.

"It isn't Theo's wedding." Jin sliced off a thin

piece of cheesecake. “Even when it is, he won’t have a say about his bride-to-be’s gown.”

Theo and his wedding. The peppermint singed Josie’s stomach. That ache throbbed into a full body sting, reminding her it was still there. Still fresh. She’d only been shielding herself from it.

“It’s quite simple really.” Helen poured coffee into a to-go mug she’d brought with her. “Josie, you don’t need to make Theo like it. You need to make Adriana fall in love with it.”

“You should see the design.” Mia spread her hands out in her front of her face as if she’d pulled it up digitally. “I already love it.”

Josie narrowed her gaze at her friends—her loyal, faithful and trusting friends. “You have to say that.”

“We don’t have to say anything.” Helen took Josie’s hand and squeezed. “But you have to believe.”

Josie cringed. Those were the very same words Theo had thrown at her last night. He’d accused her of being too scared. Too afraid to believe. Too afraid to risk.

“What do you believe?” Jin asked.

“That it’s the perfect gown for Adriana.” Josie clutched Helen’s hand and pushed back her shoulders. A shard of conviction pierced through her. She clasped onto it, concentrated on believing. Focused on the women around her who already believed. Conviction wove through her like the strongest stitch. She pushed confidence into her voice. "It is the only gown for Adriana."

"Then make her that gown," Mia urged.

Helen squeezed her hand. "Fight for yourself this time, Josie."

"Fight for your voice and your vision." Jin covered Helen's and Josie's joined hands.

"I couldn't have done this without you." Josie's cheeks were damp again. The tears were welcome this time. "I don't know how to thank you."

"We love food." Jin touched Josie's cheek. "And we appreciate being needed."

"I like to think we're very useful, too." Mia laughed.

The trio cleaned up the kitchen and gathered their supplies. Josie walked with them to the door. She gave each one of the women an extended hug. There were no more words required.

She stepped out of Helen's embrace and thanked her again.

Helen took both of Josie's hands and leveled her gaze on her. "You do know that we've been here all along. We've just been waiting for you to reach out and accept us."

"I won't hesitate again." Josie wrapped the dear woman in another quick hug and waved goodbye to the trio.

She shut the door and glanced around her apartment. Strangely, her apartment was no longer empty. She'd only needed her family to fill it. They'd brought her a wreath, presents and food. Yet they left something even more precious: their love and support.

Josie picked up the outfit Jin had requested. She had the perfect fabric at the boutique. But first she had a wedding gown to upscale and deliver.

CHAPTER TWENTY-ONE

"FRAN TOLD ME your family has breakfast together every Monday morning." Josie stood on Theo's front porch, clutched the garment bag tighter and pressed Pause on her rapid heartbeat. "She gave me your address."

Theo ran his hand through his hair, disheveling his look even more. Josie had never seen Theo in jeans. She'd never seen him quite so *not* put-together. His slight beard matched the shadows under his eyes. Behind her a garage door opened. A car alarm chirped. A dog barked. Construction workers three houses down laughed.

But it was his stillness that unnerved her. His hooded gaze that absorbed her.

"I gave my word I would have a wedding dress for Adriana. I keep my word." Josie rambled, filling the pin-drop silence. "It's one of a kind because Adriana is already one of a kind."

"The wedding was called off, as you know." Theo never moved. Never reached for the garment bag. Never reached for her.

"Their love was canceled, too, was it?" How brilliant would it be if loved worked like that? Like a canceled online order. The money returned to your credit card. Or, in this case, a refund on a broken heart. The heartache returned to the supplier free of charge.

"Excuse me," Theo said.

"Adriana and Ryan are very much in love." The forever kind she'd thought she'd found. But one-sided love only hurt one person forever. She met Theo's gaze: his unreadable, hers unwavering. "Love doesn't quit on each other."

The barest crease curved at the edge of his mouth. "Is that one of Mimi's sayings?"

"No." Josie tilted her chin up. "That one is all mine."

There in the deepest part of his gaze, she saw it: admiration. It wasn't enough. She hurt too much looking at him for that to ever be enough. She added, "There will be a wedding for Adriana and Ryan. And Adriana will have a dress if she chooses to wear it."

"I don't recall requesting a new dress." He widened his stance in the doorway.

"I'm not sure it matters what you requested."

His eyebrows lifted. That admiration sparked. "Are you certain of that?"

"Absolutely." Josie pulled out her most defiant smile, adding an extra measure of politeness to her voice. "You see, I spoke to Adriana last night. I'm here to see her, not you."

Adriana stepped into the entryway, her grin

soft, welcoming and knowing. "Josie. Please come inside."

Josie eased around Theo and followed Adriana down a hallway into a great room. A modern kitchen gave way to a surprisingly comfortable family room. In another time and place, she'd have wanted to sit down and rest her feet on the leather ottoman. Watch the flames in the corner fireplace and listen to the Christmas carols. She tipped her head. Those were Christmas carols playing over the speaker system, infusing both rooms with the cheerful sounds of the season. Only hot apple cider or hot chocolate was missing. And assorted homemade Christmas cookies.

Lilian Rose strolled into the great room from another hallway. She assessed Josie. Her smile was fleeting, but lingered in her perceptive gaze. "Josie. What brings you here?"

"I came to give Adriana her wedding dress." Josie handed Adriana the garment bag.

"For her wedding that was called off." Lilian Rose walked forward, her high heels tapping against the hardwood floors. "Isn't that a bit insensitive?"

"How long were you married, Mrs. Taylor?" Josie asked.

"Thirty-one years." Lilian Rose touched her ring finger.

"I imagine in that time, you and your husband disagreed." Josie watched the older woman. "Fought, even."

Lilian Rose laughed. "On more than one occasion."

"Yet you never gave up." Josie clutched her hands together. "Never walked away for good."

"We were meant for each other." Lilian Rose touched her chest, right over her heart. "We knew that in here."

"I think Adriana and Ryan know it, too." Josie touched Adriana's arm. "They just need a moment to believe in the strength of their love again."

"Wise words." Lilian Rose pointed at the garment bag. "Can we see the dress?"

"I'm going to leave that up to Adriana." Josie buttoned her coat under her chin and her pride.

Adriana hugged her. "Thank you."

"Don't you want to know if we like the dress?" Theo asked. "Don't you want to see her in the dress?"

"I was told once that I had to stand up for my design style. That too much compromise would dilute my worth." Josie turned around to face Theo. "I don't need to see Adriana in the dress. I believe in what I created. I believe she will love it."

He stuffed his hands in his back pockets and studied her. "And if she doesn't like it?"

"At least I will know I didn't compromise." The indifference wavered in her voice. Standing so close to him—close enough to take his hand—yet being so very far away, cut through her. She'd found herself. Found who she wanted to be. And lost a piece of her heart in the process. Jin or Helen would call that growing pains. She dared to close the distance. To test those boundaries and the expanding chasm between them. "I will know in my heart that I gave Adriana my best."

Just as she'd given Theo her best. And wasn't that all she could really do?

Theo's gaze roamed over her face. His jaw flexed. No doubt from the comebacks piling behind his teeth. He certainly had comments about always being better. Surpassing your best and climbing higher. Pushing harder when your best wasn't enough.

Josie waited. He never spoke. Perhaps that was for the best.

Josie looked at Adriana and Lilian Rose. "The past cannot be redone or erased, but we can take its best parts and build from that." Josie glanced back at Theo. "Also, one of mine."

She let herself out of the house. Let herself cry one block from his house.

CHAPTER TWENTY-TWO

"THEO, YOU SHOULD go after Josie." Adriana set the garment bag on the bar stool.

"To what purpose?" He paced around the island, opened the refrigerator and closed it. He wasn't hungry. Or thirsty. He was restless.

"To tell her that you love her," Adriana said.

Love. Theo flattened his palms on the marble island and closed his eyes.

"You do love her, don't you?" his mother asked.

"How do I know?" Theo squeezed his eyes closed. "I don't know anything about love."

But what he knew in the depths of his soul, deep inside his bones, was that he missed Josie with an intensity that suffocated him. That for the first time in his life he wanted to call someone to hear her voice. Share her laughter, not make a business deal. He wanted to have dinner not to formalize a contract or negotiate an agreement, but to enjoy the food and the company. He wanted to settle in for the night with his arms wrapped around Josie, not his laptop or his spreadsheets. Theo clenched his fists.

He loved her. He was *in* love with Josie Beck.

And miserable. Completely and utterly.

He'd let her walk away. Twice. First at the gala. Then right now here at his house. He'd let her walk out of his life. "What am I supposed to do now?"

"Win her back," his mother said.

Theo eyed her. "You don't even like her."

"I misjudged her." His mother's voice was more pensive, less polished. "For that, I owe her and you an apology. I'm very, very sorry. Oh, Theo, you don't have to look so surprised."

"It's just… I am surprised."

"Let me surprise you even more." His mother turned toward Adriana and took her hands. "I'm also sorry if any of my recent incidents caused problems between you and Ryan. That wasn't ever the intent."

Adriana glanced at Theo. He recovered his surprise first. He asked, "What was your intent?"

"I was hoping your sister would become a bit more of a bridezilla." His mother released Adriana and wandered into the kitchen as if she'd just announced nothing more significant than she wanted a second cup of coffee.

Adriana prepared herself a cup of coffee as if the additional caffeine might help her understand. "Why would you want me to be like that?"

"It makes for great video." His mother set the

garment bag on the couch. "Things like that can go viral."

"Why do you want video of Adriana going viral?" Theo poured himself a cup of coffee. A headache throbbed at the base of his neck. "Is this for the TV show?"

"No," his mother said. "But I do have thoughts about the programming and schedule that I'd like to share with you sometime this week."

His mother wanted to turn his sister into a bridezilla. And now she wanted to sit down and discuss the format of the upcoming TV show. He'd admitted he was in love. Technically that should only turn his own world upside down. The whole world should not be turning over, too. "This was all fake then," Theo said. The wedding-dress fiasco. The matchmaking. The floral shop. The bakery. He waved his hands around, unable to still his sudden irritation.

"No. I intend to have a winter wedding. And for it to be a cover story." His mother grabbed each of their hands. "And I fully intend to have my children's blessing when I do it."

"Then what was this?" Theo asked.

She picked up her phone, tapped on the screen and handed it to Theo. "It was for my vlog."

"Vlog," Theo repeated. "What is HelenTs101?"

"That's the name of my video blog." His mother took back her phone. Her grin slanted into mischievous. Satisfaction slipped into her tone. "It's quite clever. It stands for, well, me and my helpful tips and advice on a number of subjects, many related to Coast to Coast Living."

"Mother." Adriana walked to the island and took their mother's phone. "You have an active vlog? A live, real-time vlog?"

"I have quite the following." Their mother tapped a finger against her chin. "Although I haven't been able to increase my reach like I've wanted. I was going to ask you about that, Adriana."

"Me?" Adriana looked up from the phone.

"Of course. You're one of the best social-media minds at the company." She glanced between Theo and Adriana. "Don't you two ever talk to the staff?"

Theo held up his hand. "We'll come back to Adriana. Mother, what is this vlog about?"

"I started speaking about remodeling and offering simple refashioning advice. Then I grew into personal topics, as well, for the half-century group." She walked into the kitchen and poured herself a glass of water. "Now I'm offering relationship advice relevant to all ages."

Adriana set the phone on the marble counter. "Theo, she has over five million followers."

Their mother squeezed a lemon into her

water. Exasperation squeezed into her words. "It's not nearly enough."

"It's impressive," Theo said. "Why did you start?"

"To prove to you that I could be useful." His mother settled onto a bar stool and stared into her water glass. "I wanted to prove to you that I could bring value to the company and to our family."

Theo rocked back on his heels. That was his priority. That was his job. "I don't understand."

"I thought if you saw my work, you might allow me to consult on the TV show." She sipped her water.

"It's not a bad idea." Adriana moved around the island, closer to Theo. "I would like to do more at the company, as well. I have a title, but no true responsibilities."

Theo retreated. "You don't think I can run the business?"

"This isn't about you running the business." Frustration rattled through his sister's words. She pulled herself together, started again. "This is about mother and I being an active part of the business. Really contributing so you don't have to do everything all by yourself."

"You want active roles at the company," Theo clarified.

Adriana held up her hand. "I want to do more

than be your stand-in at events around town. If I'm going to give speeches and press releases on behalf of the company, I want to write those. Not you."

Their mother tapped the counter. "Adriana really should be in charge of the PR and marketing area. Ask the staff in those departments, if you don't believe me."

He couldn't believe he was having this conversation. He couldn't believe they hadn't had it sooner. Or, perhaps, he could. He'd been so busy listening to himself and his own counsel that he had failed to hear the people around him. Until Josie. Until Josie forced him to hear her. To see her. "There's something you should both know."

Their mother raised her hands. "We're going to disagree over things at work. That we should all know up front and accept right now."

"But that might not be a problem." Only Josie had disagreed with him recently. Yet she'd pushed to him to look at things differently. He was better for it. He borrowed from her now. "As long as we don't quit on each other. As long we keep talking through our arguments."

"It's going to take some practice," Adriana said.

"We're doing quite well right now." Their mother smiled.

"There's something else." Theo paused. But there was no good way to tell them. They wanted to be included. Would they back out or double down? He should've fought for Josie. He should never have backed out. "I've been positioning the company to go public."

Adriana sat down beside her mother. "When?"

"The Monday after your wedding. The day before Christmas Eve—an early Christmas surprise," Theo said. That day everything would've been perfect. Everyone would've understood. Now, nothing was perfect. Yet, it felt even more right. Sitting here with his sister and mother talking about the business felt right.

"That's why you changed everything," Adriana said.

"The potential shareholders wanted Coast to Coast to prove we could be viable in the wedding sector." Theo dumped extra sugar and cream into his coffee. He doubted the sweetness could mute the bitterness in his tone. "I never meant to ruin your wedding."

"What did you mean to do?" Adriana asked.

"Take the business to the next level. Grow the brand and the profit," he said. "Make sure you were both happy."

"You're confusing us with your father, Theo." His mother spun her water glass in her hands.

"He would never let himself be happy. Never let himself be satisfied."

"You're doing the same thing as him," Adriana said.

Theo closed his eyes. "I thought you both would want this. That you would—"

"Love you more." His mother stood and walked around the counter. "No one can love you, Theo, if you won't let yourself love."

"Love makes you weak. Love makes you content." How many times had his father repeated that flaw, reminded Theo not to become like him? Warned Theo not to have any regrets. Well, Theo had one regret. Her name was Josie.

"More of your father's wisdom." His mother shook her head. "Your father never let himself be content. He never stopped to enjoy his life. To cherish the little moments as much as the big ones. And that was his biggest regret."

"I'm not weaker for loving Ryan." Adriana came around the counter to join them. "I'm stronger because of him and his love for me."

Josie had been stronger today. Inside his house. Theo wanted to believe he had a part in that. But he knew his bigger role was in hurting her. In breaking her heart. "You've twisted me up. Turned around everything I know."

"We know we want to keep the business in the family." Adriana reached for his hand. "Run it our way. Not the way the shareholders dictate."

"You're sure?" Theo looked at his mother, then his sister. Waited for their consent. "I'm not used to giving up control."

"We aren't asking you to give up anything." Adriana squeezed his hand. "We're only asking you to let us help."

"To let us feel like we have a purpose, too," his mother added.

"I can do that," he said. He might even like it. He'd been sitting in his office alone and carrying the weight. There was something appealing about the support. About knowing it came from his family—a family who wanted to be involved. Who asked to be involved.

His mother laughed. "As long as we're on a roll, turning Theo's world upside down, Adriana, can we see the dress?"

Adriana nodded, bounced around the island and picked up the garment bag. "Mother, will you help me?"

"I'd be delighted." His mother wrapped her arm around Theo's waist and hugged him. "Wish us luck."

"You won't need it," he said. "Josie created that gown specifically for Adriana. It's her gift." She'd been his gift, too. And he'd lost her.

Theo walked to the family room and the

Christmas tree. He wanted a do-over. He wanted a replay. He wanted…

"Theo…" His sister's voice barely reached him.

He turned around. He wanted what his sister had with Ryan. What his mother had had with his father. What Shanna and every other bride of Josie's had with their grooms. He wanted what only Josie could give him. A forever kind of love.

Tears streamed down both his sister's and his mother's faces. But there was a glimmer in their gazes, a glow in their cheeks. That was the magic Josie talked about. The magic Josie created. In one dress, she granted the bride her own fairy tale.

"What do you think?" His mother's voice lacked her usual potency.

"I think it's amazing." From the illusion sleeve to the rosette-trimmed train to the delicate veil. Every hand stitch showcased his sister. Enhanced her beauty. Radiated her love. "I think it's perfect. Truly perfect."

Adriana lifted the hem. "She even embroidered our initials and wedding date in blue thread on the inside. Along with Grandmother Pearl's initials and wedding date."

His mother sighed. "There's not going to be a dry eye at the wedding."

"It's the best of Grandma Pearl's dress mixed with me." Adriana set her hands on her cheeks and squealed. "I have to get my groom back. We have a wedding this weekend."

"Let's get you out of this dress quickly." Their mother unclipped the veil and draped it over her arms.

"What can I do?" Theo asked.

His mother and sister turned toward him. Adriana shook her head. "Nothing. You need to win back your own true love."

His mother nodded. "Your sister is right, you know."

"I don't know what I'm supposed to do." Theo threw his hands up in the air. "Who I'm supposed to be."

"What if you're the man you are supposed to be with Josie at your side?" Adriana locked her gaze on him. "Why don't you be that man?"

CHAPTER TWENTY-THREE

JOSIE ADJUSTED THE asymmetrical neckline of her floor-length gown. The crimson-and-black silk chiffon was flowy, bold and confident. Josie lost her confidence at the top step of the entrance to the cathedral. She shouldn't have come.

Despite Adriana's phone call, issuing a personal invite.

Despite Mia's encouragement.

Despite her two chaperones and their insistence.

Helen and Jin linked arms and finished their climb up the cathedral's staircase. Helen touched her forehead. "I might need another hip replacement after that jaunt."

Jin laughed. "It's going to be worth it. Weddings always are."

Or it was going to be a disaster. Josie fiddled with the waist of her gown. She should've never left one shoulder bare. She'd never worn a gown quite like this one. She'd never created a gown quite like this one. Never been to a wedding like this one.

She could turn around. Going down the stairs was certain to be easier than the climb up. Mia was documenting everything on her camera as the official wedding photographer. Josie could easily relive the day in pictures and film. She didn't have to live it now. *Live.*

"I recovered my breath." Helen linked her arm around Josie's. "Now I'll be able to respond to the questions about your wedding-dress design appropriately."

"Adriana might not be wearing her grandmother's gown." Josie lowered her voice as the women entered the cathedral. "She never actually told me what dress she'd chosen."

Jin shooed away her argument. "Of course, she is wearing your gown."

"And if she isn't, I have my breath back to give her a word or two about not honoring her grandmother." Helen huffed as if she'd taken on the role of ensuring grandmothers everywhere were honored properly.

The women bookended Josie and escorted her inside the church. Christmas trees adorned the front of the church, as wide as they were tall. Candles had been lit in the historic chandeliers and their light reflected off the collection of stained-glass windows lining every wall. Inside the church, the history was revered and celebrated, while the modern was accepted. The women took seats toward the back of the church and maneuvered Josie to the end of the pew near the center aisle.

Jin leaned toward her. "This way you'll have the best view of your gown."

Helen preened at a young couple behind them and pointed at Josie. "She's the wedding-dress designer."

The couple offered polite congratulations. Josie tried not to slip under the pew and prayed Adriana wore her gown.

The pipe organ struck the first keys of the "Wedding March." The guests rose and shifted to face the back of the church. Josie gripped the pew in front of her and kept her focus on the front of the cathedral. A sweet flower girl stopped next to Josie and handed her several rose petals. The ring bearer tugged the little girl down the aisle. Four more bridesmaids walked down the aisle in deep purple dresses. Then the gasps and murmurs flowed from the back of the church, sweeping over Josie.

Jin clutched Josie's arm. Josie shifted her head and swayed. Theo was beside her, his tuxedo impeccably tailored to his frame. On his arm, his sister wore her Grandmother Pearl's upscaled wedding dress. Those murmurs continued through to the front of the church. Dazed, Josie sat in the pew and spent the remainder of the ceremony focused on Theo.

A highlight in her career. A boost for her boutique. Adriana Taylor wore her upscaled vintage gown. A Josie Beck redesign. Josie should be in the pew celebrating and organizing her business cards. Instead she watched Theo. Wondered if he looked thinner. She'd seen him five long—very long—days ago.

Wondered if he looked tired. That could be the candlelight.

Wondered if he searched the guests, looking for her. That was absurd.

If he'd wanted her at the wedding, he would've called her himself.

If he'd wanted her in his life, he would've fought for her.

Josie cried for the couple and their obvious love. Cried for herself and her one-sided affection. Jin passed her a tissue. Helen patted her arm.

Finally, Adriana and Ryan shared a kiss as husband and wife. Finally, the celebration began. Finally, Josie could escape.

She walked out of the cathedral, but strangers intercepted her. Asked about the gown. The inspiration for Adriana's veil. Asked for business cards. Asked for consultations. Helen and Jin offered their own advice. Held court on the talented Josie Beck.

Theo emerged from the church and stood beside Josie. His hand on her back almost undid her. He answered a question from a reporter. His voice sure and effective. "Adriana and Ryan's wedding is a blend of the new while honoring family and the past. Something we learned was possible from Josie Beck." His fingers flexed on her back. His next words were only for her. "You came and I'm unprepared. But I need to talk to you."

She was unprepared for the sensations coursing through her from one simple touch. She wouldn't be able to withstand the onslaught of emotions from his words. What more was there left to say?

"Theo, you're wanted for pictures." Helen anchored her arm around Josie's waist and steered her away from the crowd.

"We'll head to the reception venue," Jin stated. "Food and a glass of wine will most certainly help."

Josie wasn't certain an entire cheesecake and extra bottle of whipped cream could help her now. She slipped into the van that was ushering guests to the reception venue. Once there, she'd slip down the street and disappear into her own taxi.

Josie wove through the guests milling on the vast lawns outside the private estate and reception hall. She searched the grounds, looking for a place to escape and call a taxi. Her gaze connected with Theo. The group and family photographs had ended. The wedding party mingled with the guests.

Josie's steps slowed. Her mind paused on the moment, afraid to press Play. Fearful of the impending hurt. She spun around. Cowardly? Yes. She couldn't face him. Not here. Not again.

"Josie Beck, I love you." Theo's shout carried across the lawns. Captured the guests' full attention.

His words rooted Josie in place. She closed her eyes. Surely she'd misheard. She was stressed, imagining things. Dreams didn't come true for her.

"Josie Beck, I love you." This time Theo's voice came from directly behind her. Still an octave too loud. An octave above commanding.

Josie glanced around, took in the cameras filming and personal cell phones recording. More guests hurried across the lawn toward them. Josie twisted around. Theo righted her and gripped her hands.

He said, "Josie, I—"

"Stop talking." She searched the grounds for a private area. Tugged on his hands to pull him away. Locked her gaze on his, urging him to move.

He never budged, as if he always preferred public displays. Always preferred being the spotlight. "I have things I need to tell you."

Stubborn, stubborn man. "Hold onto them." She yanked on him again. "We can talk in private."

"I want to tell you now."

"Now?" she whispered. "They're watching. Filming. Recording."

"I don't care." He squeezed her hands, kept his gaze on hers. "Let them go. This is between you and me."

Josie moved closer to Theo. He wouldn't move to a secluded spot. But she could close the distance. Create their own private space.

"I love you, Josie," he said again. Wonder in his voice. Affection in his gaze. On his face.

His words stitched all those broken pieces of her heart back together.

He continued as if he'd always spoken in rapid succession. "I love you, but you shouldn't love me."

Josie opened her mouth.

He set his fingers on her chin, closed her mouth. "You shouldn't love me. I'm opinionated. Work too much. I don't like to share. I don't always listen and more times than not I do things my own way. I'm a terrible loser and an even worse winner. And if you ever want to win the Fiore-Reid gingerbread contest, it definitely won't happen with me."

"You stand up for what you believe in. You're

passionate about work. You're protective, confident and competitive." Josie cupped his face. Pressed her lips to his and leaned back. "I love you, Theo Taylor for all those reasons and so many more. You're not perfect, only perfect for me."

Theo lifted her off the ground and spun her around. Cheers and claps filled the lawn around them. One more kiss. More applause and Theo lowered her to the grass. Her feet might've been on the ground, but she was floating. The cloud-nine, over-the-rainbow, enchanted-fairy-tale kind of floating. And she never wanted to come down.

"Shall we test our newly acquired dance skills inside?" He laced his fingers around hers.

"Yes. We should." Together, they walked toward the reception hall, leaning into each other. Supporting each other.

Lilian Rose intercepted them outside on the terrace. "Can I have a word?"

Theo tucked Josie into his side, wrapping his arm around her waist. He said, "We were going to see if we remembered our dance lessons."

Lilian Rose grinned. "You won't forget. This will only take a minute."

Josie looped her arm around Theo's waist and waited.

"I thought you took the TV show from me,

but you took something more valuable—my son's heart." Lilian Rose motioned for Josie's hands and took them in her own. "But you gave us something even more precious—yours."

Josie searched Lilian Rose's face. Found only sincerity. Candid and genuine.

"I don't always get this parenting thing right." Lilian Rose's eyebrows quirked, a wryness wrinkled across her smile. "But I understand love. I recognize the love between you and my son. It's the same love I shared with Theo's father."

Josie swayed into Theo. His hand fell on her lower back and anchored her.

"We don't deserve you in our family, but we're better with you beside us," Lilian Rose said.

Josie spoke from her heart—one that was open and healed. "I'm better, too."

"I'm not the perfect mother. I get more wrong than right." Lilian Rose laughed. "But I'll try to be a better mother-in-law."

"I never had a mother. I never wanted perfect." Josie squeezed Lilian Rose's hands. "I only ever wanted a family."

"You have one now, if you'll accept us." Lilian Rose opened her arms.

Josie stepped into her embrace. Lilian Rose

released her and added, "I'd like to talk to you about a dress or two, as well."

Josie brushed the tears off her cheeks and nodded.

Lilian Rose hugged her son and pointed over her head. "You two should really be more careful about where you stand. See you inside for the reception."

Josie and Theo looked up. A mistletoe bouquet trimmed with red ribbon and silver bells hung over their heads.

Theo pulled Josie into his arms. "Did you know it's considered bad luck to refuse a kiss underneath mistletoe?"

Josie curved her arms around Theo's neck. "Well, we have to honor tradition."

"Let's start a few of our own, too." Theo kissed her.

And it was perfect.

EPILOGUE

"DON'T MOVE. Don't even breathe." Theo raised his hands away from his project, slowly and carefully. He tapped his shoulder into Josie's and whispered, "My walls are finally standing."

Josie chuckled and eyed her own gingerbread house. She added two more candy canes to line the walkway and surveyed her work.

Theo grinned at her and plucked a candy cane from her walkway.

"Stop sampling my display." She kissed him and eased the candy cane from his grip.

"I'd rather practice our new traditions." He pointed at the mistletoe he'd hung from the kitchen light.

Josie laughed. "Is there any place you haven't put mistletoe?"

He tucked her hair behind her ear and curved his palm around her cheek. "If there is, I'm going to have to order the fake kind. I think I bought out Baylee's entire supply."

"You never do anything half-measure, do you?"

"Where's the satisfaction in that?"

Josie pulled him toward her and kissed him again. Poured her heart and love into the kiss.

"It's a good thing someone in this family is taking the first annual Taylor-family gingerbread competition seriously." Lilian Rose's cheerful voice suspended their mistletoe moment.

Josie turned and gaped. Lilian Rose carried a cutting board with a two-story, Victorian gingerbread house standing in the center. Snow-capped trees and a sleigh decorated the gingerbread's front yard along with a chocolate-candy picket fence.

"What?" Lilian Rose's grin was infectious, her laughter light-hearted. "You didn't think I could make a good gingerbread house, did you?"

"Mother, where did you buy that gingerbread house?" Theo asked.

"I resent your implication that I cheated and purchased this gem." Lillian Rose adjusted her hold on the cutting board.

"It's quite perfect." Josie took in the straight walls, neatly cut windows and tall chimney.

"It really is." Lilian Rose grinned and chuckled. "I did mention that in addition to being a very good dancer, Kirk is also quite the skilled baker. With his engineering brain and my creativity, we put this together ourselves. No professional assistance required."

"But we agreed to all build our own gingerbread houses alone," Theo said.

"Kirk and I realized that we're stronger as a team." Lilian Rose shrugged. "And we came up with the same idea for the next new Taylor-family tradition."

"You only get to name the next family tradition if you win the gingerbread contest." Theo tapped the wall of his house, forcing it upright.

"I'm well aware of the rules." Lilian Rose walked slowly toward the kitchen counter.

"Mother, let me help." Theo reached for the cutting board.

"Hands off, Theo. There will be no sabotaging our house." Lilian Rose aimed her smile at Josie. She set her cutting board beside Theo's undecorated cookie sheet and wobbly house. "Kirk and I fully intend to win tomorrow night. You're going to love our idea for a new family tradition."

The roof slipped off the side of Theo's gingerbread house. Josie slapped her hands over her mouth and caught her laughter.

Theo never flinched. "I'm going for open-concept living. It's all the rage."

"Unacceptable." Lilian Rose shook her head and tried to hid her smile. "Everyone inside your house will freeze."

Theo stuffed cotton candy on top of his roofless house. "There. Insulation." He eyed his creation and nodded. "It's not that bad."

Josie bent down to peer inside the windows of Lilian Rose and Kirk's Victorian masterpiece. "You added candles to the windows. It's almost not fair."

"That was Kirk's idea," Lilian Rose said. "It added much-needed warmth to the whole house."

Lilian Rose's voice was warm every time she mentioned Kirk's name. The pair had been inseparable since Adriana and Ryan's wedding last weekend, then through the Christmas gatherings and celebrations. Now the New Year approached, the pair appeared even closer. Josie had heard Lilian Rose mention the appeal of a spring wedding several times.

"The competition isn't until tomorrow night, before the New Year's Eve party." Theo pulled out a mixing bowl and the flour container. He reached for the blender and nudged his elbow into Josie's side. "There's still time to challenge Kirk and mother."

"Are you suggesting that we team up together, too?" Josie asked.

"We are better together." Theo leaned over and kissed her cheek.

"I'll leave you two to your baking." Lilian Rose hugged them both and walked toward the back door. "Kirk and I are off to pick up a few more decorations for tomorrow night's party. I'll leave our house for inspiration."

Theo eyed his collapsing gingerbread. Two walls sagged into the center, the third teetered as if unsure which way to fall. "Maybe this wasn't such a good idea."

"If only you hadn't agreed to turn it into a contest," Josie said.

Theo tossed leftover flour at Josie. "I blame Adriana and Ryan for that. I think it was their suggestion after we forgot to monitor which cake was finished first at their wedding reception."

Josie dipped her finger in Theo's icing. "If I recall, we were too busy dancing to watch the dessert table." And too interested in being together to worry about a bet they'd made and declaring a winner. So both Theo and Josie got to choose something to do on New Year's Eve. Josie picked a New Year's Eve party for their family and friends. Theo chose gingerbread-house building.

How the contest came about…well, that was anyone's guess really. They'd shared a family dinner on Christmas Eve. A home-cooked meal set out on Theo's large dining-room table. Every seat had been filled—even the film crew had stopped in without cameras and their new TV star, Daphne Holland. The producers had determined Daphne's matchmaking business fulfilled their criteria for a hit TV show better than Coast to Coast Living. The Taylors had willingly stepped aside and agreed to revisit a potential TV show at another time. It'd been a lively dinner, where conversations rolled over each other and laughter filled the air. And love joined them all together.

Josie licked the frosting from her finger and wiped her hands on her apron. "I suppose we should get baking if we're going to win."

Theo took her hand, spun her in a circle and drew her into him. It was exactly where she wanted to be.

"Or we could take a moment and dance," he said.

Josie closed the distance and set her cheek over Theo's heart. The simple moments really were the most precious. Especially with Theo—the man she loved. And her new family. The ones she was going to love forever and always.

* * * * *

Psst!

Available January 7, 2020

#311 LASSOED BY THE WOULD-BE RANCHER

The Mountain Monroes • by Melinda Curtis

Franny Clark's Bucking Bull ranch needs help—stat. Enter Shane Monroe, CEO and city slicker, who's looking for answers of his own. They know they come from different worlds, but not even a rampaging bull can keep them apart!

#312 A BRIDESMAID TO REMEMBER

Stop the Wedding! • by Amy Vastine

Bonnie Windsor was the perfect maid of honor—until the groom declared his love for her! Blacklisted in town, her only ally is Aaron Cole, the bride's brother. Now Aaron's falling for Bonnie—but is that worth falling out with his family?

#313 HEALING THE DOCTOR'S HEART

by Shirley Hailstock

Trauma wounds mean Dr. Jake Masters's right arm won't move, but he keeps refusing treatment. Engaging Lauren Peterson as a companion seems like a good temporary solution, but hiring her is complicated by the secret she holds.

#314 THE SHERIFF'S SECOND CHANCE

by Tanya Agler

A string of thefts in Hollydale, North Carolina, inexplicably point to Georgie Bennett as the number one suspect. When the sheriff turns out to be Mike Harrison, an old flame, things go from bad to...better?

THE FORTUNES OF TEXAS COLLECTION!

18 FREE BOOKS in all!

Treat yourself to the rich legacy of the Fortune and Mendoza clans in this remarkable 50-book collection. This collection is packed with cowboys, tycoons and Texas-sized romances!

YES! Please send me **The Fortunes of Texas Collection** in Larger Print. This collection begins with 3 FREE books and 2 FREE gifts in the first shipment. Along with my 3 free books, I'll also get the next 4 books from The Fortunes of Texas Collection, in LARGER PRINT, which I may either return and owe nothing, or keep for the low price of $5.24 U.S./$5.89 CDN each plus $2.99 for shipping and handling per shipment*. If I decide to continue, about once a month for 8 months I will get 6 or 7 more books but will only need to pay for 4. That means 2 or 3 books in every shipment will be FREE! If I decide to keep the entire collection, I'll have paid for only 32 books because 18 books are FREE! I understand that accepting the 3 free books and gifts places me under no obligation to buy anything. I can always return a shipment and cancel at any time. My free books and gifts are mine to keep no matter what I decide.

☐ 269 HCN 4622 ☐ 469 HCN 4622

Name (please print)

Address Apt. #

City State/Province Zip/Postal Code

Mail to the **Reader Service:**
IN U.S.A.: P.O Box 1341, Buffalo, N.Y. 14240-8531
IN CANADA: P.O. Box 603, Fort Erie, Ontario L2A 5X3